"The truth is rarely pure and never simple."
  – Oscar Wilde
  (Algernon, Act 1,
  The Importance of Being Earnest.)

About the Author

FROM Dublin, Ireland; Carolann Copland has also lived in the Middle East and the United Kingdom. She writes between Dublin and Andalucia and is a mother of three children aged twelve, twenty-two and twenty-three.

As the founder of Carousel Creates Writers' Centre, Carolann works with writers of all ages and lifestyles. She has a Bachelor of Education in English and Drama and has been a teacher for sixteen years.

Carolann is happiest when she is sharing her passion for reading and writing.

Scarred is her second novel.

SCARRED

by
Carolann Copland

June 2015

Scarred
2015

Published by Emu Ink Ltd
www.emuink.ie

Cover Design by Gwen Taylour/Emu Ink

ISBN: 978-1-909684-53-9

Acknowledgements…

Scarred is dedicated to my family.

…To Neil… who holds us all together.

…To my children; David, Katy-Anna and Aoife.

…To my parents; Joe and Bridie Maher.

…To my siblings; Doreen, Joe, Siobhán, Colum and Lorcan.

…To my aunts, uncles, cousins, nieces and nephews and in-laws.

Because family is everything.

Special thanks also…

…To my heroic Castle Writers; Tara Sparling, Bernadette Kearns and Joan Brady.

…To all the workshop facilitators at Carousel Writers' Centre.

…To the writers at Carousel Writers' Centre.

…To the Irish Crime Writers' Association.

…To all the amazing authors I have met on my writing journey.

…To those I have never met, but who keep me going on Facebook and Twitter with their constant encouragement.

…To my teacher friends.

…To my best friends; Jackie Murphy and Louise Williamson, my Drama Queens and all my Knocklyoners.

…To Emer and Brian Cleary and their team at Emu Ink Publishing, for their trust in the story.

…To Jax Miller for launching my book with such enthusiasm.

…To you, for reading my book, thank you.

Part one

Chapter one

THERE had been good times over the last eighteen years, when Rory had managed to forget that Maria was murdered and that he might have stopped it. But those times were rare. He was back in his hometown in Donegal; beginning to live his life without constantly looking over his shoulder and right now, he was happy enough. Tonight's party was a fitting celebration for all that had been achieved since. Smiling over at his younger daughter handing around glasses of champagne, he let his gaze wander longingly towards the pints that Jim was lining up on the counter. He accepted the narrow-stemmed glass and held it while he made his thank you speech; praising his lovely family, his loyal friends and the best of work colleagues.

'Enjoy yourselves now.' He raised the bubbles to his guests, took a sip and grimaced. 'Terrible stuff. Here you go, Caitríona.' He handed the glass to his eldest. 'You'll do that more justice, love.' He then pecked her on the cheek and legged it towards the bar to the lovely cold, black, creamy pint that had his name on it.

Gerry was waiting on his usual high stool and he placed the pint in Rory's hands. 'Get that inside you now and leave the sparkles to the ladies,' he said, laughing with his friend.

Sitting up on his familiar stool, Rory looked lovingly at his pint and enjoyed the knowing feel of it in his great big hands. Lifting it to his lips he allowed the black nectar to slide down his parched throat. He took another gulp before finally sitting it down on the counter to settle the creamy top once more.

He sighed. 'So is this it, Gerry? As good as it gets?'

The two friends sat in companionable quiet for a few moments while the noise of the GAA club buzzed on around them. The enormous screen was blazing adverts but was turned to mute as they listened to Bon Jovi's *I'll be there for you* blazing from the music system.

'Can you credit it, Rory? You forty and me a few years more. Weren't we lads on the hurling pitch only a while back?' Gerry shook his head and lifted his pint for comfort.

'Speak for yourself. I'm not an auld fella nearing fifty like you,' Rory teased. Of all the people in Balcallan, Gerry had been the only person to forgive him his sins over the years. It was good to be back with him, training the young lads and reminiscing about their time hurling together. The Donegal team was on the up and he loved being a part of it all, but if he could have those earlier years back...

'Same again, Jim.' Gerry gestured to the barman.

'I'm away home now, Dad.' Caitríona tapped Rory on the shoulder.

'At this time?' He looked at his watch. 'It's not even nine yet. What's your hurry?'

'I've an exam in the morning and I've more study to do. I told you that this party was bad timing but Clodagh was insistent that we had it on the actual day of your birthday. Sorry, Dad. But haven't you hoards of people to celebrate with you here?' She reached in and gave him a dutiful peck on the cheek.

Rory watched her leave the club with a nod and a wave to her grandparents. He loved his daughter but he knew that would never be enough. He had a huge amount of mending to do to fix the broken life he had given her. Having her and her sister here at his party was the start of something new. He didn't have the right to call himself their father but he would keep working on it. It had taken a year of living back in Balcallan to get them to talk to him and another year before they called him dad. They'd had a few other names for him before that and all of them justified. If only he had felt able to tell them what had happened to turn his life on its axis all those years ago.

He listened to the words of the singer he once enjoyed dancing to at the discos. The only way he could be there for his daughters was to tell them the truth about what had happened, but how could he do that now without repercussions? *I'd live and I'd die for you* sang Jon Bon Jovi and Rory clenched his fists in yearning for a better life with his girls. Caitríona was gone back home where her mother would no doubt quiz her about the party and ask who was there. His wife. He had waited all these years for her to ask him for a divorce. A quick end to something that had begun in haste twenty years before when Deirdre had fallen pregnant and he had done the honours in the church before she was showing too much. Poor girl never got to show enough before she lost their baby. They should have gone their separate ways after that but then he wouldn't have had his two beautiful daughters.

He scooped up his pint glass and walked over to where eighteen-year-old Clodagh was conspiring with his sister, Rita, to get her a real drink, even though it was a school night. If he told her off she would tell him where to stick his fatherly advice. After all these years of not knowing what they were up to, it was a bit late now to be acting all concerned. Rita had a much stronger relationship with his daughters than he would ever have. He glanced up at the television screen behind Clodagh, as the adverts were replaced by a party political broadcast. That shower again. He smiled brightly at his family and sat himself down at their table. The usual awkward silence between them filled the space at first, until he pushed a few words out.

'How are you, Dad? Lovely to see you, Mam. Hiya, Rita. You're very good to come along. I appreciate it.' A nod from his mother while his father solemnly raised his glass at him.

'Happy birthday, son. Sure of course we came. Why wouldn't we?'

And that question sat between them, as they each answered all the reasons why they might not have bothered to come to celebrate the fortieth birthday of the man who had fucked up all their lives, over the last twenty years.

Rory closed his eyes briefly as the words of Bon Jovi washed over all of them. *Well I can promise you tomorrow, but I can't buy back yesterday.* If he could bring himself to tell them all the truth, then tomorrow might be a release and yesterday could be laid to rest.

Chapter two

WHEN Rory opened his eyes he was looking at the man who killed Maria.

His face froze and the years fell back like the pages of a book where you return to a remembered scene. The smile on the man's face captured the camera and flashed through the clubhouse television screen; but it was a smile that never seemed to reach his eyes.

'Rory? Rory what's the matter? What are you looking at?' But Rory didn't hear his sister or see the concerned look on her face.

The man on the screen reached his hands up to straighten his soft, lilac tie. The camera was moving on. Some other politician was making a speech but for Rory, the face was still in front of him. The glassy eyes still bore into him.

They brought him back through the pages again. Back to the squat in Dublin, eighteen years ago. Maria didn't overdose. She wanted to live. She was a fighter. For all her losses, for all that was wrong in her life, Maria knew that she would keep going. They had talked about it the day before she was killed, about facing up to her addiction. Maria was murdered. Rory knew this because he had been there... And ran.

'Are you alright, Dad?' Clodagh put a hand on his shoulder and shrugged at her grandparents' questioning look. 'What is it?'

Rory shook his head and reached for his pint, wrapping his fingers around its familiar shape. He looked back at the screen willing it to be blank but the camera had swung back to the man's face, and Rory watched the politician reach for his glass of iced water and wrap his fingers around its coldness. The same fingers that had wrapped around the syringe. The one that the politician had used to fill Maria with poison and empty her body of life.

Maria.

The man turned and exposed his left profile to the camera. The scar that Rory had given him still ran along his cheek. It was faded but there all the same. Eighteen years older; his skin was weathered by what had no doubt been a desperate existence. But there was no mistake. This man had killed Maria. In his other life. Rory closed his eyes again in an attempt to block out the picture of Maria's murderer and in its place he saw her face as she succumbed to her death. He made a groaning sound and putting down his pint, slopping it over the table; he fled from the clubhouse.

The January rain ripped at the skin on Rory's face. He pulled his shirt collar up a little more but it was no protection against the bitter cold. He dug his hands deep into his pockets trying to find warmth. He had been sitting on the rock on the hill without his coat for about an hour but this was the first time he had noticed that he was frozen. The comfort of the earlier pints not even a memory in his body. The waves smashed against the rocks beneath him in time with the rhythms of his anger. Somewhere out there was Tory Island, cloaked in rain, denying Rory its familiar comfort. The islanders were cradled in a simple lifestyle. Rory craved any one of their lives rather than his own.

'Maria!' he shouted into the wind and it carried her name across to Tory. 'I can't do this!' he screamed at the waves and they in turn slashed at the rocks in answer. 'Maria! Maria... I'm so sorry...' his voice dying to a whisper against the sound of the storm. 'There was nothing I could've done... nothing I can do now either.' The tears merged with raindrops and sea spray on his face; splashes of anger and shame. He knew that he *could* have done something back then. He could take action now, even though it would tear at his life. It would rip his family's life apart too, especially his grown up children.

8

Then the face on the television was there again and he thought, if he could bring *him* down with him, would that not be worth it? Would they not all understand why he had behaved the way he had all these years? The past would all have to come out. Not only the bit to do with the murder but the whole sordid, sorry story.

And he *was* sorry. Sorry for them all. Repentant for what had passed and what was now. Not for himself because self-pity had no place in this mess. A bit late now to be worried about Rory McGee's position in life, anyhow. He should have worried about that way back then, when he had abandoned his family after being a silent witness to a murder. Silent for eighteen years, while inside him the storm raged, destroying him; anger and guilt, wind and rain, tearing at his soul. And grief. He had never been able to grieve for Maria.

He hadn't been able to go to her funeral or to tell her family that he was sorry. He had wanted to be part of her eulogy, to let the world know that she was his life and that at one time he had been everything to her too. But the world didn't know the truth of Maria's last years.

Fleeing to London back then helped keep his distance from that terrible man who had killed his love with the push of a needle. That determination and fear held him together in those first few months and afterwards this shaped his life. He carried on that life in London all those years, drifting from one job to another, one address to another, and sending most of what he earned to Deirdre. Women came and went, while he ran from each of them terrified of what an association with him might bring on them.

He walked the world two-faced, like Maria's killer, the now politician.

What had taken them both from that life to this one? Had the politician's actions back then changed *his* life? Was he now a peace-loving man, intent on putting the past behind him and making the best of the present; making the future a place where politics played no part in murder? He probably had a family now, as Rory had, and was doing lots of good in his new life. Rory should leave well alone, move on with the life he had made for himself and allow this man to get on with his. Two years ago, Rory had come home to Balcallan having decided that if *they* had left him alone all this time that it was probably safe to presume that he and his family weren't a target. Seeing the man on the television tonight was confirmation of this. He had changed to make his beliefs work in a different way. Rory could move on too. It had all happened such a long time ago.

As he pulled his cold, stiff body from his wet seat, he blinked his eyes against the picture of the politician's cold, glassy stare. He put the image of the smugness on that face away in the corner of his head reserved for such memories; and as he walked towards the descent, he shook away the comparison to the face of the man who had taken Maria. By the time Rory had reached the bottom of the hill with his back to the still raging sea, he was worried about how soaked and freezing he was. How could he have been so stupid? He coughed his way along the beach towards the lane that would lead him back to the comfort of his new life.

This way was easier on his family. It was easier on the politician as well but he wouldn't think of that too much. Instead he thought of peeling his wet clothes from him and lying in a warm bath. He might have a hot whisky. He kept some in the press for Gerry when he dropped in. All these years of not having a stiff drink. Rory had been afraid of letting the truth spill out through drunken lips. Sure there was no harm in an odd drop of the hard stuff. It would help to forget and to put all this heartache behind him, where it belonged. It was nothing to do with his life now.

Why would you wreck everyone's heads over something that happened so long ago?

There. It was grand to see your man on the telly tonight. It had been the best thing to bring it all to a head and bury the ghosts. Rory was only forty years old. He had more than half of his life still to live and by God, he would live it.

At the entrance to the lane Rory stopped and looked back

along the dark sands. Suddenly he was remembering a summer's day all those years ago; with Maria sitting on top of the dunes, watching him whack his sliothar with his hurley stick the length of the beach, as Duffy his dog raced to collect it for him. That first day when Maria ran down the dunes and into his arms.

He was kidding himself if he thought he could ever put her behind him without making someone pay for the wasted years.

In the small hours of the morning, Rory lowered his head slowly to his pillow but the room continued to buzz. He liked this feeling. He had missed it a little. He decided that he wouldn't go to work tomorrow. From what he remembered of whisky hangovers this was going to be a big one. He closed his eyes and let the drink work its way to oblivion, but as is sometimes the way with the hard stuff, it left him wide-awake and staring into space. The events of the evening began to play tricks with Rory's memory. Those eyes. They were the last things that Rory saw when he eventually slept; the whisky finally doing its work.

Maria's rolling eyes. Her killer's glassy eyes. His own coward's eyes.

Chapter three

THE morning after his past caught up with him, Rory phoned in sick to his job at the glass factory. He lay back on the couch thinking of the hard face of the man who had killed Maria. He released the mug from his shaking hand, letting it clatter onto the coffee table. The residue leaked over the side and dripped down to yesterday's newspaper, seeping into the headline that read, *DUBLIN MURDER LINKED TO DRUGS BUST.*

These words tore at Rory and sent his thoughts hurtling back to Maria's squat. He blinked back tears, knowing it was more than the hangover and the soaking he had suffered the previous, freezing cold, night that was making him feel so wretched. He wasn't sure what he should do... if he did anything for God's sake. Wouldn't a politician be a respectable man? Was he wrong? But there was no mistaking that terrible scar. He had imagined it a million times. It was the only comfort he drew from that sickening night. Knowing that he had permanently maimed Maria's killer, at the very least. He shook his head to try to block out the picture of him now, but it was still there as he closed his eyes.

He'd been sleeping off his hangover for a while when he was woken by the phone. The vibrations had moved it to the edge of the table and he caught it as it fell towards the floor.

'Hello?' His voice came out as a squeak.

'Rory. You sound awful. What in the name of God happened to you last night?'

'Eh, I had a bad turn, Gerry. I feel dreadful. I didn't make it to work and I think I'll have to take tomorrow off as well.' He coughed in response to his friend's query.

'That bad eh? Can't say I'm feeling too good myself. We went out after you but we couldn't find you and you weren't answering your phone. So we went back in and well, your party was a great night, so it was. Isn't it well for those who can take the day off though?'

'Ger...' Rory was desperate to tell someone about what had happened.

'Yeah?'

'...nothing. It's nothing. Yeah. Drop in later if you're passing.' And he ended the call and left his friend as he had been for eighteen years – ignorant of the terrible event that had shaped Rory's life. How could he tell him now? How could he tell anyone? But equally, could he leave this politician to get on with his respectable life when he had once been a brutal killer?

Rory had been twenty-two years old the last time he had seen O'Gorman. They were about the same age. Rory was no saint back then either. Loving his beautiful Maria in Dublin, when he had Deirdre and their babies back home in Donegal. He had been besotted with the younger Maria, but he had been no murderer. He was a young man playing away from home... and most certainly a coward. Maria's killing and her killer's threats to Rory had frightened him all the way from his well-paid job in Dublin, and even further away from his family, to the grim streets of London.

Curling up on the couch, his back to the world, he began to shake violently. He held on tightly to the cushion under his head and let forgotten tears slide down his cheeks. The memory flooded him now. Maria lying in his arms, dying from the poison that washed through her body. That bastard had taken Rory's life from him when he had taken hers.

Had he gone on to live a normal life where he thought he could be a leader of people? How was that possible? Had he been in politics for a long time? How had Rory not noticed him before? He sat up suddenly and rubbed at his face and his eyes. He then opened his laptop on the table beside him and googled the words

13

O'Gorman and *Politician*.

There he was.

His first name was Fergal. He was standing for elections in Dublin and according to the piece on the internet he stood a good chance of winning.

'Over my dead body. Or *his*, the dirty shit.' Rory glared blackly at the photo on the screen.

A couple of hours later the doorbell rang. Still on his laptop, Rory closed the lid and pulled back from the window out of sight. It might be Deirdre. She had called earlier that day to say that she had heard that he had run from the clubhouse like a mad man the night before and their daughter was mortified. Had he only come back to Balcallan to shame them all again with his mad antics? Could he not piss off back to London and leave them all in peace? When he told her he wasn't well she had relented a little and threatened to drop around after work with some of her mother's soup. Rory would love some of that delicious, thick, comforting soup right now, but not when it was accompanied by Deirdre's bitter tongue on the side. He heard the footsteps moving away from the front door and around towards the back of the ground floor apartment. Rory didn't have time to close the curtains so he lay back down on the couch, closed his eyes and waited for the worst. A shout through the window made him relax.

'Are you there Rory? It's only me; Gerry.'

Rory pulled himself up and dragged his feet towards the kitchen in relief.

'Jesus, Gerry. I thought you were Deirdre, come to haunt me on my deathbed.' Rory followed this by a series of coughs. You'd be sure to get some sympathy from another fella.

'That's a terror of a dose you have there. You should be in bed with that.'

'Sure it's good of you to be concerned, Gerry. That's a lot more than I'd have from Deirdre if it had been her that was calling.'

'Sure you'd never get sympathy from a woman, Rory. You

should know that by now. You'd swear they weren't sick a day in their lives. You'd never think they drove you mad on a monthly basis and then finished up going through the change, with a mouth on them like Tory Bay.'

'You're right, Gerry. My God you're right.' Rory spoke this with man to man conviction; but this belied the guilt the statement left in his conscience. Guilt at anything that might put Deirdre down in any way had eaten at him all these years. He had betrayed her for Maria and betrayed Maria for fear. So, he had used up all his capabilities of betrayal in the first few years of marriage and, to make up for ruining Deirdre's life, tried to say only good things about her since.

The guilt just never left him.

'Ah, sure you wouldn't blame her, Gerry after all she's been through. It can't have been easy on her own here.'

'Never a truer word, Rory. You've no idea.'

Guilt was a disease. It had wrecked his life; eaten away at his head and his heart, leaving only small parts behind. These pieces had served him okay, until last night when he had seen the face. Now the disease was seeping into the good places. Those that he tried to reserve for his girls. This wasn't supposed to happen. He had held it all at bay for so long. A bad dream that had happened a long time ago, to someone else. Rory began a fit of coughing. He couldn't catch his breath. He held on to the kitchen counter to settle himself but as the breath began to reach his lungs again he realised that he was shaking and Gerry was bringing him back towards the television room and the couch.

'Sit down there now, Rory. My God I never saw the like of that for flu. You're in a terrible state altogether. Even worse than you were last night in the club with your funny turn. Wait there now and I'll see have you a whisky in the house. I won't take no for an answer. You'll have a drop this once and no arguments.'

While Gerry crashed around the kitchen, Rory lay back on the couch and took some deep breaths as he tried to compose himself. He looked at his watch. Would Deirdre turn up now to see them sitting back enjoying a whisky this early in the evening? He had to be in one piece by then. She would guess that it wasn't only a bit of a cold that was making him fall apart right now. She'd be all questions. He had to get back to being normal, whatever that was now, quickly.

Rory sat up and grounded his feet on the wooden polished floor. He would take the drink and sip it slowly. He wouldn't let it go to his head but he wouldn't refuse it either. There was no point making a fuss in front of Gerry Martin who could drink half of Balcallan dry; without missing a syllable. Rory wasn't going to loosen his tongue though and spill the beans. That was never going to happen. Not then and not now. He would put it all out of his mind as he had always done. The disciplines of eighteen years would not go to waste. He smiled up at Gerry as he came into the room and accepted the hair of the dog from his caring hands.

'Thanks, Gerry. I don't normally like to have a whisky, but sure I'll sip at this and see if it won't tide me over 'til Deirdre gets here with the soup.' Rory would have liked to tell Gerry about the skinful he'd had the night before while he tried to blot out the world. He was sorely tempted.

'You're that bad, Rory, you should see the doctor in the morning. You're shaking like a leaf.'

'I *will* go and see the doc, Gerry and see what has me ill. It was the shaking and dizziness made me rush out of the party last night. I'm sure they all thought I was gone mad or something. Poor Clodagh, after all the organising. Sure I'll have a good night's sleep and I'll go up to Tom in the morning and he'll give me something to sort me out. In the meantime, this drop'll be the ticket. By the time Deirdre comes, I'll be a new man.'

Rory had been at ease around this nice, kind man for half his life and was feeling it now more than ever. He would love to confide in him but Gerry was married to Maria's sister Fiona and he was the last person who Rory could talk to about her death.

'You were out of work early this evening, Gerry.' Rory was eager to keep the small talk up.

'I came by to make sure you were okay and that, and... well... actually... There was something else.' Gerry had an uncomfortable look on his face. 'Fiona has this idea in her head... she says as it's Maria's... you know... her sister's anniversary today, we could get a few of the neighbours together for a drink tonight. You know, only the ones that kind of knew Maria... after all these years you'd wonder at the sense in it... and of course I don't know why I'm telling you at all now, 'cause you look completely washed out, Rory, and you wouldn't be going anywhere in that state. But say it to Deirdre, will you, if she comes by? I'm delighted I was here to look after you though, with your bad turn and all. Now get that down and no talk of the demon drink or anything out of you. It's for medicinal purposes and it'll do you the world of good.' Gerry drained the dregs of his glass and stood up. 'You're looking terrible, Rory. We might have a refill to get you better.'

'No, I'm fine, I...'

'We'll have one more before I run off to the rest of the neighbours with my message. I better not have a swift few in every house though or I'll be divorced.'

While Gerry was in the kitchen again, the aftermath of the first whisky settled Rory's nerves a bit, while at the same time making his stomach churn. It was Maria's anniversary? How was that? When had he stopped remembering that it was the day after his own birthday? He should never have forgotten. Maria deserved to be remembered. And he *would* remember her. He would bring down that bastard. He snatched the second glass from Gerry with the force of a man with a mission on his hands.

'Easy now. What has you so angry all of a sudden?' Gerry had a surprised look on his face. 'Rory... remember that bit of depression you suffered from when you were living away in London. All the fear you were living under. Would it be bothering you again do you think?'

Rory's hands were beginning to shake. He so desperately wanted to tell Gerry what was upsetting him but he knew he should pull back. At least until he was sure what he was going to do. He'd have to get rid of his friend quickly before he started to probe too much.

'When I lived in London, Gerry, I had everything to be depressed about. I spent sixteen years away from my daughters and missed watching them grow from babies to children to almost adults. I have everything to be happy for now.' He took a deep breath and exhaled. 'It's a cold or flu or something like that and I'll be right as rain in no time.'

The two men sat and finished their drinks in silence. Rory knew that Gerry was thinking about the reason he had given him for leaving Ireland when the girls were babies. He had told his friend that he had gotten in with a bad lot in Dublin. That he hadn't realised until it was too late that they were criminals of the worst sort. He had let Gerry and Fiona in on the secret that he had to run to hide from some gang to keep his family safe. Part of this was true but most of it was made up. It had been enough to make them accept that he hadn't chosen to run from his wife and daughters and it had worked as a good enough reason for them to stay in touch and keep him in the loop throughout his exiled years.

Eventually Gerry stood to go. 'Well if you're sure now? We go back a long way and I've always been there for you, Rory. Don't forget that.'

Rory took the empty glass from Gerry's hand. 'I won't forget, Gerry. Sure aren't you the best sort of a friend a man could ever have? Now get out of here will you, before you have me going all soppy.'

Gerry backed out of the room and fumbled his way towards the back door, looking like he was glad to be getting away from the strange look on his friend's face.

'Cheerio, Rory. Mind yourself now,' and he was gone down to the next house, like a hare in a dog race, with his invitation to Maria Dooley's anniversary drinks.

Rory stared out the window at his retreating back. He didn't move until Gerry was out of sight, giving his message to Gallagher's down below him.

He shuffled towards the kitchen with his fingers wrapped,

once more, around the glass Gerry had given him that was still half full. His intention was to pour the whisky down the sink; to wash it away with its bad smell of past catching up with present; but when Deirdre knocked on the door, Rory was sitting at the kitchen table with the bottle of whisky, almost finished, in his hands and his back to her. When he ignored her, she pushed in the open door and he could feel her disgust at him seeping through his skin.

'Whisky, is it?'

He said nothing.

She sat down on the chair opposite him and put the pot of soup on the table between them.

'I met Mairéad Gallagher on the road, Rory. She was saying there's to be some sort of anniversary party for Fiona Martin's younger sister tonight. Well, I'll not be going, so I won't. I didn't like that wee Maria when she was alive and I'll not go down now and be a hypocrite, so I won't.'

'Yeah?' Rory didn't take his eyes off his glass but he tried to respond.

'Some people in life are best forgotten, you know. Buried away. That Maria is best let go of. She was a bad egg. She put her own mother in an early grave worrying about her, my mother says.'

'Shut up, Deirdre.' Rory spoke slowly and didn't raise his voice. 'Shut... the... wee... fuck... up.'

He didn't have to look up to know that the woman was sitting stock still with her mouth wide open and her eyes jumping out of their sockets.

Chapter four

'ISN'T she beautiful, Rory?' asked Deirdre, as they watched their younger daughter leave the room, all dressed up for her nineteenth birthday celebrations.

'She's bonny right enough,' he answered, trying his best to make conversation.

'Imagine us having daughters of nineteen and twenty, Rory.'

'Comes of getting together so early in life, I suppose.'

'I sincerely hope that they won't *have* to get married though; that they're careful in life and don't let themselves be saddled too early.' Deirdre left a heavy silence in the air.

Rory huffed his annoyance. 'They could fall in love, Deirdre. It happens. Now, do you want me to help you get on with the food for this lot? Get them fed and out – the quicker, the better, eh? There are kids in there wolfing back the booze, who I know for a fact are underage.'

'What's the hurry, Rory? Sure they've only arrived. It's a birthday for God's sake. Mind now that you might enjoy yourself or something terrible. Wasn't it sweet of Clodagh to want to invite a few of us older cronies to her pre-bash before she goes off into town with her friends?'

'Oh, absolutely. And I'm sure it was nothing to do with having free drink to top them up before they go. She's all heart.'

'Why do you have to be so bloody cynical about everything, Rory? Go and make sure that everyone has a drink and keep topping up my friends. Let them toast your daughter properly and don't be such a bloody killjoy. The youngsters'll be leaving at about ten to head to a club, so let them have their fun for now.' Deirdre stormed from the kitchen, cream scarf flying in her wake.

Rory knew he needed to get a grip on himself soon or Deirdre was going to chuck him out of their lives again. He had been like this for too long now. It had been three weeks since he had seen the man on the television. He could feel that he was impossible to be around. For two years he had been all sweetness and light to everyone in Balcallan, to try to win back favour, but now he was jumpy and narky. The lads on the counter at the factory were losing all respect for him. It was a terrible situation and he felt Deirdre was on to him. She was on the wrong trail thank God, but she knew that he was off the wall. Yesterday they'd had the grandmother of all rows.

'Are you having an affair with some married woman or something, Rory?' she had asked.

She was asking him *now*? After all these years, Deirdre was asking him was he full of guilt over something.

'Am I having an affair?' He stared in the general direction of her lap. Anything but her face or her eyes.

'Yes, Rory. I know it's none of my business but if it affects my girls then I'll make it my business. So are you?' Deirdre was calm, Clodagh's party dress sitting on her lap, the hemming at the halfway stage.

'You're having me on aren't you, Deirdre? You don't honestly think that I'm having an affair with someone? Jesus. I came back to Balcallan with enough sins to sort without trying to bring on any more guilt.' Rory tried to laugh, to make light of the leaden words. 'Sure who'd have me? Don't be ridiculous. Where did you get such notions?'

'Well you've changed so much, so there must be something. You're jumpy. You're drinking whisky now. What's going on, Rory? Do you think I'm blind and deaf and do you think the girls have no feelings? Who is it, Rory?' The dress she was altering dropped to the floor as Deirdre stood up and held on to the mantelpiece before raising her voice.

'Is it someone we know? Are you about to make a show of your

21

daughters in front of their friends? Here in Balcallan? Are you? Because they've put up with enough crap from you over the years, without having to suffer from your presence too.'

'Deirdre. I'm not having an affair. I don't even have a legitimate girlfriend. Do you? Have a boyfriend I mean? Are you trying to say that you want a divorce after all this time? Because we should, you know. Make it all legal and such like.'

'Oh, so that's what you want is it? Well no problem. That can be arranged with the greatest of ease.'

Deirdre had been worried about what other people might think.

Imagine.

So today, Rory did what he was told and mingled with Clodagh's guests.

'Can I top up your glass there, Tom? Didn't you walk over to the house, Eiley? You can have another. Isn't your granddaughter beautiful?' Rory kept smiling and filling glasses and chatting to everyone.

He was doing his best to avoid the Martins, as he had been since his discovery, but Gerry sought him out, asking did he need a hand with anything.

'You're grand, Gerry, not at all. Can I get you another can?'

'Thanks, Rory. I won't say no.'

Rory pulled the ring back off the can of Guinness and passed it to Gerry.

'I know this is not the time, Rory but I was wondering was everything okay with yourself? You seem out of sorts lately and I overheard Deirdre in the kitchen saying to her mother that you were turning into a right grumpy little sod... Her words not mine. That's not like you, Rory.' The concern showed on Gerry's frown. 'Maybe we could have a pint down the local later this weekend, and you could talk to me about it. Is it the depression thing that's come at you again? We've been friends this long time, Rory... Whatever it is, sure a chat would do it no harm. Would it?' Gerry stopped, looking uncomfortable with this new role. It didn't suit him. He liked an easy life.

Rory was slowly nodding his head up and down, his eyes fixed on Gerry's. What could he tell the man to shut him up? Gerry Martin was the last person he could tell these troubles to. He had to pull himself together.

'Grand, so.' He tried to push out a smile. 'There's nothing, Gerry, but we'll have that pint. I'll see you down there tomorrow about nine or so. Right? I'd better get a few more cans from the garage or Deirdre'll be after me.' He rolled his eyes to heaven, smiled for Gerry and moved away.

This was crazy. He made his way down the hall and into the garage at the side. He needed time out. Again. It was becoming increasingly difficult to put up a front. No matter where he went, who he spoke to, or what he did; the face of the politician followed him everywhere. He was going to have to do something about it or he would go completely mad.

Fergal O'Gorman was in his head constantly. He had googled his political party again and found that O'Gorman was high-ranking enough without being too much at the front. Handy enough if you're an ex-murderer. He was based in Dublin and Rory had travelled to the capital to see him, incognito of course. He wasn't ready to talk to the man yet and he hadn't even decided whether he would take it any further. He had gone as far as attending one of the party's clinics. Watching O'Gorman shaking hands with his public, hearing their woes and advising them on what to do about problems, promising all sorts of ways he would *look into it* for them; Rory thought he would burst with anger. The bastard. The cold, menacing little shit.

Driving back he had thought of what he might do, but by the time he reached home he had convinced himself that there was nothing he could do. Not without hurting his girls, and what was the point in that? Hadn't he done enough harm?

Sitting on a box, listening to the hum of voices celebrating inside, he relived the enormity of what he had done to Deirdre and his children by running from them with such a weak explanation eighteen years before. He had been so busy feeling guilty about what he had done to his wife and trying to make up for it, that he hadn't actually thought about how *she* felt, truly felt, about him. His recent conversation with her had answered that one. She hadn't asked for a divorce before because she wanted her family name to stay somewhat intact. Their marriage had always been a farce from the day that he had, in his youthful stupidity, thought that putting a ring on it would make everything better. She didn't want him making a fool of their children by having an affair and bringing discussion down on them. She had made that clear. She didn't want to be married to him but found, like he did, that it was easier this way, and there were the girls to think about.

So if Deirdre cared so much about him having an affair now, then surely she'd go crazy if she found out that he'd had an affair a lifetime ago. That shouldn't stop him from ousting this fella though. He should have done it long ago. Maria had been murdered and he'd let the killer get away with it because he'd been scared. The threat from O'Gorman after he killed her left him cold at the memory. He was still frightened – but he owed this to Maria. To *his* Maria.

Rory sat and thought about where he might start. He didn't have enough to go straight to the police so he'd have to do a lot of digging first. He could hire a private detective. He'd think about it.

The door opened and Gerry's wife Fiona Martin walked in with a girl of about Clodagh's age.

'Oh, Rory, I'm... eh... sorry. My cousin Emma needed the loo and the others were full, so Deirdre said to show her where the loo was out here. Sorry to disturb you...

'...Are you okay, Rory?'

Rory was staring at the girl. She looked like her other cousin. His Maria. Those eyes... Maria's eyes, stared back at him. Emma, uncomfortable with the scrutiny, ran into the toilet.

Fiona stared as Rory started to cry.

'Jesus, Rory. What's happened? Tell me, for God's sake. What's wrong?' She crossed the garage to where he was still sitting on the box.

'Maria, Fiona... it's about Maria,' he whispered. 'She didn't overdose... she was murdered.' Rory ran his sleeve over his nose and Fiona grimaced. Oblivious, he continued. 'I know... I was there... I saw it happen... and I know who did it... I saw him... I tried to stop him but he was too strong... I have to tell someone... I'm going mad... I'm sorry, Fiona. I shouldn't have blurted it out but I had to say it... I want to go to the police and tell them what I saw... but I think it's too late now... I've no evidence or anything...'

Fiona was looking at Rory like he was gone mad. Emma came out and stared at the crazy man.

'Emma. Go back in and don't tell anyone that Rory's upset,' said Fiona. 'He's had a bit of bad news. Say nothing to spoil Clodagh's party.'

Emma backed out, looking Rory up and down as if he had grown another head, and turned and ran.

'Shit. I have to go talk to Emma, Rory before she blurts this out; but I'll come back and you can tell me what the hell it is you're talking about. Stay there.' And she was gone, running out after Maria's look-alike. Looking at Emma had brought Maria back to life. Beautiful Maria whose life had been wasted by a syringe, and then he remembered...

Maria's arms had been wrapped around a small, white blanket when she died. O'Gorman had wiped his blood on the blanket after Rory had stabbed him with the needle. Somehow, Rory had ended up with the blanket and was still holding it when he ran from the house.

He had hidden that blanket afterwards. Would it still be where he left it? O'Gorman's DNA could be on it. Would there still be traces of him and maybe the poison from the needle? Would Maria's DNA still be on it? It was worth a try. He would go looking soon. First he had to explain this madness to Fiona. It felt good to let it out but Fiona's poor, crumpled face had upset him even more. Fiona loved Maria as much as Rory did and together they would nail this little bastard.

'What the *fuck* are you talking about, Rory McGee?' She was back, outraged after the few words he had blurted out about her sister's death, had sunk in.

Rory stood up. 'Not here, Fiona. Let's go somewhere else so we don't go upsetting people needlessly.'

'Are you crazy? Spit it out right now. What the hell has my sister's death got to do with you?'

'Please, Fiona. For the sake of everyone in the house can we take this elsewhere?'

'You stupid bastard!' Fiona shouted. 'Tell me what you did or didn't do. Maria. Oh, Jesus. Maria. What happened to you?' Her tears were flowing now and when Deirdre walked in on them, Rory was standing beside Fiona trying to hold on to her while she sobbed her heart out.

'*Her?*' asked Deirdre. 'Gerry's wife?' She shook her head and stared. 'You'd stoop to anything you dirty little shit. Get the fuck out of my house and don't you dare come back.'

Chapter five

RORY let himself into Eiley Sharkey's house using her daughter's key. It had been easy to slip it into his pocket when Deirdre had dropped it in the scuffle that had followed the encounter in the garage. She should've known better than to walk around with a key that said *mam* on it.

This morning he watched Eiley toddle off down the road to mass and he sent a little prayer of thanks upwards for keeping her pious on a daily basis. Eiley never missed morning mass and sometimes they had decades of the rosary afterwards. Then she always had tea with Father Jack. By the time she said her goodbyes afterwards, he reckoned he had about an hour and a half to look for the blanket.

'Hello? Anyone here?' It was easier to make sure the house was definitely empty than to be bumping into any ill-timed visitors that Eiley might have.

He had walked in this door eighteen years ago when he had sneaked back to see his family before going to London. They had been sitting around the table in the kitchen; Eiley, old Barty and Deirdre with toddler Caitríona on her lap and baby Clodagh in the pram.

Eiley and Deirdre had sat and stared at him, in silence. He was in danger, he had said. Got in with a bad crowd and he had to run. He didn't want to endanger them too so there was no time to spare. He'd be going to London and would send money from there. The two women were unable to pretend that they were unhappy to see the back of him. Deirdre had obviously been enjoying her single state and Eiley had never had time for the pup that had made her daughter pregnant and forced her into marriage. As far as they were concerned London wasn't far enough.

Barty had eventually come to the rescue and filled the silence.

'Rory, I've a job in the attic that I need help with while you're here and we'll leave the women to their nursing while we're up there. Eiley wants some boxes shifted and I need a hand with carting them down. Come on now and the girls'll put the kettle on and throw a bit of tea together before you go. Are you right?'

Rory had yearned to stay in that kitchen, to pick up his babies and hold to him. It had also crossed his mind, for a fleeting moment, to take them and run to London and hide away with them. But he had found himself floating behind Barty and climbing into the attic. He had the small blanket tucked away inside his coat from earlier in the week. He remembered slipping it into a box of old school books up there; staring at the pure whiteness of it, tarnished with the bastard's bloodstains, nestled beside the Leaving Certificate poetry book. The sight of it there had stayed with him for a long time after. He was always going to go back and get it when the time was right but...

Now he retraced his steps up the stairs and located the pole to pull down the attic door. Hopefully boxes would have been left there from years ago. He climbed on the banisters and pulled himself up. He was nearly in when he lost his footing and fell backwards, hitting his leg on the corner of the banister.

'Fuck! And double fuck!' Rory held onto his leg and squeezed, as if he could push the hurt out of his body. What excuses could he give Eiley if she came back from mass and found him sprawled across her landing carpet, having fallen out of her attic?

Well you see, I told Fiona all about the fact that Maria was murdered and in the end she didn't believe me, thought I was completely off my rocker, and I thought it would be a good idea to come and see if the blanket was still where I hid it, to show her, and...

No. He had to shake off the fall and deal with it later.

Fiona had been inconsolable at the party when he had explained to her the reason for his outburst. At first she had been furious with him. How could he have kept silent after all this time? Then she told him he was a lying bastard and it was the worst thing anyone had ever said to her in her life and she ran from the garage, pushing past Deirdre as she went. Rory had run out after her but stopped when he registered the key. He knew then that he would be able to prove it to her.

Time enough when he had some proof for Fiona, to go dealing with the likes of Deirdre and Gerry and then the Gardaí. The blanket was the first step but how to get up to the attic had been the problem, so he had come up with this plan. Now here he was on a freezing winter's day, climbing in and falling out of attics.

He hauled himself off the floor and gingerly moved his leg back and forward. It hurt like hell but it didn't seem to be broken. Rory glanced at his watch. Ten minutes gone already and he wasn't even in the attic. He pushed open the door of Eiley's bedroom. It was immaculate with nearly everything coloured a dusty pink. Eiley was once a girly person. When she married first she was probably different. Rory couldn't think of her going into a shop and ordering all this pink fabric. It was well faded now – like it's owner.

Under the dressing table was exactly the thing he'd been hoping for. If he could put that stool on top of the table out on the landing he could reach the attic without having to try and haul himself up. If he fell from that though, he would definitely break both legs and a few other bones for good measure.

Five minutes later he was up and in, shining the torch that he'd brought around the dusty, scattered mess. Eiley's spotlessly clean facade didn't extend to attics obviously. Where would he find the box he was looking for? It had been way at the back years ago. In the corner. It was a box of old school books that must have belonged to Deirdre when she was a girl. Was Deirdre ever a wee girl? He couldn't visualise her. No more than he could the mother.

Rory didn't remember it being this untidy. When Barty was alive he must have kept a bit of order up here. Eiley probably threw everything up that was in her way in the rest of the house.

Out of sight, out of mind. It had a look of someone being up here not too long ago, though. There were certainly boxes that had been moved around recently and marks where belongings had been dragged through the dust.

He started to pull at bags and boxes. It was chaos. Next to where he thought the books should have been was a torn, cardboard box of old photos. Curiosity pulled him down on his knees beside a pile of pictures of his wife as a young girl. So that was what she looked like then. Pretty. Like his daughters were. Delving deeper he pulled out some more of Deirdre as she was getting older. There were none of her since she had met and married Rory. None downstairs in the sitting room either. As if marrying him was such a big mistake that there shouldn't be a record of it anywhere. Eiley, in her badness, had felt something right for once. Rory McGee and Deirdre Sharkey was indeed a match made in hell. He had spent half a lifetime making her miserable, and he hadn't even been around. How utterly stupid. He would insist on a divorce after all this was out in the open and make her move on with her life.

Realising he had wasted time looking at the bloody photos, Rory pulled at a few more boxes. He would have to give up soon and put everything back on the landing. Make himself scarce before the dragon returned, breathing fire on the world. He crawled his way towards the hole in the floor. Near the entrance he put his hand on a book. A poetry book. *An Anthology of Irish poetry for Leaving Certificate.* Rory opened it and started to read a poem by one of Maria's favourite poets, Patrick Kavanagh. He could hear her voice through the words of the poem. Time passed again. Why was this not in the box with the other books? It was lying near the entrance to the attic. It wasn't covered in dust though. Had it fallen from the box when Barty or someone was clearing it? But why would he be clearing that box? There were other memorabilia that he could see had been around for even longer than that and hadn't been touched. Where in God's name was the box? Ten minutes to go. Shit. He'd never be out of here before Eiley returned. He scrambled through the entrance, closing the hatch. He then lowered himself onto the stool below and stopped still as it teetered on the edge of the table. Rory gingerly put a foot back on the table, the stool fell from under him and he went clattering to the floor once more.

A cluster of expletives spilled from his mouth as he rolled back on all fours and pushed himself to standing. He could hear Eiley's voice in the distance. She mustn't have stayed for the tea. Shit. Shit. Shit. Rory threw the stool back under the dressing table and put the other table back against the wall as Eiley turned her key in the door. Jesus, she was coming straight up the stairs. He ran back into her bedroom and flung himself under her bed, just as he saw her two feet come around the door. Thank God for the frilly looking valance thing that surrounded him. Eiley sat on the bed and Rory took a deep breath. She was on her mobile.

'How can you be sure, love? Men go through funny stages when they get older. Your father did. And I could swear to you that he never so much as looked at another woman. I suppose it's a bit like when *we* go through the change. And at the end of the day, it's really none of our business what he does.'

Silence while Eiley listened to whoever was on the other end. Rory was intrigued. Who could she be talking to? There was definitely a bit of village gossip flying around.

'Well, look... if he *is* having an affair with Fiona, you'd better be careful. Leave it with me. I'll keep an eye on him. And would you ever get a move on with the divorce and make sure that you're sorted legally. I'm not having that fella inheriting anything belonging to me.'

It was Deirdre on the other end, and the silly cow was still harping on about him off bonking some married woman. *Fiona*? The stupid bitches. If they fed that idea to his daughters he'd... A thought started to form in his head. What if he was to come out from under the bed right now and scare the living daylights out of Eiley? She'd have a heart attack and keel over and die before she had a chance to change her will. But that said, she'd have to have a heart first. Even so, wouldn't it be wonderful to come out now and tell her that he'd been using her house, every morning for the past couple of years, to carry on his affair while she was out at mass? He had to stifle a laugh. It was getting hard to stay still. He could hardly breathe. There was such a horrible stench under the bed. Was Eiley a bit incontinent at night?

'Look, Deirdre, I've to go and change out of these heels. Will I never learn? The consequences of vanity. I'll see you soon. Bye now, love.'

Rory froze. Eiley's ancient, pink slippers were lying not far from his nose and were one of the reasons that he was feeling sick. He closed his eyes and resigned himself to discovery. At least he would give her the biggest shock of her life.

He almost banged his head with fright when Daniel O' Donnell's latest hit came pouring out of Eiley's mobile and barely managed to stop himself from shouting out.

'Ah, fuck off Deirdre and leave me alone. I wish you'd never given me this fucking mobile phone. Am I never to get a minute's peace from you?' The music stopped and Eiley's voice changed. 'Hello, sweetheart. What's up?'

Rory swore that whatever happened in the next few minutes... if Eiley found him and screamed mercilessly at him and told everybody in Balcallan what had happened... it would be worth it. Rory had heard Saint Eiley Sharkey swear *and* put her daughter down all in the one sentence. Life was worth living. In fact, life was glorious.

'No, Deirdre. I don't think you should tell my poor granddaughters that their father is having an affair. You don't know for sure that he is yet. I told you. Leave it with me. If he's up to anything, I'll be sure to find out. It'd be selfish of you to share your suspicions with the girls before you know anything. He's their father at the end of the day and he's somehow managed to wheedle his way back into their lives, after all these years of neglect. You can't take that away from them now. They've waited long enough for a father, for what he's worth.

'Now you say you rang him at work and Rosemary said he was sick and gone to the doctor? Mmm... Well, when I was passing the factory this morning on the way to mass, his car was parked in its usual spot in the car park. So if he *is* gone to the doctor he'll be back to work shortly or come to collect the car to go home. So I'll tell you what I'll do... I'll go and park nearby and I'll watch out for him. Okay? I'll ring you back later. Now, don't be worrying yourself, Deirdre. I have no time for that eejit but I can't see him having an exotic affair with a married woman somehow. I mean for God's sake, who'd have him? I'll talk to you.' Eiley turned the phone to off and flung it on the bed.

'Does she think I've *nothing* else to do with my days but play private fucking detective to her fucking ex? Does she care that I'm going to be eighty in a couple of months? An affair is it? In this village? Sure you couldn't fucking fart without that lot out there analysing it and turning their noses up at you... Right... Off we go again. No rest for the truly good. Fuck her anyway.'

Rory breathed out as she left the room, her heeled shoes clicking as she went, still safely attached to her swollen feet. He couldn't believe his luck. When he heard the front door bang closed he allowed himself to let out a bellyache of a laugh. Imagine Eiley Sharkey being so privately attached to the word *fuck*. He had never heard her say anything untoward in all the years he'd known her. He wondered had she had such a vice when Barty was alive. And she was going to be eighty this year... Seventy-five she'd been telling everyone. Wouldn't it be a great laugh to hold a surprise party for her? Invite the whole village. He shuffled his way out from under the bed and gasped a few, slightly fresher, breaths. All he could think of was getting out of the house as fast as he could. One hurdle jumped over. Now, what was he going to do about his car? He wished there was someone he could confide in to ask for advice. He was going to have to go and talk to Fiona again.

Rory climbed over the back wall and into the field behind. He would intercept Eiley by coming out of the doctor's as if he really had been there. He made himself literally bump into her and ask after her health. When she had finished telling him exactly what she thought of him, thinking that he had the right to go asking after her like he was a member of the family or something, she couldn't resist asking him what it was that had sent him into the doctor.

'Oh, a touch of depression, Eiley. Been very down recently. Women trouble and the like. You know yourself. See you now.' And he was gone down the street and up to the factory to where he'd left his car that morning before he'd told his boss he had a doctor's appointment.

So he and Eiley had something in common after all. Both were playing private detective on separate cases, one fictitious, both going great guns at it. Well Eiley was. But Rory was running out of steam already. He didn't like all this sneaking around. It actually *was* depressing and a bit scary. He had used the excuse of suffering from depression with Gerry and Fiona in the latter years, as his reason not to come back to Donegal, and it might come in handy again. If things didn't get a bit better for him soon then he *might* need the help of something that the doctor could give him. No pretences.

He kept going.

It was a while before he realised that he was walking towards Gerry and Fiona's house and away from the factory. Gerry would be at work and hopefully Fiona would be home. He had to talk to her or he'd go mad.

Chapter six

'YOU took your time.' Rory was in a strop with Fiona. He was freezing. The weather forecast had warned everybody to stay indoors unless it was urgent. Rory couldn't ever remember seeing snow like this. It kept falling, icing over, then snowing again. It was treacherous to drive but walking hadn't been any simple task either.

'It wasn't easy to get out you know.' Fiona was clapping her gloved hands together and stamping the snow off her boots in an attempt to get her circulation moving again. 'Gerry kept asking me why I wanted to go for a walk in this weather. He must think I'm completely mad. I told him that I was going crazy being cooped up inside all the time. I had to get out. Then he wanted to know who was on the phone. I could hardly tell him it was his friend, Rory, and he wanted to meet me to go breaking and entering into the parish hall. I told him it was Anna. That she called to make sure we were coping alright in the snow.'

'God but you women are great at the old lies, so you are. Where do you get the training in that?' Rory was impressed but wary. It was only twenty-four hours since he and Fiona had sat in her kitchen where she had listened in agony to the story of her sister's last few hours of life. He had persuaded her to tell no one else until they had located the blanket. He was sure it held the proof they needed to point a finger at O'Gorman. The one good thing that had come from his talk with Fiona was that she now seemed as determined as he was to put O'Gorman behind bars. She was still furious with him. She might never forgive him for keeping it to himself for so long. But she recognised the need to work together for now.

'What exactly are we doing here, Rory, with a crowbar? What could you possibly want in here?'

'A box of books, Fiona. I found out what happened to Deirdre's old school books. Eiley sent her handyman up into her attic to bring down a whole load of old rubbish from up there. She donated the box to the Christmas fair last month and the leftover stuff is still stored in the back room here. I mean who would have wanted a load of old school books? They were shoved in here afterwards and were supposed to be moved yesterday but due to the bad weather...'

'And you think that the dirty old blanket will still be sitting in the bottom of the box, even though it's been moved from Eiley's attic into her car and sat around the hall for the fair; and that hopefully the box might not have been tipped over at some point and the contents strewn around the floor? And that some old biddy might not have baulked at the sight of an old blanket with eighteen years of dust and dirt on it, and thrown it in the bin immediately..? I'm away home, Rory. I can't believe you dragged me out here saying that you knew where it was when you hadn't a clue...'

'Wait, Fiona. Let's give it a go. We've nothing to lose. And no one else will be out tonight so we won't be spotted.'

'No one else would be mad enough you mean. It took me half an hour to do a ten-minute walk. And how are you going to explain the broken door to the priest tomorrow?'

'I'm hardly going to own up to it, am I? I'll give you an extra few bob to put into the basket on Sunday to cover it. Come on now. Stand back and I'll get this door open.'

Rory didn't have much problem forcing the rotten lock. He was probably doing the parish a favour. It needed changing and now they could claim on the insurance. He should break up a few other ancient pieces in here while he was at it. They could do with a new kitchen for a start. There was no lock on the storage area at the back of the hall and Rory and Fiona were in there with the torch quickly. Boxes and bags of all shapes, sizes and colours were thrown every which way across the floor and piled on top of each other, some reaching as high as the ceiling.

'Oh, Mother of God, would you look at the state of that. We could be here for a week!'

'We could, Rory, but we're not going to be.' Fiona leaned back against the door and folded her arms.

'What? You mean you're leaving me to do this by myself?'

'No, Rory.' A smile started at the corners of Fiona's mouth and worked its way upwards. 'Your box of books isn't here. It's gone to the library. I remember when I used to help out with the Christmas fair a few years back, all the leftovers *were* stored here afterwards, but all the left over *books* were sent on to the library. They would sort through what they wanted to keep and then the rest would be dumped. Recycled. So we're looking in the wrong place.'

'Now she tells me. There was no chance that you could have remembered that before I broke the bloody lock off the door? Now what do we do?' Rory slammed the storage door shut.

'I don't know. We can go to the library when it reopens and see if they still have the box with Deirdre's books. It's worth a try. I mean who would want to buy a load of ancient school books?'

'But the library won't want them either. They'll probably have dumped them by now.'

'No. I don't think so. They're short-staffed and, chances are, Mairéad won't have had time to do anything with them yet. She told me herself that she was waiting for the transition year students to come in, in February, and help her to catalogue a whole load of books – so we could be in luck. You go into Mairéad as soon as she opens up again and make up some cock and bull story about wanting one of the books back if it was still around. She won't mind you having a look.'

'Sure... And Mairéad Gallagher won't be going telling everyone else who comes in that I was looking for Deirdre's old school books... And Deirdre won't find out and ask me what in God's name I was looking for those for... And I suppose Father Jack won't put two and two together and realise that it might have been me who broke down his door looking for some old book and...'

'For God's sake, Rory you've a wild imagination. The reason men are such bad liars, you see, is they don't know how to keep explanations simple. It's like this... *You were remembering this old poem you used to know at school and you couldn't remember the lines and it was annoying you and Deirdre said that it was in one of those old books that her mother gave away and well, here you are to look.*'

'Actually, Fiona, the poetry book is still up in the attic. I saw it when I was up there before.'

Fiona stared long and hard at Rory and shook her head in despair. 'Yeah... Well... You're right... I'd better go myself...' and she turned on her heels and marched out into the snow again, muttering about men being thicker than planks and some planks being thicker than others.

***

The following Monday the snow had thawed enough for life to resume as semi-normal. The talk in the library was all to do with the break-in over in the parish hall two days before. Fiona listened in amused silence while she waited to speak to Mairéad.

'I heard it was some poor soul who was looking for shelter from the snow. The poor creature. Isn't it bad times we live in when a person can't find shelter, on a night like that, in a town like Balcallan?'

'And nothing was taken. Nothing was even tampered with, so it can't have been vandals.'

Mairéad was enjoying the conversation over the counter. 'Can I help you there with anything, Fiona? Everyone seems to be in to stock up on books to get them through the long old winter days.'

Fiona saw an opportunity. 'Actually, listening to you talk about the parish hall reminded me of the leftovers from the Christmas fair, Mairéad. I was talking to Deirdre McGee about school yesterday and we were remembering a poem that we learned but we couldn't remember the lines. We tried googling it but we didn't have enough information. Then Deirdre recalled that her mother gave an old box of books to the Christmas fair and that the poem was in one of the books... Don't you get all the leftover books here, Mairéad? I'm sure those old books would never have sold. Could I have a quick look do you think?'

'Of course you can, Fiona. I've a key to the room upstairs where all those books are. There's a lot there though... Eh, you know, I'm sure I did see a box of school books going up there now that you mention it. Old... About twenty or thirty years I'd say. Recognised a few of them. Brought me back a bit... Anyway, feel free!'

Fiona walked up the stairs with the hairs standing up on the back of her neck. The box was here. She could be minutes away from finding the evidence that was going to fix that bastard.

It didn't take long to find what she was looking for. It had hardly been touched as it was so obviously full of books that wouldn't sell. Fiona recognised the box logo from the old supermarket that used to be on the Main Street in Balcallan. She pulled back the ancient cardboard and pushed aside the books on top.

It was nestled in among Deirdre's books, exactly as Rory had said he remembered. Fiona reached in gingerly and wrapped her fingers around the off-white, stained cloth. She took it out gently and stared at the last thing that her little sister had held in her hands before she had been killed. What was it about this that was so important to Maria? She held it to her face and inhaled what she hoped would be a familiar smell but all she could get was the musty odour of eighteen years of rest.

Holding it up and turning it around, Fiona could see what looked like rust stains on the blanket.

O'Gorman's blood.

Chapter seven

DEIRDRE was miserable. She sat in her kitchen stirring her cold cup of tea. Again. Nothing was getting any better. She had called Rory after Clodagh's party and told him to stay well clear of her girls. He was nothing but trouble. They had managed perfectly all these years without him and would do so again. She didn't want to hang around waiting for them to be mortified by the town's gossip. He had done enough to wreck their lives and she would have nothing more to do with him now, except to file for a long overdue divorce.

Her mother hadn't been able to find anything on him. In fact she had as good as told Deirdre that she was being paranoid and that the man was only going through a funny stage. A bit depressed or something. She hadn't been to see her for days either. It seemed everyone was avoiding her. The girls had hardly been in the house since the party. Maybe everybody else knew what was going on except her. Perhaps Rory's fling was already the talk of Balcallan. She had no sway over Rory's movements but after everything he had done to them could he not have got himself a decent girlfriend, instead of stealing someone else's wife?

She was sure her mother was wrong. Then, as if she'd conjured her up, she walked in the back door.

Eiley filled the kettle and turned it on. She made a great play of getting the cups out and rinsing the teapot. She then sat down heavily on a chair opposite her daughter but still she said nothing.

'I suppose you've come over here to tell me I'm off my rocker again?'

'No.' Eiley took a deep breath and jumped straight in. 'You were right, love.'

'What?' Deirdre wasn't sure she wanted to hear this. She liked it better when her mother thought she was mad.

'I'm almost one hundred percent sure that Rory is having an affair.'

'Ah, Jesus, Mam... And is it who I thought?'

'You're not going to like this one bit, Deirdre.'

'For God's sake, Mam. You're telling me that my girls' father is about to make a show of them in front of Balcallan! I'm hardly going to *like* it.' Deirdre stood up and leaned on the table for support. Her voice came out as a whisper. 'Who?'

'Look. I'll tell you what I know so far and you can tell me if I'm imagining it. Last week when you said that Rory was not at work when you rang. Do you remember?'

'Yeah. Go on.'

'Well, I said I'd go and check it out and I told you that I bumped into him coming out of the doctor's. But I think he may have fabricated that. Mairéad Gallagher saw him shortly after heading into Fiona's house – and he didn't come out for hours.'

Deirdre was nodding feverishly, wishing her mother would get on with it.

'Then this morning, Bríd Mc Menamin came to tell me something in confidence after mass. She said, on the night of the bad snow she'd been running next door to the presbytery with some milk for Father Jack, when she actually *saw* Rory break into the parish hall with a crowbar. She said she'd been carrying the secret around with her since, not knowing what to do with it. She didn't want to tell the priest. She said she was shocked enough herself at the idea.'

'What in God's name did he do that for?'

'Well... There was a woman with him... My guess is they wanted somewhere in out of the cold...'

'Who, Mammy? For God's sake will you spell it out?'

'She couldn't see who it was with him. The woman was all wrapped up for the snow but she described her coat.

41

'Well I still wasn't exactly sure, but this afternoon I was at the library and Mairéad said that Fiona had been in earlier looking for an old box of books that I had donated to the Christmas fair. She said that she was after the lines of a poem that you learned at school. I mean even I know that you can google these things.'

Deirdre sat back down. 'Well Fiona's always loved poetry, Mam. Remember we went to that creative writing course together. She was always looking for the perfect lines.'

Eiley didn't look convinced but Deirdre couldn't listen to her mother's drivel anymore. She hadn't shown any signs of senility up to now but there were threads of this tale that she couldn't make sense of. 'Mam... What on earth are you on about? What has all this about doctors and break-ins and books to do with Rory having an affair?'

'Ah, Deirdre, do you not see? When Rory left the doctor's he didn't head for the factory but took the road up towards Fiona Martin's house. Bríd Mc Menamin described *Fiona's* coat to me and Fiona was after the lines of a love poem. Don't ask me why... something to do with romance or some such nonsense I wouldn't wonder, but it's there in black and white. It's absolutely true that one of your oldest friends is having an affair with that dirty little toerag. Plain as day. As bold as you like.' Eiley waited while Deirdre took in what she had said.

'Would you like a fresh cup of tea there, love?'

Deirdre sat stock still as her mother reached over and filled her cup. She couldn't mean this. Fiona Martin? She had her suspicions after seeing them in the garage but was still presuming that there was another reason for their argument.

'Are you absolutely sure, Mam..? How could she do that..? I mean, Gerry and Fiona have always been so close. They didn't *have* to get married like Rory and I did... and if they fancied each other that much, why wait all this time to get together? It seems crazy.'

'Well, look love... I went around there to talk to her this evening, to make absolutely sure before I told you, and she wasn't there. Now you might say it was none of my business but

42

I was hoping to appeal to her to drop the whole thing before my beautiful grandchildren got dragged into any more difficulties in their young lives.

'Gerry said she was gone to *Mary Mac's* to meet a friend for a drink. Well I'd been there myself, you know. I thought I could do with a swift hot port to warm me and to give me courage to talk to Fiona and... well, as you can guess, she wasn't there at all. So I sat Gerry down and I told him my fears. At first he was fuming and nearly threw me out of the house, but then he seemed upset and he started to tell me about Fiona and how she'd been acting strangely lately. Since the day of Clodagh's party actually. He was nearly in tears when he told me that Emma, Fiona's cousin, had told him that Fiona was in the garage with Mr McGee for a long time that evening.

'A few days later he found Fiona sitting crying on her own when she thought he was gone out, and when he tried to ask her what the matter was she made up some story about being upset over her sister, Maria. *Maria* who's been dead for the last eighteen years? Now, honestly... You'd think she'd think up a better excuse than that but I suppose she felt she had to come up with something. He's down in the house now waiting for her to come back so that he can confront her... For God's sake, Deirdre, would you stop looking at me and biting your lip and say something. Are you alright?'

Deirdre stood up once more and went to the window. She looked out at the garden she and her daughters had cultivated together for all the years of her struggle through single motherhood. She had used the garden as therapy to help her through the hardship of being an abandoned wife in a small town society. Twenty years of it and she had let that bastard back into her daughters' lives as easily as she had first let him into her bed. It had finished for them as suddenly, and as stupidly, as it had started. But *Fiona Martin*? The wife of the only man who had stuck by him through all the crap that he had dished out over the years. Then again, who had gone along with her husband to see Rory on every trip, but his faithful wife? Poor

Gerry. He must be broken-hearted. Rory McGee should pay for everything that he's done. She would certainly start the divorce proceedings but there must be something else she could do to him to get even.

***

Having lied to Gerry that she was going to *Mary Mac's* to meet a friend, Fiona had gone to meet Rory. She threw her coat down beside her and sat in front of the glass of red he had ordered for her.

'I could have done without this, you know,' she told him. 'All this cloak and dagger business is beginning to piss me off. And a pub two towns away is pushing it a bit. In any case it's about time we told Gerry about it. We need his practical nature to help solve all this.' She picked up her glass and threw back half the contents in one gulp.

'You're right,' Rory replied. 'I can't seem to recognise the wood from the trees the way I am at the moment. I'm falling apart to be honest and it would be good to get another brain working on this. You and I were too close to Maria. Gerry will see it from another perspective.

'We're further on than we were when we started the search though.' Rory was shuffling some beer mats with the excitement of knowing that Fiona had found the blanket. It was years since he'd played cards. He liked the feel of them in his hands. He might take it up again. At least it would get him out of his lonely apartment.

'Not much, Rory. We have a blanket now but no way of knowing if it's still any use to us as evidence to nail my sister's murderer. There's little we can do and I want it over. It's time to stop creeping around and let the Gardaí take it from here.' Fiona sniffed. 'There's a part of me wishes you'd never told me about this. I feel like she's died all over again and now I have to go through a different kind of grief. But after tonight I don't want to pussyfoot around anymore. Okay?'

'It's all I can think about at the moment, Fiona. Ever since I saw that guy on the television. He won't leave me alone. I'm plagued by the whole thing. I haven't slept properly for weeks and I can't manage it all on my own. I've had to get the doctor to certify more time off work as I can't face anyone. There must be some way we can prove it...'

'If there is, Rory, you can let the Gardaí at it.'

'But all these years later, Fiona, will it be enough evidence? We have to have more on him than my say-so, to get them to believe that he did it.'

Fiona looked over at Rory.

'You must have loved my sister a lot to feel like this all these years later. Poor Deirdre.'

'Yes. Poor Deirdre. She's suffered too much from all this. She called me the day after Clodagh's party and told me to stay clear of the girls. She keeps harping on about me having an affair with some married woman. As if I didn't have enough problems in my life without going looking for more.'

Fiona downed the rest of her drink and stood up. She put on her coat with the distinctive buttons up the back.

'I'm going home to my husband and I'll not lie to him for one more moment about what I'm up to. I've had enough. He'll tell us to go to the Gardaí. So that's what we'll do now.'

Rory watched her walk out, to drive back to her lovely home with the fire blazing; where her adored husband was waiting for her. He wished he'd had such a lovely life. Lucky Gerry. The best thing Rory had going for him was his family, and he wouldn't let Deirdre keep him from his girls so easily – not after everything he had done to get them to forgive him. Maybe it was time to go see her and tell her the truth about what had happened when she was a young bride all those years ago. She deserved a proper explanation. And maybe, in time, he would be able to explain to his daughters how he had left them for their own safety. That it was Fergal O'Gorman who had taken him away from them. They would understand that it was time to make him pay.

Chapter eight

GERRY sat in his sitting room. What else could he do? He couldn't put his thoughts together in any coherent form. He wanted to tell himself that this wasn't happening; that it was all in Eiley Sharkey's imagination. There was *another* reason behind all the rubbish that Eiley had told him. But what about all the differences that he'd noticed himself? He knew his wife for most of their lives and he knew that she'd been keeping something from him. What other explanation could there be for all the time that she'd been spending with Rory McGee?

If it was true, then what could have brought this on after all these years? Rory and Fiona had known each other forever. It had taken a lot to get her to trust Rory all those years ago, on the back of what he had told them about his reasons for leaving Deirdre and his children. But she had relented and given him the benefit of the doubt.

Whenever they had gone to London they had always called to see him, giving him news of his family and watching him crying over photos and stories of his girls. Deirdre and Fiona were friends. Poor Deirdre had always used Fiona as the go-between for getting in touch with Rory when needed. And he himself looked on Rory as his best friend. Was Fiona going to leave him? And what about their daughter? What about Deirdre and Rory's girls? Did they have any idea when they were starting out on this *affair* that it would affect so many lives?

For God's sake... Now he was even thinking of it as if it was actually happening. Believing that his wife, who he worshipped, didn't love him anymore? That she might leave him to live with another man? What was it all about... all those years that they had grown together, if it wasn't to grow old together?

Gerry loved Fiona. He had never loved anyone else and he had never believed that she would either. He leaned forward in his seat and put his head in his hands. Tears came and his body shook. Suddenly, he heard Fiona's key in the door and he tried to pull himself together; but thinking of talking to her about all this made him worse, and he cried harder.

'Oh, Jesus Christ, Gerry... what's the matter? What's happened? Tell me...' Fiona was with him in seconds. She put her arms out and took his hands. 'Has somebody died or had a bad accident? Please don't let it be one of our own,' she said. 'Come on, Gerry, for God's sake, tell me.'

Gerry looked up at her and the look he gave her was not one of grief, but of fear... He pulled his hands from hers and took her by the shoulders, staring hard at her.

'It's not true. You tell me that for sure, Fiona and I'll believe you.' He stood up and walked towards the drinks cabinet. He poured himself a large whisky and downed it in one. He poured another and turned back to his wife. Fiona was sitting on the floor by the chair he'd vacated; a look of confusion on her face.

'What's wrong, Gerry? Tell you what's not true?'

Gerry walked across the room and stood over her. 'Did you enjoy your drinks in *Mary Mac's?*' He frowned at her. 'All your friends well are they?' He looked down at Fiona's face as it began to redden slightly at the neck and then work its way up to her cheeks. Was this confirmation? No way. He had known in his heart, until now, that this was nothing but another way for Eiley to stick her oar in to other people's business. But the look on Fiona's face was definitely telling of something.

Fiona spoke to her husband's distorted face, her words filled with panic. 'I wasn't in *Mary Mac's*. Gerry, I was going to tell you soon... I've finished with it anyway. I told Rory tonight. I don't want any more to do with it. It was all a big mistake to try and go it alone... It's time to involve everyone now. It was...'

'What?! It was *what?*' Gerry's drink splattered over the rim of his glass.

The only time Fiona had ever seen him so annoyed was when she had gone off looking for information on Maria after her death. Was this all about Maria? He had never liked her when she was alive and he had always thought that Fiona should put her death behind her and get on with her own life. Maria had been the only thing that they had argued about over the years. And now here they were again. But this was different. Fiona had never seen Gerry acting with such aggression.

Gerry turned back to her and she could see that he was crying again. This was crazy. This was all out of proportion to what she had been doing. It wasn't that bad. And if he hadn't had such a bee in his bonnet about everything to do with Maria, she would have been able to tell him in the first place. She pulled herself up, reaching for the coffee table to steady her. She would sit him down and talk to him. She walked over to where he was standing by the fire; staring at the dimming flames. Fiona reached a hand and put it on his shoulder.

'I'm sorry, Gerry. Let's sit and talk about it. I've told Rory to leave it now. It's gone. It's finished. I've hated all this going behind your back. I'm glad it's all out in the open now.'

'Out in the open?' Gerry stood with his eyes closed, gripping the mantelpiece for support. He pulled himself free of her hold. Opening his eyes again he glared at her and raised his voice. 'This is not happening. I can't believe that you would stand there and apologise and say it's all over, as if that would make it all better. No. You're talking rubbish. There has to be an explanation.'

Fiona backed away. She started to cry too. What was going on?

'Gerry, I don't understand. What are you saying? You're upset. You're not making sense.'

'I'm upset?! Of course I'm goddamn well upset. Sit down on that chair and tell me exactly what it is that you want to get off your chest. Tell me that Eiley has it all wrong.'

Fiona's tears stopped. She looked at the expression on her husband's face. She started to smile and then to laugh at the mention of Eiley. 'Eiley has what all wrong? I'm sorry but if Eiley Sharkey has something to do with your strange humour then we must be at cross purposes. Sure what could she know of what me and Rory have been trying to do?'

Gerry's face lost a little of the fear but then he registered what she'd said. 'What you and Rory have been trying to *do*? For God's sake what is it, Fiona? What's going on?'

Fiona let out a long sigh of relief as she explained the bones of the story about Maria and Rory and O'Gorman. The more she said the better Gerry looked. When she was finished he seemed to be delighted with himself. This wasn't what Fiona had been expecting at all.

'You seem happy that my sister may have been murdered. What did you think I was going to tell you, Gerry? What did Eiley tell you I was up to?'

'Of course I'm not happy to hear that. Eiley had it all arseways anyway. I knew. I told her that there would be a perfectly good explanation for what she thought she saw. But she was adamant. I hope to God she heeded my warning and didn't mention it to a soul.'

'Eiley Sharkey not mention something to the whole town? What was it, Gerry, that you told her not to mention?'

So Gerry went on to tell her about how he had felt over the last few weeks, knowing that there was something up, and then about Eiley turning up and telling him all that crap.

'Oh, Gerry… Where in the name of God did she get an idea like that? *Rory McGee*? Are you mad or what? He's one of your oldest friends. What's going on?' But the smile began to fade from Fiona's eyes, then from her mouth, and a look of apprehension came over her face.

'Who dreamed this up, Gerry?'

'It wasn't only what Eiley Sharkey said. You've been acting so strange and as she said herself… everything leads to the time you and Rory have been spending together.'

'You can stop right there, Gerry.' Fiona was getting angry now. 'I've given you a perfectly good explanation as to why I have been spending so much time with Rory McGee lately and you can rest assured that it has absolutely nothing to do with us having a bloody affair! The very thought... I've only ever put up with our visits to him because you two go back through the hurling team. After all these years how could you give credence to something that Eiley Sharkey, of all people, conjured up?'

'Ah, but I knew she was wrong, Fiona.'

'You did not! You were crying when I came in.'

'That was shock. Once I realised how ridiculous it was I was fine.'

Fiona felt an anger creeping into her stomach and moving its way up towards her throat. She felt sick. Everything she had ever held dear in their relationship was being mushed to pieces.

Her husband didn't trust her.

Fiona ran from the room and barely made it to the downstairs loo where she threw up. Holding on to the cistern with both hands, she tried to steady herself. She reached over and pulled a piece of toilet roll to wipe her mouth. A wave of despair fell over her, pushing all thoughts of Maria and Rory out of her mind. She flushed the toilet and put the cover down, then sat on the seat and leaned her forehead on the cold sink. The only thing that mattered was the trust that she and Gerry had always had for one another and now it was broken. Fiona sat and cried, letting her thoughts relay one on to the other until she had a whole team of negative ideas washing around in her brain.

Gerry stood where Fiona had left him. Fiona wasn't having an affair. Of course she wasn't. Fiona... his beautiful, loving, caring wife would never do that to him. What had he been thinking? And she was so upset. He could hear her in the bathroom. What had he done? As soon as she came out he would go to her. They'd pour a drink. They'd talk it over like they always did if they ever encountered a problem. He heard her coming out of the loo and heading up the stairs. She was gone into their bedroom, so he followed her up. He knew that he had a lot of making up to do. If Fiona ever accused him of having an affair he would be very upset too. But whatever it was that she *had* been up to with Rory she should have included him. That was the kind of marriage they had. He pushed open the door with trepidation. He wasn't sure, exactly, what he had been expecting but Fiona in the middle of packing a bag was the least imagined scenario.

'What are you doing?' Gerry looked at his wife in disbelief.

'I'm going to Dublin to stay with Anna. I need to clear my head. I can't believe that my husband thinks that I'm having an affair.' Fiona continued to look for toiletries, shoes and clothes while she spoke in a monotone voice to Gerry. She was in shock.

'Excuse me, Gerry,' she said, after she had zipped up her bag, and moved to pass his stunned figure in the doorway. He couldn't believe that he didn't even try to stop her as she stomped down the stairs to her car.

Gerry was astounded. Maria had managed to come between them again; eighteen years after her death. Rory was a witness to her murder? What was she talking about? This was ridiculous. This kind of behaviour was for young ones. Senseless arguments that led to giving up on relationships before they'd even had a chance to develop. But walking out on a marriage that was cemented in trust and love and dependency. That was incomprehensible. She wasn't walking out though, was she? She was going away to stay with their daughter for a few days to clear her head. Isn't that what she had said? Let her off. It was a good idea. He needed time to get over his own shock anyway.

He stepped back and let her go.

Chapter nine

DEIRDRE stood up from the kitchen table. She had sent her mother away an hour ago. No point both in them sitting in vigil over their findings. She had refused her mam's offer of a drink but she was beginning to think that it might be a good idea. Eiley had called as soon as she arrived home, to report that she had seen Fiona roaring out of Gerry's house, down the road with a face on her like thunder. She was obviously not pleased about being rumbled.

Had Fiona called Rory to warn him that the game was up? Were they already heading off somewhere together? She wouldn't put it past him to leave without actually telling her daughters he was going. Did he think so little of them though, that he'd leave it to somebody else to tell them what a disgrace he was?

She heard the doorbell as she was pouring her gin into the glass. She ignored it, the rage inside her making her pour twice as much. She was going to need it. She went to the fridge to get ice and orange juice. She felt him come in through the back door, into the kitchen behind her, and heard him clear his throat. Preparing for a confession? Her hands clenched around the glass; her neck and shoulders tense.

'Sorry I let myself in, but I knew you wouldn't answer the door if you thought it was me. I needed to come and tell you something. I have to clear the air between us once and for all. I think we should get a divorce. But before we go down that road I want to get you to promise that what I'm about to tell you won't interfere with the relationship between me and the girls.'

What did he say? Was he *serious*? He expected her to stand back and allow him to break up someone's marriage and tell

Caitríona and Clodagh that this was normal behaviour. Deirdre felt tears of rage rise up and she blinked them away. She wouldn't shame herself but she was getting angry already. She backed away from the fridge and closed the door.

'You'll not see hide nor hair of my girls, Rory.'

'You're wrong, Deirdre. They're grown adults now, capable of doing what they want. I did wrong by them all their young lives but I'll not mess up what I've built now.'

Deirdre turned around, the full glass in her hand. He was leaning against the back door and staring straight at her. He didn't look at all ashamed of his actions. On the contrary, he looked proud, as if what he was about to tell her was all that was needed to explain his life away.

Rory gasped in shock at the bubbling waterfall that cascaded on course to his face, before the cold ice hit him all over like bullets.

He fell forward, knocking the bin to the floor, dripping gin and orange all over the place; coughing and spluttering and then staring in disbelief.

'Deirdre! What the fuck was that for? Are you gone *completely* mad?'

Deirdre saw Rory's look of disbelief, as if she had no right to fling her drink in his face. She had no choice now but to give in and let the tears take over. She slumped down on the nearest chair, gripping the empty glass. It was okay to cry. It was to be expected. But Deirdre knew that she was crying for what had gone before and for the shame her girls would have to go through when everyone heard about this. That their philanderer father had done it again – except this time on his own doorstep, with Fiona Martin. The gossips would have a day and a half.

Rory reached over for the kitchen towel and dried himself off while staring at Deirdre. He didn't take his eyes off her for a second.

'I came today, to tell you the truth of what happened to me eighteen years ago and you go mad before I even open my mouth about it. So whatever it is I'm supposed to have done, other than what I've come to tell you, I'm sorry.'

He was sorry? Just like that? And he didn't even have the grace to let her know that he realised what was wrong with her? That she knew. He was going to make her spell it out? Well she wouldn't give him the satisfaction. She held up the empty glass and letting out a primeval roar, threw it hard. She hadn't meant to actually hit Rory. She was so full of anger and she wanted to throw something, and if Rory hadn't moved suddenly towards her she would have missed, as she had meant to. But now he was standing there screaming obscenities at her and there was blood spilling out of his head and *Jesus*, what had she done?

'What the fuck is wrong with you, Deirdre Sharkey? For fuck's sake get something to hold against my head.' Rory held his fingers over the cut to try to stop the blood. 'Jesus, there's something in it. There's probably glass embedded in it. What the fuck have you done?' He grabbed hold of the towel that he'd forgotten was soaked in alcohol and shoved it against his head before letting out a roar.

'Agghh! Fuck it! And *Fuck* you!' Rory swerved as the alcohol and acid from the juice on the towel seeped into his wound, and then he dropped down.

Deirdre looked at her husband lying on the floor of her kitchen, more blood coming from him now that he had fallen into the broken glass. My God, she'd need an ambulance. She ran to her bag, pulled out her phone and somehow managed to give the details to the person on the other end.

She sat on the floor beside him, oblivious to the splinters of glass that were digging into her legs. She felt his pulse. He'd be okay. Had some glass been pushed in further when he had held the cloth to his head? She was afraid to hold anything else against the flow of blood in case she did any more damage, but it was still coming. She stood in the kitchen staring at her handiwork and found herself wondering how her life would be if Rory didn't regain consciousness. You could die from head injuries. The thought jolted her from her reverie and she knelt beside him and began to talk.

'Rory... Rory, you're scaring me half to death here. Come on. Wake up, Rory. I didn't mean to hurt you. I don't hate you that much. I don't want anything that bad to happen to you. Can you hear me, Rory? ... It was the shame of it all, you know?'

Deirdre reached over and took her husband's limp hand. 'When I thought that you were seeing a married woman I was mad for the girls' sake, but you know, when I heard about who it was... well I completely lost it and... well for God's sake, Rory... Fiona bloody Martin of all people. I can hardly believe it of her. I've known her all my life and she's never put a foot wrong. Ever. She always made me feel inadequate or something. Well she's certainly played a blinder this time.'

Rory opened his eyes. He moved his head and tried to pull himself up. He was dizzy but he was going to be alright. Was it the mention of Fiona's name that brought him around? Deirdre let go of his hand and pushed herself back up to standing. By the time the sirens blasted their way into her driveway she was composed once more.

She rushed outside to meet the paramedics, only to find Mairéad Gallagher was coming running from her house with a stream of people behind her – most of whom had the decency to hang back a bit.

'What happened, Deirdre? Who's sick?'

Deirdre stared past the ambulance at Mairéad and allowed her voice to be heard by the spectators. 'It's Rory. He's had an accident. He fell on broken glass... on his head.' This last bit was directed at the ambulance crew and she ushered them into her house and her kitchen and stood back while they worked on Rory and carried him out on a stretcher.

The crowd had moved nearer to the house. Mairéad's family get-together had just become a lot more interesting. Deirdre looked nervously at them and stood as near as she could to the stretcher. She caught Rory's eyes as he was moved towards the doors of the ambulance. They seemed to be reassuring; that he wouldn't say what happened. Or were they blurred and dizzy? It was hard to tell.

'Has he had a lot to drink?' one of the paramedics asked her.

'What? No.' What was he talking about?

'There's a terrible smell of alcohol off him. Are you sure?'

'Yeah. I'm sure. It was, ah never mind. He's not drunk.'

But the damage was done and the Gallaghers would have a field day with the story.

Later, Deirdre sat by Rory's bed while he slept off the pain in his head. The surgeon had assured her that he had removed all of the glass from the wounds and that no permanent damage had been done. Rory would have scars, some of them for life, but that was the extent of it. Scarred for life, like their family. There was no going back from this. Deirdre stared at the man she had referred to as her husband when the ambulance crew had arrived.

What the hell were we trying to do, Rory, getting married for the sake of social niceties? You thought you were great to stay with me. So like Rory McGee to stand by the woman he knocked up. ...If you hadn't though Rory; if you had abandoned me then; it would have been better for us both. I would have had a better life... I would have found someone to love me.

Immediately she shook the thought away. How could she even think about what life might have been like without her beautiful daughters?

A nurse had been trying to get Deirdre to go and have a cup of tea or something. Her husband would stay asleep for a while, she had said. No way. Deirdre was sitting right here until he woke up. She had told the doctors and nurses that he had fallen on glass and she was sure that they believed her. She had to know that Rory said the same thing. Would he believe her that she wasn't even aiming for him or could he think that she would be angry enough to do that to him on purpose? He would have to be persuaded to stick with her story. He owed her that much at least, after all he had done to her.

Deirdre looked up in utter amazement as the door of the ward was pushed open and Gerry Martin walked in. He looked around at the other beds until his eyes settled on her. He stopped and looked towards Rory in the bed. He shook his head from side to side. Was that a look of compassion? Deirdre didn't understand. Surely he should be delighted that the man who was trying to run off with his wife was lying in a hospital bed recovering from head wounds. She watched him move hesitantly towards her, then looked away. How were you supposed to react in front of the husband of the woman your ex-husband had been having an affair with? There was no manual. He sat down on a chair on the other side of the bed and leaned over Rory.

'Deirdre... What happened?' he whispered. 'Tell me it wasn't a fight. Mairéad Gallagher next door said that Rory was drunk and had fallen on broken glass. Why was there broken glass? What in God's name went on? Is he okay, Deirdre? Tell me he's going to be alright.'

'He's fine, Gerry,' she whispered back. 'He'll be fine. More's the pity the dirty little bastard. How could you sit there and be all concerned for the man that deceived you anyway? I never meant for *this* to happen but I can tell you and nobody else that I'm not sorry.'

Gerry leaned back in his seat and stared at Deirdre. The woman thought that Rory was having an affair with Fiona. Of course she did. He had almost believed the same himself a few hours before. She had probably thrown the glass at Rory. He wondered would Deirdre feel as bad as he did when she found out the real story. He lifted his hands and rubbed at his temples. This day couldn't get any more complicated. Now he was going to have to prise Deirdre away somewhere quiet to explain to her the reasons why she should never have hurt the man, because apparently he was completely in the clear. Gerry had wondered in the course of the evening what on earth Rory McGee had been doing anywhere near Maria when she died, but he was more worried about the row with his wife to give it too much thought. Deirdre would be much more interested in that part of the story. He supposed as Rory had been living in Dublin he must have run into her at some point.

'Deirdre. Come and have a coffee with me. I need to talk to

you.' He watched her look nervously at her husband. 'Don't worry. He'll not say anything to anybody if he wakes up. Come on. This is all going to sound a little bit strange but you know it's so crazy that Fiona couldn't have made it up.'

In the morning, Deirdre was woken by the noise of her mobile. She jumped up, thinking it was the hospital but then she saw her mother's number come up on the screen and she lay back down on her pillow. She couldn't face Eiley yet. Obviously the antics with the ambulance had spread around the village like wildfire.

Her mother had told her that she was imagining it. That Rory McGee would never be having an affair. But then she changed her mind and she had managed to persuade Deirdre that he was. Eiley had managed to convince poor Gerry too and now Fiona had left him to go and stay in Anna's. And *she* had nearly killed Rory because she was so full of anger with him and blamed him for every sorry event in her life. Was she that shallow?

Deirdre answered herself and buried her head under her pillow.

Chapter ten

ST Bridget's Day – officially the first day of spring in Ireland. Birds singing, blue skies, buds on trees, lovers loving and all's well with the world.

When Rory woke up that morning in his hospital bed he felt like shite. His head was thumping. He could hear the rain bucketing against his window. He had spent the night dreaming of men with glassy eyes coming at him with syringes – but at least he was decided.

He was going to oust the bastard that had fucked up his life.

When he had woken late in the night, Gerry had been sitting in the chair beside his bed, ready to tell him all the details of the day. Now Rory realised why his wife had put him in the hospital. He also realised why he should never have married her. Why he should have followed Maria twenty years ago, after Deirdre had lost the first baby. And why he had to tell the whole truth about what had happened eighteen years ago, no matter who was dragged under. If Deirdre thought he might have shamed her with the bit of an affair he was supposed to be having, she'd have an apoplectic fit when she caught up with this lot.

This last bit made him smile.

He had been discharged from the hospital and Gerry was coming to pick him up. He would stay with his friend for a few days while he was recovering. While he waited, he sat on the bed and picked at the breakfast with one hand while he tried to straighten the hospital gown over his rear end with the other. The sooner Gerry arrived with some clothes...

'Any of that left? I'm missing Fiona's cooking.' The voice behind Rory made him turn and smile. That wasn't all that Gerry would miss from his wife. He was going to need some support over the next few days while Fiona recovered herself and came back to the man who would be lost in life without her.

'Throw us over those clothes, quick. I feel naked in this garb. Exposed to the world.' Rory pushed away the food trolley and swapped it for the plastic bag that Gerry had thrown some of his own clothes into. Thankfully there wasn't too much difference in their sizes. Rory's own clothes were destroyed with blood and glass and he had asked a nurse to throw them in the bin for him. He wanted no reminders of Deirdre's mad antics the night before.

An hour later he was sitting in the Martin's sitting room listening to Gerry explain to Deirdre on the phone that Rory would prefer not to speak to her for a few days but yes, he would go along with the idea that he had fallen on glass in the kitchen. She was not to worry on that count.

'No, Deirdre.' Gerry continued. 'I haven't heard from Fiona yet. I expect she's still licking her wounds and will be for some time. What I suggested to her last night, expressing my lack of trust in her, was far worse than what you did to Rory. I imagine he'll get over his injuries a lot quicker. I still can't believe that you and your busybody mother managed to plant even a seed of doubt that Fiona would betray me like that. It wouldn't be possible. In future you can try to sort out your own problems without dragging other people down with you. Goodbye, Deirdre.' Pressing the red button, he flung his mobile down on the floor.

'Will you have a drop, Rory?' Gerry moved towards the drinks cabinet.

'It's ten-thirty in the morning, Gerry.'

'Does that mean no? All those years you wouldn't touch anything but a pint. You have a lot of catching up to do. I need a hair of the dog.'

He poured a large one.

'It wouldn't react well with all the medication that the nurses have me on.'

'Ah, shove your medication in the bin and get that inside you. It's much better for you.'

Gerry poured another large one for himself and put the bottle down on the fireplace where it would be handy. He pulled the heavy curtains and lit a fire and the two men sat back in their easy chairs and raised their glasses.

'Now, there you are. It's evening after all. I'm not answering the door and I'm not answering the phone. Cheers.'

They sat in comfortable silence for a few minutes. Rory was the first to reach over and pour another whisky. He took a sip. 'It's a great help to the head.'

'Don't be making excuses. Drink and enjoy.'

Another silence. Not so comfortable this time.

Rory knew that Gerry wanted to talk but he felt that talking about Fiona would only upset his friend more. So he brought the conversation away from her to himself, and the big issue that had brought them to this situation in the first place. He told him about Maria. Not everything, but enough to explain why he had been working with Fiona so much.

'And you kept that to yourself all these years, Rory. Giving me a false reason why you couldn't come home to Balcallan. That you were running from a bad crowd and you needed to keep your family safe. Bloody Maria. I can't believe that a sensible man like you would ever have had anything to do with her. When she was alive everything she touched turned bad. She could upset the world with a look. And since she died, well the only properly cross words Fiona and I have ever had were always because of something or other to do with Maria. She was bad news. She still is.

'The only time she ever did anything useful was to give birth to Anna and to abandon her after. Thank goodness she didn't even do that right and Fiona and myself were able to find her and adopt her ourselves, after she died. And there's nothing of her mother in our Anna, thank God. She's more like her grandmother. Sonia Dooley. Now there was a lovely woman. Not many men say that about their mother-in-law. Maria was more like their father I think.'

'I may have met her birth father, Gerry. Anna's I mean. His name was Dónal. Maria was in a relationship with him in Dublin for quite a while I think. She never mentioned the baby but O'Gorman had Dónal killed before Maria died. I hated him because it was his fault that we lost Maria. I loved her, Gerry. I loved Maria.' Rory stopped and sat back while his friend absorbed this. The last time Gerry had seen Maria she had been a wild young thing.

'When *you* knew Maria she was a troubled teenager,' added Rory. 'But she was beginning to grow up... before she was killed.'

'But I don't understand that. Who would murder her? Why? And you say that this guy is a well-known and respected politician now. And what were you doing there? Are you sure you have all this right? It's been a long time.'

'Pass the bottle, Gerry. I'll tell you what happened. And tomorrow, when I'm feeling a bit better, I'll go down to Dublin and talk some sense into that wife of yours.'

Chapter eleven

ANNA Martin pulled the little red Fiat into the car park of her apartment. College had been tough all day and she was in need of some time out. She knew she was privileged to be staying in her uncle's flat in Dublin while he was working in the States, and to have his car too was a dream. A big change from last year's student accommodation and public transport. She was spoiled and loving it but she was dying to send her mother back to Donegal and get her newfound independence back. For now though, she had to go in and listen to a third evening of Fiona crying about leaving her father and never being able to trust him again. And the news that Fiona had delivered to Anna about Maria had caused Anna to cry herself to sleep last night, while she listened to her mother cry in the next room.

Adopted from a young age, Anna had grown up knowing that Maria was her real mother. She knew that she had died young and Fiona had brought her sister's daughter up as her own. As Anna had matured, asking more and more questions, Fiona eventually had to tell her that Maria had died of a drug overdose. There had been mention of Maria's boyfriend but when they tried to trace her birth father they came up against a dead end.

Now her mother was telling her that Maria may have been murdered. It was like losing her all over again, her mother had said. Anna felt like that too. Dealing with this, and the fact that the couple least likely to was talking about separating, was more than she felt she could cope with. This is what happened to other people.

She dragged herself out of her car and locked it. She then started towards her door but stopped dead. A man was lying with his back to her, across the front doorstep of her ground floor apartment. His head, which was covered with a bloody bandage, was resting on a plastic bag stuffed with clothes. He had a long black coat draped over him.

She was about to turn and run when the man turned over and Anna realised that it was her father's friend, Rory McGee. Her hand went to her mouth.

'Is my mother okay?'

'I don't know Anna, love.' Rory sat up a little. 'She won't open the door though I know she's in there and I've been freezing my arse off out here for the last two hours.'

Rory looked at the doubt that fell over Anna's face.

'Your father sent me. He's upset.'

'I'm sure he is, the stupid eejit. Imagine thinking that Mammy would ever have an affair. Are you not upset yourself?'

'It's an ill wind and all that, Anna. The relief of finally having an excuse to live a life of truth is immeasurable. We could talk out here all day if you like but I'm freezing and my head hurts like hell. I... eh... fell on glass... or something.'

'My mother'll go mad if I let you in but come on. It's stalemate otherwise.' She helped Rory up and turned the key in the door.

'I knew you'd let that troublemaker in, so I'm leaving to stay in a hotel.' Fiona was inside with her packed bag in her hand. Then she saw Rory's head and her caring instinct took over.

'What in God's name happened to you, Rory?'

'I...eh... fell on glass... or something. Fiona, stay for a few minutes. I need to talk to you.'

'Stay, Mam.' Anna took hold of her mother's arm and gently turned her around towards the kitchen. 'I want to hear what Rory has to say. About Daddy... but about Maria as well. And I need you to be here too.' She looked at her mother beseechingly.

Fiona looked at Rory. He looked a wreck. His eyes were all bloodshot. The wound on his head certainly needed looking at. And she couldn't believe he had left Donegal for Dublin carrying his belongings in a plastic bag. Rory saw where her eyes were focussed.

'They're not even mine. They're Gerry's. I stayed in your house last night. I was in hospital the night before. Deirdre knows the truth now.'

Fiona put her bag down. 'You've come clean about Maria and you think you're in a good position to come here and lecture me. Sure. Good one, Rory. Sit down and let me have a look at that wound. Tell me exactly what happened.'

'I'm not entirely sure but I think Deirdre threw a glass at me. Or in my general direction anyhow and then to make matters worse I fell on the broken glass. But the official story is the one I told you first.'

Rory sat down in the kitchen and Anna threw her handbag and the day's newspaper down on the table, before setting about making a cup of tea. She fancied something a bit stronger. A good night out with her pals. She wondered how much longer her mam would be staying. Did Rory think he was staying here too? Where would she put him? She put the mugs out and filled the teapot. Her mam liked it all done properly. The apartment was immaculate. It was nice to come home to, but... well; she preferred to do her own thing in her own way.

'Wouldn't you agree with me, Rory, that mammy should at least go back to Balcallan and talk to Dad about what's happened? It was a complete misunderstanding. That Mrs Sharkey is a right old interfering cow. I can believe that Deirdre went along with what she said. It *was* her mother after all. But for dad to believe her so easily.'

An uncomfortable silence swept through the kitchen. Rory was staring at her mother and waiting for her to speak. Fiona was staring at the front page of the newspaper refusing to say a word. Anna opened the fridge. No milk. She could pop out to the shop for a few minutes and they might get on with talking, instead of sitting there staring at nothing.

'I'm going out for milk. I'll be back in a jiffy. Neither of you are to move from there 'til I get back.' Anna headed towards the kitchen door as her mother reached for the remote control and flicked on the six o'clock news. She looked determined to give

Rory the silent treatment.

'Do you think you could turn that crap off for a few minutes and listen to me, Fiona?' Rory's head felt like it might explode. Since Fiona had *sorted* out his bandage for him he hadn't been able to think straight. How was he going to get her to listen to him pleading Gerry's case? He had to get on with working out his own life.

'Fiona...'

'Shut up, Rory. I'm listening to this.' Fiona was glued to the television. That girl was in the news again. Looked like all those crazy reports about her were about to be wrapped up. He zoned in on the story.

...and thus ending the nightmare that has been Shona Moran's life over the last few months. A spokesperson for Ms Moran said that she was delighted with the result of the charges being dropped against her but not surprised, as she has always insisted that she was completely innocent and that there was never any evidence to suggest that she had played a part in any crime.

Eighteen-year-old Ms Moran's relationship with the terrorist Jameel Al Manhal, and her disappearance after the attempted bombing on the 8th of August in St Stephen's Green, brought authorities to believe that she was involved in the attack in some way. Her spokesperson has asked for Ms Moran and her family to be left in peace, to get on with their normal lives...

Fiona was still staring at the television.

'It's a strange story all the same, Fiona. No smoke without fire, I'd say. She's a shifty-looking one, that one, wouldn't you say? There's something about her... I dunno...

'Fiona...' She was still staring, even though the story had moved on to something else. Rory reached out and pressed the off button on the remote. 'Fiona... what are you staring at? Would you turn around and talk to me? You have a crisis on your hands and you're ignoring it and we can't, love. We have to talk about Gerry... Fiona...'

'The 8th of August she said? The woman on the news...' At last Fiona was responding. But what was she talking about?

'Stick with me here, Fiona. Anna'll be back in a few minutes and I want us to talk about Gerry while she's gone. The poor man is sitting at home by the telephone waiting for a call from you to say he's forgiven. He's a thick eejit. You're right there. To think that you and me would ever be having an affair. No offence or anything like that but we've known each other for most of our lives, Fiona, and you're Gerry's wife and all that... and well, I don't fancy you.' He thought that might get her attention but she had only turned back to the table and was reading the front page of the Irish Times. Unbelievable. Here was he, down on his knees begging her to go back to Gerry, and the woman was reading the bloody newspaper!

'Fiona! Are you listening to me?'

'It says here that Shona Moran is eighteen years old, Rory.'

'Yeah, right, Fiona... now about Gerry...'

Fiona looked up at Rory; her eyes brimming with tears. She was listening to him after all. She turned the paper around and pushed it towards him. She prodded the picture on the front page.

'Look at her, Rory.'

'Yeah, she's a sad-looking little thing alright.'

'No, Rory. I mean *look* at her. You of all people must see the likeness. Her eyes... and her smile... and the way she's kind of biting her lower lip even. Who does she look like?'

'I don't know, Fiona. I suppose she's a bit like Anna. Yeah, she's a lot like her. Is that what it is? Is it because she has a look of Anna about her?'

'The woman said, Rory, the woman on the news, that Shona Moran is eighteen years old. And I heard somewhere else that the bomb was planted on a day she was on her birthday outing. I never connected with her before. I suppose it's all this talk of Maria lately and all that you've been saying about how she died. Well I haven't been able to stop thinking about her. And that time after she died...'

'Fiona, would you ever stop rambling and tell me what you're trying to say, 'cause I haven't a clue what you're on about.'

Fiona shook her head and said 'you're right, Rory. You're absolutely right. It couldn't be her. And she *has* a mother and father. I saw them on the news. But it's the dates. They're absolutely spot on, you know, her age and all... and she looks like her... but you're right... she couldn't possibly be hers and anyway, I don't even know for sure if Maria *had* another baby...'

'Maria had another *what*?!' This from Anna standing in the door with her eyes boring a hole in the back of her mother's head.

Rory turned to look at Anna, and Fiona tried to hurriedly dry her eyes. Rory threw Fiona a warning look. He didn't have a clue what she was concocting in her damaged head but he felt that whatever it was, it had to wait. Anna Martin had been through enough shocks lately. She needed a break.

But Anna wasn't going to let it hang. 'I heard you saying that Maria had another baby, Mam. What are you talking about? Jesus Christ! The one thing you've said to me all my life was no secrets! Yesterday you tell me that my mother didn't overdose. That she was murdered. Now you're talking about another baby? A sister or a brother? For God's sake what else haven't you told me over the years?'

'Anna, Fiona's not herself at the moment. She doesn't know what she's talking about...'

Anna locked eyes with her mother. 'No lies you said.' Anna's look challenged her mam. 'Maria was my mother. If she was murdered and Rory has any proof that this happened, then I won't stop until I've uncovered everything I can about it. But, Mam, I want you to know if I find anything out on the way that might say that you've lied to me over the years, even by omission, then...'

'I've never lied to you, Anna. That's the truth...'

Rory interrupted. 'Fiona, this is definitely not the time to go telling Anna mad thoughts that're going on in your head and have no substance whatsoever.' But he knew by the look of determination on the faces of these women, that whatever was going on was about to be aired and God help the consequences.

'Fiona! Leave it!' Rory was pissed off now. The whole Maria story was getting out of hand. 'Fiona! If Maria had another baby, I would have known. This child you're talking about... I was with Maria in the days before she died. If she had recently had a baby I'd have *known*! There weren't even enough months in the time that Maria was gone to have two babies before I found her. So stop there, Fiona. Alright? Anna, your mam has had a few shocks over the last while and she's not thinking straight.'

Fiona looked back down at the picture of Shona Moran on the front of the newspaper. 'You didn't know back then that Maria had had Anna, Rory. How would you have known whether or not she'd had a second? I don't know, Anna love. I don't know that Maria had another baby. It was only a hunch... Something one of her flatmates said to me.'

'But Anna was born less than a year before that. Weren't you Anna? She wouldn't have gotten pregnant so soon again after giving birth,' said Rory. The two women went quiet.

Fiona closed her eyes and thought back to that time... Her darling baby sister... She would have to explain to Anna... No secrets... She'd promised...

Chapter twelve

'OH Maria…' Fiona sat at the table and clutched the newspaper with the pictures of Shona Moran to her chest. Eighteen years on and her heart wasn't finished disintegrating yet. Eighteen years since that knock on the door.

'Mrs Martin?'

Fiona stood stock still.

'Something's happened to Gerry,' she thought. 'Oh please, God no.'

'Can we come in?'

'Of course, sorry.'

'Let's sit down, Mrs Martin.'

'Of course, sorry.'

'Mrs Martin, it's about your sister, Maria.'

Fiona was so relieved to hear that Gerry was okay. And here they were saying that they'd found Maria too. Her smile filled her whole face.

'Oh my God, you've found Maria. Oh thank God. Where is she? Did you bring her home? Is she alright?'

The Gardaí shuffled uncomfortably in their seats.

'I'm so sorry. There's no easy way to tell you this.'

'We've found a… girl that fits Maria's description. Mrs Martin, the girl was found dead in a squat in Dublin, having overdosed on heroin. I'm… so sorry, Mrs Martin.'

Fiona sat still in her chair. They were wrong. It wasn't Maria. Maria loved life. She was wild but she enjoyed living. She would never do this to herself.

'Where is she; this girl?'

'In Dublin. In a hospital morgue.'

'Mrs Mar... Fiona, we need someone to go to Dublin. You know... to...'

'Yes. I'll come. I'll need to make some arrangements. I'll drive down this afternoon.' Fiona couldn't believe how calm she was being.

'We'll tell them to expect you. We're so sorry.'

All the way to Dublin, Fiona convinced herself that it wasn't Maria. It couldn't be her. Maria was too strong. She was too full of life to be...

When she was finished with the business of looking at this poor girl, she would resume her search for her missing sister. Her beloved Maria. There had to be something they hadn't thought of. Somewhere they hadn't looked. If anyone could feel their way to Maria, she could. Two years was so long. She must be ready to be found now.

'I'm coming Maria. I'll find you. I'll bring you home.'

A few days later she *had* brought her beautiful baby sister home. For a week Fiona had practically lived by her graveside; talking to her. Two years of talk.

'Why did you leave us Maria? What could have been so bad that you couldn't face us? We loved you so much. Where did you go? Why did you hide? We tried so hard to find you Maria. Where were you? Were you punishing us Maria? Were you punishing yourself? Where were you...?'

'Eighteen years later and all the hurt is still there; still raw. When will it all stop?' Fiona placed the newspaper back down on the table. The memories wrapped around her like blankets, each one suffocating her more.

'I wanted to find those *missing* years, Anna. I went back to Dublin. Now that Maria had actually been found and wasn't trying to hide herself; it was easier to retrace her steps. I started at the beginning and found you, Anna. So quickly.

'You had been fostered twice from the home but they hadn't

been able to have you adopted. They hadn't been able to find your birth mother. Of course there was a lot of red tape to go through, but once they ruled out the chance of finding your father, we had no problem with adopting you. We were a long time going up and down to Dublin, and while we waited I ploughed through the rest of Maria's time away. What I found... it was terrible...

'Maria had lived in so many different places, under so many different names. She had made herself invisible. Impossible to find. I wondered at the time how she had fed her drug habit. She never seemed to have a job and hadn't applied for social welfare. She had never been in trouble with the police for stealing. Was there a wealthy man out there who had been supplying her with drugs, Rory? In return for what? I had so many questions that would never be answered. The drug scene was a closed world where people asking awkward questions were never invited in.

'But Maria's last squat had been the most distressing. Her *friends* there had slurred something about her being pregnant. They thought she was but she would confirm it to nobody. Then she disappeared for a while. When she came back she wasn't pregnant. That was a month before she died. She hardly came out of her cloud after that. Then one day she didn't wake up.

'I tried everything I could think of to find out if there had been a baby. There was talk of a boyfriend but he had disappeared without trace and was wanted by the Gardaí. There had been a few leads, but so many name changes brought me to dead ends again. Eventually... I gave up. If there *was* a baby I knew I might never find it. Then I wondered if there had been but Maria had miscarried. I thought that this could have been what had driven her to overdose. Too many maybes, though.

'But one certainty. *You* Anna. Gerry and me brought you home. It filled the gap. It covered up some of the hurt. For eighteen years you've been *my* baby girl. And you still are. I've often thought about the baby that might have been. But eventually I convinced myself that I was wrong.'

'And you're still wrong, Fiona.' Rory was looking pale. The bandage was seeping again. She would have to bring him to a hospital if it didn't stop. 'You said yourself that this girl in the paper had parents. You saw them on the news. She wasn't brought up in a home or something. She isn't Maria's baby.' He looked over at Anna. 'Or *your* sister, Anna.'

Anna picked up the paper and studied the photo of Shona Moran.

'Mam. This is all too much. She does look like me and like the photos you have of my mother... and there's one other thing.'

Fiona and Rory looked worriedly at Anna, both thinking that she probably couldn't take any more of this.

'What, Anna love?' Fiona dried her eyes with her sleeve.

'This girl... you know when someone is trawled through the media... they print out all sorts of trivia... like they said she has a baby girl called Ruby by a guy called Tommy who she doesn't live with... well... *she* was adopted, Mam... I know because it was the one part of her story that I zoned in on.'

'It still means nothing,' Rory wanted to get off the subject. He grabbed the paper from Anna and threw it on the table. Then he picked it up again, peering at the first paragraph. 'Jesus.'

'What, Rory? What do you see?' Fiona moved in to look over his shoulder. Rory was pointing to the first line in the write-up.

All charges were dropped against Shona Moran today...

'Shona. It's like...'

'God you're right, Rory. If Maria had a baby, she could have called her after our mam... Shona's the Irish version of Sonia.'

'But she had me first, Mam. She called me Anna. You said that you were told that my mother had given me my name.'

'Yes, love,' Rory said. He had a faraway look on his face. 'Your mother's name was Maria Anna Dooley. She did give you her own name.'

Fiona picked up the newspaper with Shona's picture on it. Shona's face. Anna's face? Maria's face? She closed her eyes and spoke to her sister.

'Maria, tell me what to do.'

Anna shook her head. 'Jesus, Rory. You've already opened up a crazy can of worms with your talk of my mother's murder. This is all too much.'

'Maria *was* murdered, Anna. I was there. I saw it happening and I couldn't stop it. Afterwards I ran away. I'm not proud of the fact, but I was scared. I ran all the way back to Balcallan and on to London to hide and never looked back. Until now. I tried to forget and I nearly managed. But now I've found the man who killed her. I have to do something about it. I can't leave it anymore.'

'But how could you have been there, Rory?' Anna was looking exhausted. 'You would have been married to Deirdre at the time. Your daughter Caitríona is my age. What were you doing in Dublin when Deirdre and Caitríona were back in Balcallan? My mother was five months pregnant with me when she left Donegal. Did you know her then?' Anna reached for the chair and sat, not taking her eyes from Rory who had gone pale as this question began to sink in.

'Anna… you were born at the same time as my daughter Clodagh. Gerry wrote and told me that… after you found her, Fiona.' Rory was shaking.

Fiona was looking from Rory to Anna. 'Jesus, Rory. Anna was born the same time as Caitríona, not Clodagh… Rory? Were you with Maria before she left for Donegal? Jesus, tell me you weren't the bastard who got her pregnant and let her run off to Dublin on her own…'

Tears stung at Rory's eyes as the significance of what Fiona was saying began to sink in. 'Maria was pregnant when she ran away? No, she couldn't… she would've told me… And she had Anna a few months later? So Anna's not Dónal's child…'

Rory felt like he was going to vomit as he realised the significance of what was happening.

'I didn't know she was pregnant, Fiona… I swear Anna; I never knew why she left…' His eyes pleaded with them to believe him. 'I went to Dublin after her and looked for her everywhere. I knew that before she left she had overheard that Deirdre was pregnant with Caitríona. I thought that she had run because she was so angry with me about that. But I had no idea that she was…'

He let the tears flow and a howl of pain left him.

Anna stared at Rory and even as she said the words she knew…

'Tell me you are not my birth father. For fuck's sake.'

'I swear to God, Anna love. I never knew. By the time Gerry told me that they had adopted you, I thought that you were Dónal's baby. He said that you were born the same time as my own daughter and I thought that he meant Clodagh. Jesus, Fiona… Maria *could* have had another baby after all. She and Dónal were certainly together for a while. I'm sorry… Anna, sit down. Please. I'll tell you what happened. I'm so sorry we've had to find out like this.'

Anna let out a whimper and Fiona moved to wrap her arms around her daughter but she flung her away.

'Leave me be! You told me you had no idea who my father was…'

'Oh, God, I meant it, Anna. This is the first I knew that Rory was with Maria before she went away. I thought they'd got together in Dublin.'

'You're both lying! You knew this. You had to have known. It's as plain as anything.' Anna went to push past her mother.

'Where are you going, Anna?'

'Anywhere away from here. I never want to look that bastard in the face again. He's a lying piece of shit!'

'Stay and hear me out, Anna. Please.' Rory was begging.

Anna picked up the nearest mug and flung it at the wall, then sent the other two crashing beside it. She wailed her distress and ran towards the door, leaving the milkless tea residue dripping down the walls.

Fiona and Rory stood still for a moment and by the time they shook themselves and moved after Anna, she was speeding down the street away from her adopted mother and her birth father. Rory turned to reach out to Fiona but she screamed and dived at him with her fists.

'If I find you had anything to do with my sister's murder; if there're any other secrets you have tucked away, I'll fucking kill you, Rory McGee.'

He caught her two arms and steadied her.

'I only knew what I told you, Fiona.'

'You bastard liar! You knew you'd been fucking my sister before she left Donegal.' She shook his hands away from her. 'God help me but I'll find out the truth about what happened to Maria and you'll damn well fill me in on everything you know.'

'I didn't know about Anna, Fiona. I never had any idea.' Rory shook his head and wiped tears away. 'Whatever I do know I'll share it all with you. And with Anna too when she's ready. I know I've lied in the past. At first it was from fear. Then it was to safeguard the new life I'd made when I came back to Ireland. But no more lies now. I'll tell you what I know of Maria's time in Dublin and we'll try to fill in the gaps.'

As Fiona ran to the bathroom, Rory dropped to the floor of the hallway, hugged his arms around himself and rocked back and forth.

'Maria,' he sobbed.

Part two

Chapter thirteen

I SIT on top of the dunes, hugging my knees, looking down at Rory on the sand. I'm beginning to feel cold, but I won't give up my seat in the *Gods* of this outdoor theatre. August is withering away to make room for September and although the evening sun looks radiant in its orange cloak, there's little heat left in it. The dying light is catching the tips of the waves as they make their way in towards Rory and as they seem about to reach him they race away again. *Tripping the light fantastic* as they go. Now where's that from? Something by Milton? Rory's right. If I'd paid any attention at all to my schooling I'd have done well.

If school was only for learning it would've been fine but the nuns and all their rules made me dread the daily ritual. I've spent most of fifth year in trouble with Sister Ignatius, in trouble with teachers, in trouble with my parents and in trouble with my friends' parents. I'm the talk of the town. I can almost hear them as I'm passing on the street.

'Did you hear about the antics of that Maria one this week? No? Well, wait 'til I tell you...'

My poor mother.

When Mary Carr introduced me to a little weed this year *to take the edge off life* I was ready and waiting. Drinking and smoking with the best of them and the worst of them, I was a walking mess. Dropping out of school was inevitable and God knows where I would have ended up if I hadn't become friends with Rory.

I watch his hands now, gripping his hurley stick with a look of fierce concentration on his face. Each time he whacks the sliotar down the beach, I hear him let out a loud, frustrated grunt. Then his collie, Duffy, sprints after it, spraying sand every which way in his wake before tearing back to his master, ready to drop it at his feet and earn his undying love and gratitude. Then he does it again; each time with more effort; each strike, a blow against the world. How much anger and frustration can fill one man? The sound of his ranting rises up towards me.

'To hell with the lot of you, you waste of spacers!' Another wallop of the sliotar.

Balcallan beach is a favourite haunt for both of us and this summer has been the start of something lovely between us. He's the only person who makes me feel like an adult and I suspect he enjoys my company because it makes him feel closer to the youth he's been forced to let go of. Bumping into Rory on the beach at the beginning of this summer has been the best thing that's happened to me. I hate the crappy *receptionist* summer job he put me forward for in the glass factory where he works though. More like general dogsbody and tea lady. But I get to see Rory every day and I hug that feeling close to me as I watch him now with his dog.

We were the only two people mad enough to be out walking in the lashing rain that day in early July, and it was easy to strike up a conversation. We found in each other a willing listener. Many liaisons later, I've decided that Rory's the closest person I've had to a proper friend for years. He's persuaded me to stay well clear of Mary Carr and her cronies. He tells me that an intelligent girl like myself should be out there working towards going back to school and showing the world what I'm made of.

'Never mind anyone else,' he says. 'Do it for yourself. Look after yourself.'

And I am. With Rory there to guide me I can rule the world.

Such a shame he's married, I think, as I watch him flex his well-honed muscles for another bash at the sliotar. Years of training for hurling and Gaelic football have given him the body of an athlete. I've never taken up any sport. In fact I've never managed to let a hobby take more of my time than the occasional passing fancy. I suppose I could take on a bit of camogie. My family'd be delighted with that. Rory could train me. I've never picked up a hurley stick in my life, though. Never even went to cheer on my school at their matches. I could have a go. Why not?

'Hey! Rory!'

I enjoy watching his downturned mouth turn upwards in a smile at the sight of me running down the dunes towards him. When I hit the bottom I can't stop and he has to reach his arms out to break my run. I let my hands rest on his shoulders. I like it like this. It's only a friendly gesture but it feels nice. I'd like to let my hands keep going. Slip them around his neck and pull him close.

Looking at his face though, I'm not sure yet if it's what he wants.

'I've been watching you from up there, Rory. What's with the bad temper?'

He lets go of my shoulders and turns away. 'Ach, you know. Domestic stuff. Nothing you'd know anything about, Maria.'

'Are you sure about that? Being the youngest in my house means that everybody thinks that they have every right to tell me what to do and when to do it. Believe me, I know about it. I'm living my life for the day I can leave home.'

Rory drops onto the wet sand and I drop down beside him. He takes my hand and I feel all the warmth of him travel through me.

'I thought like that only this time last year,' he says. 'Now I've swapped my mother telling me what to do for Deirdre telling me what to do. And *her* mother is the devil himself. Making us get married because Deirdre was pregnant was such a stupid thing to do. My own parents were dead against it. I wish I'd listened to them now. I feel *well* trapped.'

'Would you feel the same if Deirdre hadn't lost the baby? I mean, I know when my mam lost babies my sister said she was hell to live with for a long time afterwards. Won't Deirdre be better when she gets over the miscarriage?'

I don't want him to say that she will.

'I'd like to think she might, Maria... but... at the end of the day... well... I know I'm such a bastard for saying this... but I don't love Deirdre enough to be married to her. It all happened so quickly. I wish to God I could get up and leave but you know what it's like in this town. You get up and get on with it. Leave your pipe dreams for watching drama on the television.'

I squeeze his hand and smile. 'So that's why you're trying to send that sliotar into outer space?'

'Only if I can go with it... I came straight from the training ground today. I was dropped from the county team at the end of the league and now I've been left on the bench by the manager of the Balcallan team. Deirdre stopped me going to training too many times with her constant weeping and wailing. Apparently I've become unreliable. Not a *team player* anymore. I've lived for hurling, Maria. Nothing else mattered when I was growing up. It's all that's kept me in Balcallan. If I've to spend the rest of my life going to my dead-end job and coming home to Deirdre, then outer space wouldn't be far enough.'

I try to keep the panic out of my voice. Rory here with Deirdre is better than no Rory here at all.

'If they saw you hitting that ball they'd never let you go. There'll be nothing left of that sliotar by the time you and Duffy are finished with it.'

Duffy, at the mention of his name, jumps all over me, his new pal, and slobbers across my jeans.

'I've had to leave poor old Duffy with my parents since I married. We've been inseparable all these years but living in a flat isn't any use to an active dog like him. I miss him.'

I reluctantly pull my hand away from Rory to concentrate my attention on the dog. I stand up and pick up the sliotar before throwing it far, and Duffy legs it down the beach again.

'You've a great throw, Maria. Have you never done any sport?'

'Not if it involved movement, Rory,' I laugh, 'but I was watching you with the stick and the walloping. It'd be a great stress buster. Would you give me lessons?' I know my look has a dangerous glint to it. I've been perfecting it.

'Well, you'd have to join a team, Maria, to play properly but I could certainly get you started. Teach you the hold first and a bit of balancing the sliotar.' Rory bends down, picks up the sliotar that the dog has dropped at his feet and puts it in my hand.

'Yeuk! It's all covered in dog slime and sand.' I throw it for Duffy again.

'Okay.' Rory grins at his reluctant student. 'Let's try the hurley. This is how you hold it. Which is your dominant hand?'

'My what?'

'The hand that you write with.'

'Eh, my left.'

'Oookay. Let me try and turn everything around here. *There's* a challenge for me. Now your left hand is going to grip the top of the hurley stick and your weaker hand is locked underneath. Okay?'

'Yeah… why?'

'Just do it, Maria.'

'Oh, I love a man who's being masterful.' I let him see that glint again.

'Are you going to take this seriously? You need to hold it like that to help you when you're striking the ball. Here let me show you.'

Rory stands behind me while I hold the stick. He puts his hand over my left hand and moves it so that we're both holding the same part.

'This part here is called the top.'

'You don't say.'

'I do.'

He moves his hands down the stick and as he does he moves closer to me. He puts the lower part in my right hand. 'Down here is called the bas.'

'You mean the base.'

'No. I mean the bas. It's in between the toe and the heel. The toe is thin to allow you to pick up the sliotar from the ground and the heel is thick to give strength to your strike.'

I'm not actually listening to the end of this. Rory's whole body is pressed up against my back and his gorgeous, strong hands are wrapped around mine. I never want to be anywhere else for the rest of my life. I can feel his heartbeat through his t-shirt and I imagine what it might be like if he reached down and kissed the back of my neck. The idea makes me shiver with delight.

Rory lets go and I turn around in surprise.

'You're cold,' he says. 'Did you not bring a sweater? These evenings are beginning to get a bit chilly and your clothes are wet from the sand. You should get away home now and keep warm.'

I feel myself deflate. I'm angry with Rory now. I know he doesn't deserve it but it's there anyway. I've no right to expect anything more than friendship from this man but it's hard not to. And hasn't he told me that he doesn't even love his wife; so what was all that about? *If* he doesn't... I turn on my heels and start to walk away. There are tears stinging my eyes and I can't let Rory McGee see that he's upset me.

'I'll see you soon then, Maria. Make sure you go home and get changed.'

'No chance, Rory. I'm away into town to hang out with Mary Carr.'

'Maria...'

'See you sometime, Rory.'

And I run away up the dunes and down the road I came only an hour ago, when I was feeling so full of myself. I let the tears stream now. I remember a time when I was small and the top had fallen off my ice cream. I'd wailed, and all the older members in my family had roared with laughter, which made me cry more. By the time my howl became a full-blown tantrum they were splitting their sides at the spectacle. That was the last time that Maria Dooley has ever been the source of entertainment for anyone.

Rory McGee's a little shite. As bad as the worst of them.

Chapter fourteen

RORY lay in his bed about a thousand feet away from his wife who was lying about a thousand feet away from *him*. He felt that if they accidentally touched it might result in physical pain. He couldn't figure out why they were still sleeping together. He was sure that Deirdre felt as repulsed by him, at this stage, as he did by her. She hadn't let him touch her since she had lost the baby and that had been three months ago. Not that he wanted to touch her in any romantic way but he had tried to comfort her by holding her hand or putting his arm around her once or twice; and she had snatched herself away from him with one of her withering looks that left him feeling sick. Four months married seemed like a lifetime and the future stretched in front of him like a life sentence. Rory wanted to talk to Deirdre about them sleeping separately but he was afraid to mention it. He should move into the spare room himself. Why should he ask her opinion? He could slip out now when she fell asleep. She probably wouldn't even notice.

He looked over at Deirdre and, as usual, was surprised to see that she was actually a pretty girl. When she was sleeping and her face was relaxed, losing all those vexation creases, she was almost beautiful. Those big, long eyelashes she'd inherited from her father's dark looks were like curtains gone down on an extravaganza. But he knew as soon as she woke she'd take on her mother's pinched face and those green eyes would glare accusingly at him. For *what* he was never sure. All Rory had done since the day that Deirdre had told him she was pregnant was tell her that he would look after her. Whatever she chose to do he was right behind her. She had chosen marriage. The baby had died shortly after, along with any feelings that Deirdre and Rory had for each other. If the baby had lived they would be getting closer now to being parents and there wouldn't be that big gaping hole to fill.

And Rory wouldn't be lying here trying to think of something; anything; that would take his mind off a certain dark-haired, bright-eyed beauty. He had spent two months telling himself that he only needed a friend... and that Maria needed a friend. They had talked so much about their respective lives and dreams and they had become close. Maria had only turned eighteen but she had a grown up's head on her shoulders and was often able to put life into perspective. It was from growing up in a house where she was the youngest. Sonia Dooley must have been getting on when she had her second daughter and it was difficult for Maria to relate to her mam. The generation gap was momentous. And of course Sonia was originally from Spain. So there was a culture gap there as well. And as for the father... the village drunk. No wonder Maria had grown up wise.

So he had to remind himself that she was still a kid. There were only a few years between them but Maria was going to go far when she pulled her head together. Rory was stuck in a dead-end marriage with a sales job. So why shouldn't he lie here and dream about Maria? That afternoon at the beach had been completely explosive. When Maria had her hands sitting on his shoulders and her lovely face turned up towards his, he had never desired anybody as much. So much for being friends. Rory had had to use every form of denial in his make up to stand clear of her. Those eyes... Where Deirdre's pushed him away and tore him to shreds with one stare, Maria's eyes invited him in to paradise. And paradise was where he was for a few moments when he had his arms around her and his body pressed against her back during her hurling *lesson*.

Oh, Maria, Maria, Maria... Six months ago he would have been free to pursue her and the gap between them wouldn't have seemed much. He was a big deal in the town. Captain of the local team and selected for the county team where he was beginning to show what he was made of. His job wasn't terribly exciting but his boss had been talking about sending him to do his sales exams at night. Girls were falling at his feet. He was Rory McGee and he was *somebody*.

Six months later he was dropped from both teams and he was hanging onto his job by a thread. Deirdre was a distraction – but the wrong kind. Rory knew that if Maria had been his distraction he would have been filled with a drive that would have put him at the top of his sport and given him the wings he needed to fly high in his career. But instead, he was well and truly landed in a load of crap he couldn't manage to claw his way out of.

He wanted to be with Maria and to protect her from all the harm that life could throw at her. He had spent the last two months helping her to realise her own self-respect, while Deirdre had worn him down slowly but surely. He had persuaded Maria that she was clever enough to go far in life. All she had to do was go back to school in September and drop that Mary Carr, and it had been working too. She hadn't seen Mary for weeks.

Until today.

What was it that had pushed her in Mary's direction again? Had he made her think that there was more to their relationship than friendship? Had she felt the desire in him sitting on the sand holding her hand? They had held hands a few times before, but today he had found it impossible not to show her how he felt about her. Maria, his beautiful Maria, could have feelings for him too and he had pushed her away. But did she not realise? He wasn't available. He was married to Deirdre. Father Paddy had said *Do you?* and he had said *I do* and here he was *forever and ever 'til death do us part.* Rory shivered.

There was no point trying to stop himself thinking of Maria. He had to have something nice in his head or he would go mad. So he allowed those thoughts to have free reign. Him and Maria on the beach the first day they had bumped into each other in the pouring rain. Taking shelter in the rocks beneath the cliff face. Later in the summer, walking out towards Muckish Mountain, breathing in the freshness of the heather after the soft sprinkle of rain. Standing beside Deirdre at mass on Sundays, catching glimpses of Maria standing beside her mother. Small smiles noticed by nobody but the two of them. Maria and him, driving out of town all the way to Letterkenny in his dad's car on a Sunday afternoon, when he had seen her at the bus stop and offered her a lift. Letterkenny, where they could stroll through the streets unnoticed and unknown. And today. The picture of Maria running down the dunes and into his arms. Well, that's how he liked to think of it. And holding her. Having a legitimate excuse. Who was he kidding? Maria no more wanted a *hurling* lesson than he wanted to give one. And then he thought he had seen someone up on the hill looking down at them and he had used her shiver to let her go. To send her home. He knew by the way she had run that she was hurt. He should have run after her.

Walking through town later that evening he had seen Maria laughing and shouting with a group of teenagers on the corner, by the chipper. He had kept his head low and tried to go unnoticed but Maria had shouted some abuse over the road at him. She was well and truly high at that stage. He had wanted so much to go over to her and insist that she go home and to smack that Mary Carr over the head with his hurley. Once should do it. It wouldn't take too long to wreck the few brain cells that were left. But he had no say over what Maria did or didn't do. He had no right to interfere in her life. So he had to leave her to her fate.

He wondered had she managed to get home. Was she safely in her bed? Hopefully her sister, Fiona, had found her before her mother did. Or worse, much worse, her father. He wished he knew. He wanted to be part of Maria's life; to save her from herself and to hold her and kiss away her worries. He imagined what it would be like to be there for her, to stick the broken pieces back together when they shattered, caressing her back to smiling, stroking her beautiful face and easing away the worry lines and...

Rory took a deep breath and sat up suddenly in the bed. He tossed his feet over the side. He needed a cold shower. He stood up and felt his way in the dark, groping for the handle before opening the door. The bedside light flew on and his wife sat up. One look at Deirdre's condemning eyes was all the cold shower that Rory needed.

'I think I'll go out for a walk, Deirdre.'

'In your pyjamas?'

Rory looked down at his attire and smiled. Before he married Deirdre, he had never worn pyjamas in his life. He had come home one evening and found them laid out on the bed. Nothing was spoken but Rory took it as an understanding that this is what Deirdre wanted him to wear. Like everything else he had gone along with it. If he kept up this attitude he would go mad. Life had to change.

'No, Deirdre. I was opening the door to let in a little light to find my clothes. I was trying not to wake you.'

'Well you failed in that. Like everything else. What are you going out walking for at this time of the night? It's half past eleven.'

He smiled again. Before he married Deirdre he would never have been anywhere near his bed at half past eleven on a Friday night. He was turning into a right auld fella.

'I can't sleep, Deirdre.'

Brushing past the end of the bed his thigh touched her foot and he pulled back and felt his leg burning. He bent down and picked up his clothes where he had tossed them on the floor earlier to annoy her.

'I won't wake you up when I get back. I'll eh... kip down in the other room; so as not to disturb you. I'll come in like a mouse.'

There. It was done. He had moved into the spare room.

She was lying on the side of the road. The one that led down towards the beach. He thought that she had been knocked down at first; the way she lay like a rag doll; unmoving. But when he ran to her and turned her over she started to mutter something ridiculous and he realised that she was stoned out of her head. He lifted her up in his arms like she weighed nothing and carried her in the direction of her house. Her mother would kill her but she couldn't stay out like this all night.

Coming around the corner Rory saw, or rather heard, Manus coming up the road towards his house. From the state of him, Rory knew that Maria's father would make minced meat out of his daughter and ask questions later. He did a quick U-turn and walked towards old Molly's farm. He would put Maria in the barn and then go and see if he could get her sister's attention, without getting any attention from the father. Molly was so old now she never looked to the leftovers of her farm at all, so the barn was unlocked and unused. The perfect place to hide a stoned teenager. He laid her down on the ground, wishing he had a torch. God only knew what was beneath her.

'Stay here, Maria. I'll be back in a few minutes.' He kissed her forehead and stood up to go.

Back in the barn half an hour later, Rory had found a torch in Maria's father's shed but he hadn't been able to get hold of Fiona. He would stay with Maria until she started to sober up. Was that the term you used for coming down from a high? Rory hadn't a clue. A few years ago Balcallan hadn't a notion of drugs. Rory and his teenage friends had been out of their heads on pints of Guinness. That was good enough for them. But this lot were a new breed of teenagers. With Mary Carr as their leader they could only follow the path to destruction. Looking down on Maria's face, under the torch light, Rory felt a true sense of protectiveness towards her.

'I'll mind you, my beautiful Maria. Mary Carr'll not get her filthy hands on you. Not if I have anything to do with it. I'm here for you girl. I'll always be here.' And Rory lay down beside Maria and put both his arms around her. When she woke up she would know exactly how Rory felt about her. He would never hurt her again.

Chapter fifteen

'THE Christmas lights are beautiful, Rory. Letterkenny looks transformed into fairyland.' I squeeze his hand and feel my excitement shine.

'And you, my dear, are the fairy princess,' he laughs. 'You could sit on top of the tree over there and look down on all your subjects.'

'Ouch. That sounds painful. All those prickly pines sticking up your arse.' I break into a fit of giggles. Rory always brings out the happiness in me. I reach up and throw my arms around his neck.

'I love you, Rory.' Every time I hold him, I can never rid myself of the feeling that it might be the last time. He never replies with an *I love you too*. He holds me tighter as if he can feel the transience of us. I try occasionally to bring the conversation around to what's out there but he always looks uncomfortable, promising to sort it all out sometime. And then he changes the discussion around to something more neutral.

'Let's get in out of the cold, Maria love. I'm freezing and gasping for a nice hot cup of tea.' He takes my hand and leads me into a café and we order a pot for two.

'So are you glad you went back to school, Maria?'

'I think I am, Rory, but I've given up on one or two of the subjects I was doing before. Like Home Economics. Sister Maria said I am to marry a rich man and get a servant to do my cooking and sewing for me. She said I am a dead loss. And Biology. I haven't a scientific bone in my body. I threw up every time Miss Ferry dissected an animal. I don't know why I chose that subject in the first place. Mammy said I had to have a science. Yeuk. That's left me with six subjects and that'll be fine.' And on I rabbit... I want to talk to Rory about something that matters more but I know he's stalling on *that* subject and he'll keep changing tack until he's good and ready... whenever that might be.

'That's brilliant, Maria. You'll get an A in English and you'll definitely get into journalism with that. Where would be your first choice? Dublin?'

I don't answer. He's sitting there as happy as you like asking me am I going to run off to Dublin and leave him here with his Deirdre. Does he honestly not give a shit what I do? Would he not go crazy if I wasn't around? It's hard enough not seeing him at work every day, much and all as I hated the job. I can't imagine life without Rory in it. Nothing matters as long as I can get to see him at some stage during the week. And when I leave him I'm filled with such a sense of purpose that anything's possible for me.

And I'm being good for my mother and staying far out of my father's way. I'm spending a lot of time with my sister, Fiona. I'd love to confide in her about Rory but I know that she would go mad. She's kind of friends with Rory's Deirdre. I hate saying that. *Rory's Deirdre*. Deirdre's older than Rory and she was at school with Fiona. I can't for the life of me figure out why Fiona'd want to know her. She seems to make Rory's life a living hell.

One day, I overheard Fiona talking to her husband Gerry about Deirdre's problems. She said that Deirdre was having a tough time getting over her miscarriage... that the doctor told her that she was having a bit of postnatal depression and she'd get over it eventually... that it happened to lots of women and there was no reason why they couldn't have another baby. Deirdre had apparently gone to Father Paddy, and he told her to stop moping and to concentrate her energy on being there for her husband. He actually told her that a baby conceived now that they were married would have a much better chance of survival than a baby conceived in a state of sin. Fiona was saying that she thought that Deirdre seemed to be in a terrible way and it was a shame in this day and age that more wasn't being done to help women like her.

I listened to all this and had the decency to feel guilty, but not guilty enough to finish with Deirdre's husband or to even tell Rory what I'd overheard. I guess the reason Rory isn't moving our relationship on at all, has a lot to do with Deirdre's present state of mind. So I'm keeping my mouth shut. I don't think that Deirdre loves Rory, and I know that Rory certainly doesn't love Deirdre.

But does he love *me*? I'm not sure of that either. He's never said the words. But those kisses and caresses say it all. Don't they? I feel the love is there even if he won't admit to it. I reach across the table for his hand and give it a little squeeze.

'I might try Queen's University in Belfast, Rory. It's nearer to you.' And I smile my widest smile. There. I've said what needed to be said. I'm going nowhere far from Rory's side. I'm building my future around him. Now the ball is well and truly in *his* court.

'Don't narrow your choices though, Maria. You're young. You have years of college ahead of you and some exciting job out there waiting. You'll be a famous journalist. Don't be tying yourself to Balcallan.'

I'm furious. I know the tears will start now. I always try my best to put a brave face on our relationship but when he's dismissive of me, as he seems to be now, it's too hard. I know it's childish but I snatch my hand away from his.

'Don't be upset, Maria. We were having much too nice a day to ruin it with an argument. Come on now. Let's pay for these teas and get on with our lovely evening.'

Rory puts a note on the table and I stand up and march towards the door. He runs after me, but by the time he catches up I'm at the bus stop for Balcallan, in deep conversation with my neighbour Mairéad Gallagher. I know that Rory won't dare come near me now and expose us in front of someone like Mairéad. The bus pulls up and as I follow Mairéad onto it, I wave over at Rory. Then I think better of it and when Mairéad's not looking, I stick up my two fingers at him. Rory's right. I shouldn't waste my life waiting for a loser like him to make up his mind about leaving his wife.

But as the bus pulls out of Letterkenny, I catch sight of his distraught face looking up at my window, and I'm able to make out the words he's mouthing at me.

'I love you.'

The bus pulls into the main street of Balcallan and slows to a stop. Mairéad hasn't shut up for a minute during the whole trip and I'm delighted that my job as listener is coming to an end. And on she goes… but her last sentence catches my attention.

'Ah, there's poor Rory McGee holding up the wall of the pub. Terrible business that with wee Deirdre. They're in a right old mess from what I hear. Don't you be getting yourself into any business like that now, Maria. Poor Deirdre. Sure her life is over before it began. That Rory's a young pup for getting her into that mess in the first place. But at least he stood by her. And now look. They've nothing at all to show for their efforts…'

How has Rory made it back to Balcallan before us? There isn't another bus due until much later. I smile up at Mairéad and decline her invitation to walk back home with her. I tell her that I've some bits that need dealing with in the town before all the shops close. I make a pretence of walking over to the gift shop but double back on myself when I see Mairéad disappear around the corner.

'How did you do that, Mr Magician?'

'Ah, you know that old fashioned trick of taking a lift off someone? Tracy Ferry, your dissecting biology monster, was getting into her car as the bus pulled off. I told her I'd missed the bus and I asked her for a lift. If she dissects animals as fast as she drives cars then no wonder you feel sick. The legs are shook off of me.'

'You might need to be nursed back to health then?' I smile up at him but don't touch him. I know better than that on Balcallan's Main Street. I whisper an answer to what he told me in Letterkenny. '*I love you too.*' We stand in silence for a minute, gazing at each other. A comfortable quiet that shuts out the rest of the town.

'Rory?'

'Yes?'

'My sister's away at her in-laws and I have the key to her house. It's pitch dark around there. No one'll see you come in. Give me twenty minutes to make sure the coast is clear. We'll be warmer chatting there than standing here in the street.'

I walk away up the road and try not to think of the doubt I'm sure I saw in his eyes; the reservations around the downturn of his mouth; the guilt that emanated from his breath. Inhalation desire. Exhalation guilt.

'It's make your mind up time, Rory McGee.' I cross the fingers on both hands as I whisper to myself.

An hour later and I'm still sitting in Fiona's kitchen making, yet another, cup of tea. I know I should've left after half an hour. I'm practically throwing myself at that married eejit when I could have the pick of Balcallan and beyond. What's the attraction anyway, or is Mammy right and I only ever want what I can't have? Oh wouldn't my mother be over the moon if she knew about Rory and his rejection of her daughter? Wouldn't she be delighted to be able to say, *I told you so*? Sonia's favourite words. She knows everything that woman. Well she'll never know how much of a complete fool her daughter's made of herself. I'm out of here and Rory's history. I stand and walk to the sink to wash out my cup but I let it drop with fright when I see a face pressed up against the kitchen window.

Rory comes around to the back door and I unlock and open it.

'I'm leaving. You've had a wasted journey.' I shove past him into the garden but he gently catches hold of my arm.

'Wait, love. Wait. I wanted to come. Maria if you only knew how much I want to be with *you*. How much I need you. I can't stand living in that house another minute with that crazy witch. I swear. But it's you, Maria. I have to think of you. You have everything going for you right now but if I leave Deirdre for you, your name will be mud all over Balcallan. And you'll be going to college eventually, so where do I come in then? It's not worth it for you. Wrecking your life for me.' Rory sinks down onto the back doorstep and I drop down beside him.

'It'll freeze the arses off us out here,' I say.

'Beautiful night though,' he says. 'Look at those stars. Incredibly bright. They look like they're making a circle.'

I smile upwards. 'The *Winter Circle*. That's an asterism.'

He shakes his head and smiles too. 'I didn't know you knew about stars.'

'We did it at school only this week, so it's clear in my head. The *Winter Circle*. The *Summer Triangle*. *Orion*. It was interesting. I might write about it all when I'm a journalist.'

We edge closer together for warmth and Rory puts his arm around me. 'It's very pretty alright,' he says. 'I could sit out here all night and watch the stars.'

'It's too late to pull back now, Rory,' I say gently. 'I can't suddenly unlove you because it doesn't fit in with life's plans. I might go to college and I might travel but you have to let go of Deirdre and be with me. I know she's not been too good since she lost the baby, but the longer you leave it the harder it'll be. I'll wait for when you're ready but don't be too long and don't give up on us too easy. We're worth everything you and me...' I pause for a second, then add, 'So... are you in or out? I have to know for sure.'

He turns and wraps his hands around my face and his eyes tell me that he's never going to leave me.

'You're right, Maria. Do you see that circle of stars up there? That *Winter Circle* is our eternity ring. As long as those stars are in the sky, that's as long as I'll love you. And the moon in the middle? That's how perfect we are together and as long as the moon is shining, I'll be right here.' He follows this with a kiss that would melt an iceberg and I ruin it by laughing.

'What's so funny?'

'Rory, will you promise me you'll never be so bloody soppy

ever again?'

'Feckin' cheek of you. I'm professing my undying love and you think I'm hilarious.'

I jump out of his way as he pretends to throw a clout in my direction.

'Come on inside,' I say. 'My backside has gone numb with the cold of that step.'

We go into the kitchen and I open the door into the sitting room. I lie down on the rug on the floor and Rory lies down beside me.

The house is chilly but we never notice.

Chapter sixteen

I POUNCE on the alarm clock before it makes any more noise and disturbs my mother. Sonia would wake if you turned over in your sleep. 5am. Time to move. I feel over the side of my bed for the bulk of my rucksack. I think I've packed too much. I'll be carrying it myself for a long way, as I can't risk hitch-hiking near my own town. I'll walk through the fields at first, coming back out onto the roads only when I'm sure I won't be recognised. Sunday morning's a good time to travel. Everyone who knows me will be in their beds. Not many will be on the road to Dublin. As soon as I feel the usual tears start to form, I blink and throw back the blankets and shake them away. Not today.

Having slept in my tracksuit bottoms and oversized t-shirt, I only have to pick up my runners and sneak down the stairs. I know which ones are creaky and creep over them quietly. On the way out the back door I stop by the kitchen table. A cake. Beautifully created by Sonia. *Happy 19th Birthday, Maria.* I swallow hard. For a few moments I think about staying; confiding in my mother. 'I'm sorry, Mam,' I whisper. I gently open the back door while rubbing away the tears that seem to be constantly ready to fall these days. I read somewhere that being pregnant has that effect on you. Mixed with teenage hormones, I know I've been impossible to live with for months. I've hated everyone. Even my mother, definitely my father, and absolutely despised the eejit of a bastard that knocked me up in the first place.

But mostly, I hate myself for the way I've treated my family, especially my sister, Fiona; the only person who still stands by me. I've no one here who I can call a friend. I was half tempted to go to Mary Carr but what good would she be?

I thought that Rory was the only friend I'd need. He was so good to me and so good *for* me. I lived for our meetings though they were always a secret; in fact especially because they were a secret. And Rory was such a gentleman. Not like the other boys my age, who think that the wild Maria Dooley is fair game for them all when she's had a bit of the hard stuff. I knew Rory for six months before he made love to me, being oh so gentle and caring. It hurt a little that first time, but I loved it and loved him all the more because of it.

The early morning dew on the grass soaks through my runners before I've left my house far behind. I let the tears fall freely now. I don't need to see my way through fields that have been my childhood playgrounds. I want to be strong about this; to be grown up; not the blubbering ten-year-old that my pregnancy seems to have turned me into. Then again, having an affair with a married man whose wife is also pregnant could have that effect on you.

How could that bastard have professed his undying love for me? Have made me feel that I'm the only girl he would ever be with; *could* ever be with. He had said all that to me, when all the time he was having his cake and eating it with fucking cherries on top. My virginity. I've given it up for that little shite, and have a bun in the oven for my troubles. Nineteen years old today; I should be out partying with friends; young and free with an exciting life ahead of me.

I fall on my knees beside the fuchsia bushes. I feel winded, like I've been kicked. I haven't realised that I've been running. I rub at my eyes, furiously to try to rid myself of the constant tears. The fuchsia spreads out before me; reds and pinks and purples; the colours of my shame. Not shame of my unmarried state. That isn't bothering me. I'm not like Deirdre. It's the shame of what I've let myself become with Rory McGee. But never again. No matter what he might say to me now, he's part of my embarrassing past and that's all. I'll never forget or forgive what he's done to me.

That day at Fiona's house changed everything. I'd finished work and had gone there to chill out. When the doorbell rang, I'd opened it all smiles and joy with the world.

Deirdre was standing there.

'Hi, Maria.'

I stood there, staring and still. I couldn't speak. I'd spent the past year trying to avoid this woman and I'd more or less succeeded, but here she was now standing at my sister's door expecting me to invite her in.

'Is Fiona around, Maria? Could I come in do you think?'

Fiona came along then.

'I thought I heard your voice, Deirdre. Are you not stopping?'

'Eh, I'm not sure. I think so.' And she eased herself around my statue, looking at me strangely. I shivered as she brushed against me on the way past.

'Cup of coffee?' Fiona was obviously delighted to see her friend.

'No, Fiona. No coffee. It makes me want to throw up all the time.' Deirdre was grinning from ear to ear.

Fiona caught hold of her friend's shoulders and hugged her.

'No! You never are? That's wonderful, Deirdre! Oh, congratulations! I'm so happy for you. How long?'

'About four months. I know I should have told you but I was worried that you'd be upset with not getting pregnant yourself and all that. But I couldn't hold back any longer…'

'Never mind me for goodness sake. Our day will come too. Are you well?'

'Fine. I didn't want to tell anyone at first so I've only told my mother. Nothing's going to go wrong this time. I know that. But…'

'Don't even think like that, Deirdre. Sit down there now and put your feet up. Mind you, you're probably over all that sickness by now and settled into the whole thing and I suppose Rory is over the moon?'

I never heard Deirdre's answer to that. I was gone out the front door. Running. Running. Running.

I'm still running.

I have to get up, have to get on. I need to go to Dublin... Dublin because it's far away... Dublin because it's where people run to... Dublin because nobody there knows who you are. It's a place to get lost in. I grab a branch and haul myself up. I pull a clump of fuchsia from the bush and stick it between the pages of a book in my bag. My favourite flower. The only thing I'll take with me from Balcallan. Apart from the baby.

Out on the road to Letterkenny it doesn't take long to hitch a lift. As luck would have it my chauffeur is going all the way to Dublin. I could do with a bit of luck going my way.

'I'm travelling back from a weekend with an old college friend of mine. Had a few days away from the wife and kids. It should have been peaceful but you Donegal lot spend far too much time in the pubs. I couldn't keep up at all. I'm wrecked. How about yourself? It's a funny time to be going to Dublin.'

Shit. I'm going to do it again. If I even attempt to open my mouth I'm going to burst into tears. I remember a story I heard at school sometime, about a little boy in Holland who held a dam from bursting using nothing but his little finger. I know how that boy felt. But I'm not doing as good a job as he did. I take a deep breath and try to speak.

'My friend died. In Dublin. In a car accident. The funeral's on Tuesday.' And then the dam bursts.

I wonder where that came out of. Mind you, I feel like I've been run over by a bus myself and I might as well be on the way to my own funeral. My life is as good as over. The man pulls into the side of the road.

'Jesus,' he says. 'I'm so sorry and me prattling on about nothing here beside you. Look. Put the seat back there and lie down and rest. I'll shut up for the rest of the journey. Unless you want to talk. Then let me know. Alright?'

I shake my head and then nod. I don't trust myself to speak. I pull yet another tissue from my bag and blow hard. I do as he asks me and lean back in my seat and close my eyes. I hear and feel the car start and we're on our way again. I let my body relax and feign sleep.

It's hard to have all this time on my hands and nothing to think of but what I'm going to do in Dublin or how I'll manage for money. I can't bear to worry about what I'll do when the baby's born. No. Don't dwell on that. Anything but that.

I hadn't realised I was pregnant until I was almost starting my exams. I'd been sick on and off for a while but I'd put it all down to nerves and studying. I'd known deep down that I would be okay doing the Leaving Certificate but that hadn't stopped me feeling hassled about it. When I missed a period I put that down to stress as well. Rory took precautions each time we made love. Except that one time when he forgot. A few beers too many. Once was all it took.

I know I should've been worried sick but I wasn't. I was delighted. This was what we needed. Rory would have to leave Deirdre now. We'd go and live in Dublin or London or New York. Nowhere was far enough away from Balcallan. I was having Rory's baby. Rory was mine now. Completely. I had decided not to tell him until after he had finished his long-awaited sales exams. A double celebration. I was over the worst of the sickness by then.

I've never told anybody, not even Rory, but what I really wanted was to be an author. I'm already halfway through my first novel. I could finish that from home and mind my baby. I had it all worked out. I'd hugged it all close to me.

That day in Fiona's house, I'd been figuring out in my head exactly what I was going to tell Rory that evening. I'd known he would be delighted and that, of course, he would go along with all my plans. We were as good as together for life.

Until I opened the door to the blooming, beaming Deirdre.

'Are you alright, love? Would you like to pull in and have a cup of tea or something?'

I haven't realised I'm crying again. Will it ever stop?

'No. Ignore me. I'm fine.'

'Did you not have someone who could travel with you? It's too hard to be going all the way to Dublin on your own in that state.'

'I'm okay. The friend is from Dublin and no one at home knew her. I think I'm still in shock about it. That's all. She was so young.'

'So where in Dublin was she from? Where's the funeral? Where do you need to be dropped when we get there? Tell me and I'll bring you straight there.'

God, will he never stop asking questions? I follow the lies with more. It's good practice. I'm going to need to do a lot of lying from now on.

'I need to get into the city and I've to ring her brother when I get there. He said he'd come and get me or at least tell me which bus to get.'

'Why don't we stop somewhere and ring him? Tell him that I'll give you a lift to wherever you want to be.'

'He won't be up right now. He said to ring him this afternoon. Thanks. But don't worry. You're very kind.'

'Okay, but if you change your mind...'

I see him look at his watch. It wasn't that early now. Not for someone who had just lost their sister. I'd better be a little less imaginative and more pragmatic with the lies.

'I'm Jim Molloy by the way.'

A name. I have to think of a name. Why haven't I thought all this out before I set out on this crazy adventure? I look down at my bag, at the book of Patrick Kavanagh's poetry that I shoved in.

'Mary Kavanagh. Nice to meet you and thanks for the lift and for your concern.'

He looks like he might be about to speak again but Mary Kavanagh decides she'll get in there first. God knows what he'll ask me next and I haven't the energy to make up a full history of myself right now. But I'll have to soon enough.

'Do you mind if I lie back and sleep now? I didn't get much shut-eye last night.'

'You go on and don't be worrying about anything. Okay? I'll wake you when we get to Dublin and you can ring your friend's brother and tell him I'll bring you out to where he lives. You don't want to be bothering him when he's upset after his sister.

Go asleep now.'

I lie back and close my eyes. Why have I been picked up by someone so bloody kind? And there was I worried sick about what gobshite pervert might be driving along the road. It's nice to know though, that there are still some good guys left in the world and that they aren't all bastards like Rory McGee. I'll think of an excuse between here and Dublin. All I can do now is close my eyes. I can't wait to be in a town where, by my mother's reckoning, nobody knows anybody else and nobody cares. I can be invisible and do whatever I like. There's one small problem. In a few months I'll be giving birth to a baby.

What the fuck am I going to do then?

Chapter seventeen

'HAVE you thought of any names, Rory?'

Deirdre watched her husband stare at the television and tried again.

'*I* have. Thought of some names that is. If it's a girl we could call her Caitríona after my granny on my father's side. She was a lovely lady. Then if it's a boy we could call him Tomás. I've always favoured the Irish version of Thomas. I had an uncle called Tomás too, on my mother's side, but much older than her. He left for America. I've never even met him... So what do you think, then?'

No answer. The television was obviously much more important than naming his child. Deirdre picked up the remote and switched it off. He still stared. She watched his fists clench as he took a deep breath in.

'Rory!' she shouted. 'Are you listening?'

Rory exhaled. 'I am now, Deirdre. What was so important that I couldn't even watch the All-Ireland?'

'I'm sorry. I hadn't realised it was your precious football you were watching.'

'It's not *just* football, Deirdre. It's the All-Ireland Gaelic Football Final in Croke Park. I should be there. I've always been there. But this year I'm here. Listening to you.' Rory's voice was deadpan. The one he always used when speaking to his wife.

'But you're not listening. Are you? You don't listen to anything I say. You don't listen to anything anyone says. You get up in the morning and go to work and come home and watch the telly and stay in bed half of Saturday. Then watch the telly. And now it's Sunday and you wouldn't even have the decency to come to mass with me. Do you know how embarrassing that is, having to sit there on my own every week with everyone wondering where you might be? And there you are watching the telly again. We're having a baby, Rory. Had you noticed? Do you care? Will you care about the baby when it's born? Do you care about *me*? Have you ever cared? What are we going to do, Rory? We can't keep going on like this.'

'Ah, Deirdre. Of course I care, but I'm having a hard time getting my head around it all.'

'Do you love me, Rory?' Deirdre knew by the look on her husband's face that she should never have asked. Her mother had always said, what you don't know won't hurt you. But it *was* hurting her. That her husband had never told her that he loved her was a big thing to her. She needed to be loved. Didn't every woman? She was trying hard herself to love Rory but the man would try the patience of a saint and Deirdre wasn't thinking saintly thoughts about him.

When they had made love, that one time after her cousin's wedding, she had thought that their relationship would improve – and it had. Rory was much kinder to her, overly attentive almost, as if he was making up for the terrible time they had had when she had lost the baby. He was even being friendly to her mother. He was a happy man. He hadn't actually moved back into their bedroom but she had been sure he would eventually.

When she had found out she was pregnant she had been over the moon. Surely this was all she needed to bring her husband back to her?

But he had been horrified. He'd said he wasn't ready to go down that road as yet; that they had only jumped in the sack because of the fun they'd had at the wedding; the few drinks and that. *Jumped in the sack...* The bastard. Oh what a charming husband she'd landed herself with. Well she was pregnant now and he could damn well be good and ready, because this baby was going nowhere but out of her and into her arms.

She couldn't wait.

But since then, since he knew she was having their baby,

he'd become more distant than ever. Deirdre was so lost in her thoughts it took time to register that her husband had said something.

'What's that? Sorry?'

'I said I've lost my job, Deirdre. They've let me go in the glass factory. There's not enough work. It was last in, first out. I didn't finish the sales exams in the end, after all the training they sent me on, and they were pissed off with that too. I've been looking. There's nothing around here. There. I've said it. You've no idea how hard it's been for me. Look at you standing there with your mouth open. Deirdre Sharkey with nothing to say for herself. Now there's a lovely sound.'

Rory pushed past her and walked out of the house.

Deirdre sat down in his seat. Her husband had no job. Deirdre had left the post office when she married. Her husband was going to look after her and the baby. Of course he was. She had married a man with a great job. A career with prospects, he had boasted. Rory McGee was someone in this town. Deirdre didn't know the first thing about sport but she knew that the mention of her husband's name brought on great admiration. He didn't even have that now. Who was going to pay the rent on the flat? A flat above a shop was no great shakes but it was a roof over their heads. She was having a baby for God's sake.

Deirdre pulled her knees up as far as the bulk of her stomach and hugged them into her. She started rocking backwards and forwards. All she ever wanted was to have a husband and a family but she wanted a husband who loved her, and who she loved. Her mammy had said when she was getting married that the baby would bring them together. That they would grow to love each other. The baby had died and they had grown to hate each other. Now there was another baby on the way, there was a lot more work to do if they were to manage to live in the same house, never mind love one another. *Love?* Forget love from that self-centred eejit. Since the day she had told him that she was pregnant, Deirdre had felt that he had completely detached from her. He seemed to be looking around him all the time. As if he'd lost something and he couldn't keep going until it was found. He was only a few years younger than her but he acted like a teenager most of the time. Whatever it was he was looking for, it wasn't her.

Deirdre would have all the love she needed in life from her beautiful baby. She felt a kick in response to her thought. It sent a pain up her back but she somehow found the pain a delicious sensation. Like she had with the sickness and nausea, the food cravings, the swollen feet, the early butterfly movements that had grown into great big punches. She had savoured it all. Being pregnant. Having this baby. Nothing else was important.

So Rory didn't have a job. No more than a lot of people in the country. Other couples were getting by and so would they. Lots of men around Donegal had to go to Dublin and London to get jobs, so that's what Rory would have to do. Send money back to her. She could give up this pokey little flat. Go back and live with her mam and dad. Her mam would be delighted to have her only daughter back and a grandchild to fuss over as well. Rory losing his job was a blessing for everyone. When he came back she would tell him about her plan. She stopped her rocking and released her feet to the floor.

Funny thing was, she was sure that he wouldn't be upset about it either. She had a feeling that he would go willingly. Deirdre made a mental picture of Rory walking towards the bus for Dublin with his rucksack and felt herself let out a long-held breath.

Rory pushed his way into *Mikey's* pub. The television was on as loud as it could go but there was such a crowd around it, it was hard to see what was going on. Jesus, was he never going to see this match today? He had a key for his parent's house so he could head for there. There was nobody at home with everyone gone to Dublin for the game. He shoved his way back out of the pub. There wasn't even anyone to have a pint with. Every one of Rory's associates was in Dublin. Where else would you be on the day of the final? Rory passed Gerry's house on his way and was surprised to see him in the front garden having a quick smoke before the second half. He and Fiona seemed like the perfect couple; they certainly looked like the happiest couple Rory had ever met. Twenty-eight years old, well and truly married, and they were still mad about each other. But it was easy to see who was in charge. Fiona had ordered Gerry's 'filthy habit' out into the garden since the day they got married and Gerry said it was a great idea as it stopped him smoking too much.

'Rory McGee! Am I seeing things or what? Did you not make it to the Big Smoke for the game?'

Rory pushed open the little gate. 'Hiya, Gerry. Eh, no. Deirdre wasn't feeling too great. She thought it might be better if I was nearer to home.'

'So are you not even watching it on the television?'

'Em, well. You see she wanted a bit of quiet and she asked me to turn down the television and I was thinking of going up to my dad's to watch the second half there. There's no peace in *Mikey's*... I'm surprised you're not at the game yourself. But would you like a bit of company here? Would Fiona mind if I joined you?'

'Not at all. Come on in.' Gerry stubbed his cigarette out on the ground and went to walk away, but thought better of it and scooped it up. 'Best not to leave that there. Don't want to give Fiona anything new to be giving out about. Sure God love her, she's like the devil himself since Maria went missing. That's why I haven't gone to Dublin myself. Any mention of the capital makes her think of her sister's disappearance.'

Gerry walked ahead and didn't see Rory start to shake at the mention of Maria's name. By the time they were in the sitting room he had calmed himself a bit.

'Will you have a little something in your hand?'

'Lovely, Gerry. A cup of tea.'

'Would you go away with your cup of tea? You like a drop of Jameson, don't you?'

'Oh, that would be lovely, Gerry. Will she not mind? In the middle of the day like.'

'Not at all. Sure with the bit of company it might entice her to join us. It'd be good for her.'

Gerry went for his wife and the whisky. Rory wasn't feeling too comfortable around his friend since he had been left off the Balcallan team. He felt such a failure. He wasn't sure that he wanted to see Fiona either. He would have to ask after her sister. To talk about Maria without shaking and crying and generally making a fool out of himself. Too late. There she was. Looking sad and thinner and not herself at all. Rory felt the lump come to his throat and swallowed. He knew how Fiona felt. Someone they both loved had disappeared off the face of the earth. Gerry was handing him the whisky and it was all he could do not to throw it down in one go.

'Fiona. I hope you don't mind me gate-crashing the match. I was passing, on my way to my dad's, and Gerry was in the garden and I thought it would be nice to have some company...'

'Not at all, Rory. It's good to have you. We haven't seen you for ages. Yourself and Deirdre will have to come over to us one night before the baby comes. After that you'll need babysitters and all.'

Babysitters. God, why did people keep bringing up the baby? He didn't want to talk about that.

'Any news about Maria, Fiona?' Rory wasn't sure if it was good to bring up her name, but at this stage he was desperate for news.

'Not exactly, Rory. Supposedly a neighbour spotted her in St Stephen's Green in Dublin. But she disappeared again before the Gardaí were able to do anything. To be honest there's little they can do as she's an adult and, as they keep telling us, she's entitled to disappear if she wants to. If Dublin's where she is, it'll be a nightmare trying to find her. The Gardaí say the place is swarming with people from all over the country. We've been down a few times, myself and mam, but sure it's a minefield. She could be anywhere.

'I keep asking myself why. Why would she go? She seemed so settled in herself for a good while. She seemed happy. She was finished her exams and she had everything going for her. She did brilliantly in the Leaving Certificate and there are college offers waiting for her; she's that clever when she puts her mind to it.

She could have achieved anything she wanted to. I wonder did we do or say something to upset her. It keeps going round and round in my head.'

'Drink up your whisky there, love and don't be upsetting yourself over it again,' said Gerry. 'There was nothing you did to send your sister away and you know it. No one could have been kinder or more loving to her than you over the years. She'll be back. When she gets over whatever it is. She's a teenager. A law unto themselves. You wouldn't know what was going on in their heads.'

Rory kept swallowing but the lump wouldn't go away. He downed his whisky to help stop the shaking. There was Fiona beating herself up about something she never did to Maria when all he could do was sit there and listen to her. He couldn't tell anyone that he knew exactly what had been going on in Maria's head. How could he tell them that she had run within a few days of finding out that her boyfriend's wife was having a baby? When the same boyfriend had told Maria, time and again, that there was nothing between himself and his wife of that nature and that he was only waiting until he could leave her in the kindest way possible. By the time Rory had realised that Maria had been in her sister's house when Deirdre went to tell Fiona her news, Maria had already upped and left.

This whole mess was Rory's fault. Maria could be in danger. She might have no money. She might have nowhere to live. Rory didn't think she knew a soul in Dublin. But she was resourceful and intelligent and she could charm her way out of anything. That man had come forward saying that he had given Maria a lift to Dublin. He had said that she had fed him a story of a dead friend and a funeral and that she had been so distraught all the way on the journey that he had believed her. Rory knew that Maria could lie to get what she wanted. He hoped it was helping her to get by. Even if he came clean and told them why Maria had left them, what good would it do? It wouldn't bring her back but it would open up a huge can of worms for him and he wasn't sure that he could deal with all that, on top of the trauma of losing Maria.

'She'll come back, Fiona. Gerry's right.' But Rory didn't feel the conviction of his words.

'There we go, now. The second half's starting,' said Gerry.

The Artane Boy's Band was walking off the field and the enemy colours were jogging back on with a look of battle about them. Gerry turned up the volume of the television. 'Let's see if they can't make a comeback against the golden boys. Will I top you up there, Rory?'

Lying in bed the next morning, Rory tried to piece together the evening before. He knew he had been a bit drunk when he left Gerry's house. But not out of it. Had he come home? Yes. He'd come home and Deirdre and her mother were sitting in the kitchen of the flat. There had been some sort of meeting in which he had been told exactly what he was going to do with his life. What was it? Oh yes. He was to go to Dublin to start a job. Eiley Sharkey had been on to her cousin in Dublin and he had something for Rory. He tried to remember what it was but it wouldn't come. He was to go after the baby was born. They would have worked out the notice on the flat then. Deirdre and the baby were going to live with her parents and he was to save like mad and send all his money back to them. Where did they say *he* was going to live? He couldn't remember that bit either. Maybe they hadn't worked that out for themselves yet.

Apparently he was a disgrace. His mother-in-law's tongue had lashed out and no doubt she had shared everything she had been holding back since the day he met her. There was nothing Eiley Sharkey liked better than a good *I told you so*.

He had left them to it and gone down to *Mikey's* for a few more pints to wash down the whiskies. And now he was here. No doubt he would never find out what had happened in between. No loss. He pulled the covers over himself again and closed his eyes. At least he didn't have to get up and make the pretence that he was going out to work. That match was something. He should have been there.

And Maria... Maria was in Dublin. He would go there and search until he found her.

Chapter eighteen

THE rain pours down in splashes on the halves of couples waiting under *Clerys'* clock. Saturday night is Saturday night in Dublin and no amount of water is going to rain on the parade of young wans waiting for young fellas; their mascara running down to greet their lipstick. I feel sorry for the girls that are left standing, until their umbrellas can't take any more and fall apart. How can they make fools of themselves like that? Waiting and waiting, looking at their watches, checking the time with the clock above them, realising they're synchronised, looking up and down O'Connell Street, shaking their heads. One more minute... then they're definitely going. One minute later the ritual starts again. Have they no pride?

There was a time when I was as bad. Don't I know what it's like to be waiting for someone who *couldn't make it?* Haven't I listened to all the excuses and forgiven each one of them? Never again. I'll never set eyes on Rory McGee again. I wouldn't survive the shame of it. I step out into the street from my shelter once more. I'm soaked through anyway. One more wetting won't make any difference.

'I'm sorry to ask you, but have you the makings of the bus fare home? He's after standing me up and I didn't expect to be needing to get home on my own.'

The girl looks at me, her face all concern, her own abandonment forgotten momentarily in the plight of the pregnant girl whose husband or boyfriend hasn't turned up to meet her. There are worse problems than being stood up. She hands me a pound note. The third one tonight. The rain makes people feel sorrier for me and there've been lots of them left there. Girls always make it in for the date no matter what the weather but lads are harder to be pushed out in all conditions. I have four pounds and sixty-two pence in my pocket. Not bad for an evening and definitely enough to get by for another few days. I turn and make my way up O'Connell Street.

Some of the others in the squat get by on stealing for a living but I feel better this way. It isn't even begging. The girls go home thinking they've done something worthwhile for somebody and they probably feel better for it. I've a different story going in other parts of Dublin on certain nights. Sure the place is so big anyhow and there are so many people that I'd never be remembered. I dropped the *Mary Kavanagh* when I went to the squat in North Great George's Street; a place steeped in writing history. I decided that *Mary Joyce* would be an apt follow on to *Kavanagh*. Next I'll take on *Mary*... Ah... Jesus... there's that pain again. It's not like the other ones that are tight around my middle; no more than uncomfortable. This one is sending pain messages throughout my body. What do they mean? Is this it? I'm only about eight months pregnant.

I've been into the *Ilac Centre* library a few times, to look up books about having a baby. I've taken down some notes and now have a vague idea what might happen but I've never been to see a doctor. I know I should have but it's too risky. There'd be too many questions. No one in Balcallan knows that I was pregnant when I left, least of all Rory, and that's the way it's staying. He'll never know he's fathered a child with me. I'll never tell him. Let him be a father to Deirdre's child. That's surely enough for him. I smile at the idea that Rory is having twins in his own perverse way. Then the smile is ripped from my mouth when another onslaught of pain strips every thought from my mind, except that I'm in agony. I fall to my knees at the foot of Parnell's statue. My baby isn't waiting out another month. The books were wrong about the pain too. It isn't bearable. I curl up into a ball and hear a roar come from some deep primeval part of me. The pain begins to drift away and in its place is another type of pain. Loneliness. I want my mam. Sonia and all her pragmatic ways. Sonia would know what to do. Sonia would have forgiven me everything, as she had so many times before.

'Mammy...'

A lovely couple half drag me, half carry me, the short walk that feels like miles to the Rotunda Hospital and leave me in the hands of a nurse who sits me in a chair and takes my details.

'Name?'

'Mary. Mary Beckett.'

'Address?'

'The Bungalow. Hare's Road. Letterkenny. Co. Donegal.' I made that up on the way up the stairs. It doesn't sound half bad. I'll have to remember it though.

'Husband's name?'

Mary Beckett hadn't figured out the answer to that one yet.

'Em...'

'Boyfriend's name? I'm sure the baby must have a father somewhere. In Letterkenny..? Okay. Father unknown... Age?'

'Twenty.'

'Doctor's name and address?'

I make that up too. I'm getting good at this.

'Date of birth?'

In my confusion I can't figure out whether to add or subtract a year but I'm saved from having to answer by the ambush of the baby pushing a little further down the birth canal. The questions change.

'Is this your first baby?'

'When did the labour begin?'

'How far apart are the contractions?'

'Have your waters broken yet?'

These are all questions that I can answer with ease.

'Yes. The first.'

'About an hour ago.'

'About ten minutes apart.'

'Waters? Em...'

'You're probably ages away yet, love. First babies have a habit of waiting an obscene amount of time before they make an appearance. You should go home for a while and get out of them wet clothes. Have a hot bath and come back in when your contractions are nearer together.'

I look up at the nurse in terror.

'Not to Donegal obviously. Where are you staying in Dublin? You shouldn't have been so far from home when you're so near confinement. Is there someone I can ring for you?'

'It's okay. I'll ring myself. My boyfriend's here in Dublin. I was staying with him for a few days but I was on my way to the bus station to catch one back to Donegal.'

'At this time on a Saturday night? Well ring him now and tell him to come in and get you and bring you back later when contractions have moved on a bit. You'd be bored hanging around here. Babies come quicker anyway when you're moving around the place rather than sitting down doing nothing. The phone's down the corridor. We'll see you later.' And she's gone to the next woman who, from her screaming, is obviously ready to drop at any minute. And anyway, her loving husband is having nothing else but a bed for his darling wife. Immediately.

I make a pretence of heading for the phone but I find a quiet corridor in a place that is the out-patients clinic during the day. I lie down on a row of chairs and let the tears flow. I want my sister. Fiona loves me more than anybody in the world. How did I think that I couldn't tell her what happened? She would have made Gerry beat the shit out of Rory McGee. They would have sorted it out. Fiona always had all the answers. As soon as this present contraction subsides, I'll go to the phone and call her. She'll drop everything and drive through the night. She might even make it to the birth. I can feel my sister's arms around me and this lessens the pain and it ebbs away. I'm so tired. So exhausted from the strain of it all. I'll let Fiona take over. I close my eyes.

'Fiona...'

I wake up, sit up and scream. The noise carries down the halls and into the lobby of the hospital. A nurse grabs hold of a porter and they come running in the direction of the horrific sound.

I stand in the corridor looking at the liquid running down my legs and gathering at my feet. The nurse and the porter stare at the sight and the porter breaks into fits of laughter.

'Jaysus, we thought that you'd died down here or somethin' and all you've done is break your bloody waters.'

'Shut up, Johnny and clean up.'

Johnny's smile vanishes.

'You come up with me,' the nurse continues. 'We'll have a look at you. I never heard such a big raucous for such a little reason in my life.'

I'm shaking. I'm still wet from all the rain earlier and now I'm soaking from the waters thing. It's frightened the life out of me; the gushing feeling and the noise of it hitting the floor. I wasn't expecting it. I look back at the porter who's there with a bucket and mop and whistling a merry tune. How can he think that's funny? This nurse doesn't think it's funny. I've obviously rubbed her up the wrong way and I know from my months of making my own way in Dublin that it's best to try and get on her good side.

'I'm sorry, about the mess and the shouting. I was frightened. I didn't think it'd be so strong.'

'Never mind that. There's much worse to come so you better start practicing your breathing exercises. We'll get you up on a bed and changed out of those clothes, into a hospital gown.'

Twenty minutes later I'm lying down under the covers shivering, waiting for the nurse to come back. She's pulled the curtains around me and I've left them like that. The pains are coming about every five minutes now but I'm not screaming out like I was earlier. I'm in a kind of rhythm with it. I know when they're coming and I know when they're going. This must be why the book called them waves of pain. I try to put myself on Balcallan Beach to watch the waves come in and out; but when I do, I see Rory standing there, so vividly, and the next wave that comes over me hurts so badly that I call out...

'Rory...'

The curtain is pulled back.

'Is that the baby's father? Rory?' This is a different nurse. This one is all smiles. Like a daffodil in early spring.

I stare away from her, allowing the tears to come.

'Let's have a look at you then.' I hardly notice what's going on with the nurse down below. I'm still on the beach... in a different type of pain.

'You're about six centimetres dilated!' The nurse seems to think this is wonderful news but she might think everything in her job is wonderful news. 'I'll get you moved up from this ward to the labour ward and get you sorted for an epidural. It'll be a while yet I'd say but you're well on your way.'

I wonder what she's talking about. Epi whats? Dilated? What's that? I'll have to go along with whatever they tell me to do. The nurse said it'll be over within a few hours. I'll manage whatever it takes to get the baby out.

But what then? One problem at a time, I tell myself. Deal with that when it comes.

I'm out in the middle of an ocean of pain. With every wave, I know that this is the one that will kill me. I'm giving birth to a broken bottle or a pile of hot coals.

Rory did this to me. That's all I have to tell myself. That's all I need to build up the wall of hate between us.

I have a baby with a mop of black, curly hair. I'm nearly there. They've been saying that for hours. It feels like days. One more push the nurse says and one more and one more should do it. I feel the next wave come over me and take over my whole body. I roar the baby out of me and then fall back. I'm still crying. Will I ever stop?

'You've a beautiful baby girl, Mary.'

And there she is. Up on my chest, looking like she swam through a sewer to get here. I stare at the mop of humanity lying across me. The baby lets out an almighty howl and all the nurses and doctors are smiling and congratulating me and each other. The miracle of life. I've seen calves and lambs being born and been deeply moved by the scenes. Now I'm looking at my own first-born child and feeling... scared. Scared to death.

'She's hungry, Mary. Why don't you give her a feed to soothe her? Get to know her a little.'

I don't know what to say. I turn my head away from the baby. Rory's baby. I won't feed it. I won't get to know Rory's baby. It wouldn't be fair. Not to the baby and not to me. I hate Rory and I hate what he's done to me. This child with Rory's mop of curly, black hair. Why isn't he here with me? Why am I on my own? It isn't fair. I would've loved his baby. I would've loved *him*… but not now.

'Please, nurse. I can't. Please give her a bottle. I'm so tired.'

The nurse looks unimpressed and shakes her head. 'Okay. For now. I'll take her and clean her and bring her back to you. Rest for a while. The porter will wheel you back down to the ward. Have a wash and change your gown. What are you going to call her, love?'

Maria had chosen her own second name that she hardly ever used. Nobody would relate it back to her.

'Anna.'

'Lovely choice. Is her daddy coming in later?'

'He can't make it until the morning. I never expected to have her so early. He'll come as soon as he can get here on the bus.'

'That's great now. I'll tell you what. If you're so tired, why don't I feed her and put her into the nursery until the morning and you get some rest until your eh… her daddy gets here?'

'Would you? You're so good. I'm so tired. I never thought it would be that hard… Nurse, where are my clothes and shoes?'

'Well they're probably in that locker beside you, but you'll not be wearing them anywhere with the state that they're in. Make sure someone brings you a change of clothes in the morning. And the stuff for the baby. Get some sleep when you're sorted now.'

'Thanks, nurse. I will.'

I try not to think of how kind the nurse is being to me and I turn my head from Anna as she's wheeled out of the ward away from me. I don't want to think of how much the girl in the next bed smiles at me and congratulates me when I'm wheeled into the main ward. As soon as she's asleep, I'm going to borrow the girl's clothes. We're about the same size. I hope my money is still in my pockets. I'll need all I can get.

When the girl stops staring at her newborn son and falls asleep, I'm going to raid her locker. It'll be easy to slip out. This is the best way. As soon as I set eyes on Rory's baby I knew I'd never be free of him. Every time I looked at her I'd see Rory and I'd feel the shame all over again. If I keep my baby I'll have to go home and be pitied by my family and friends for what I've let her father get away with. The poor child would grow up knowing that other baby, the one that Rory wanted... No. This is for the best. For both of us.

I have to make plans. I can't be linked back to here. Nobody who matters has any idea that I was pregnant. I won't go back to the squat. If they hear about the baby and put two and two together... well. I'll write a note to Carol and slip it in the letterbox. Carol thinks my baby is due *next* month. I'll tell her that I've decided to go home to my parents so that the baby can be born in stability. Carol will go with that and then she'll tell that to anyone who asks her. I've chosen my housemates well. They accept whatever life throws at them and rarely question anything.

The mother in the next bed is fast asleep now. I sit up and put my feet over the side of the bed to test my legs. When I went for a shower earlier I was very unsteady. I feel a bit better now. The doctor said that I'm lucky I didn't need any stitches or anything, but I'm bleeding heavily and what the nurse gave me won't last long. I creep over to my neighbour's bed. If I wake her I'm going to apologise and tell her I'm dying for a smoke and I caught the whiff of fags off her earlier, so I'm hopeful. In fact if she does have some cigarettes, I'll use that excuse if anyone asks me why I'm going outside. I don't know exactly what time it is but it's nearly morning and the hospital is rousing itself. If it's like any other hospital there'll be a changeover at 8am. The place will be noisy then. Nurses busy with handovers and lots of comings and goings. I open the girl's locker and am delighted to find everything out of its bag and neatly folded on the shelves. Jeans and a blue jumper, socks and runners – a size too big but who's complaining? – and everything that a new mother could possibly need in the way of toiletries. I try not to look at her baby's tiny clothes, beautifully folded, on the other shelf. There's a packet of fags, so I take one though I'm not actually going to smoke it... and the lighter... I'll take that in case I need to light the thing for authenticity.

Back in my own cubicle I'm dressed in minutes. They'll be looking for someone wearing the stolen clothes so I take my own bag with me so I can wash *them* and wear them as soon as I can.

I'm surprised at how well I feel. Resolve gives me energy. Plenty of time for collapsing in a heap later. The buzz in the hospital is definitely getting louder. Now's the time to go, before the nurse comes back with my baby. I walk down the corridor past the empty nurse's station. The handover is taking place in an office within.

I talk to myself all the way out. Don't look around for her, Maria. Don't even think of her. She doesn't need your mess. She deserves better. Don't cry now. You're doing the best thing, Maria. Go on now. There's the door and the security man's not looking at anyone going out. Keep going. Out the door. Never mind the legs. They'll hold out. So will you, Maria. So will you.

Chapter nineteen

'HOW can you bear to go away to Dublin and leave her, Rory? She's a wee dote, so she is. Do you think Deirdre will mind me coming to see her when you're gone?' Rory's sister Rita cuddled her two-week-old niece into her.

'I'm sure Deirdre will want a babysitter the odd time, Rita. I'll tell her you offered and she'll be delighted to see you too, Mam. You can go and see baby Caitríona any time you want. You know that.'

'Indeed and Deirdre'll not be delighted to see me,' said Éilis. 'Her mother hasn't had a kind word to say to me since the day you married her princess. You'd think it was me had put her daughter in the family way and not my wee brat of a son.'

'Ah, Mam. Don't let's go down that road again.' Rita was keeping the peace as always. 'Rory's away to Dublin tomorrow. Can't the two of you quit the clawing and be civil for a few hours?'

The silence roared in the kitchen and the baby woke up.

'Here, give her to me and I'll soothe her while you get her bottle ready. Don't make it too hot now. We had the devil's time with cooling it down earlier.' Éilis gave her son another hard stare. There was no doubt who she blamed for that one either.

'Paddy.' Her husband looked up from the paper and jumped to attention. 'Bring that fella down to *Mikey's* and have a last-minute chat with him. See if you can't talk some sense into him at all. Rita'll get a bit of dinner on while I'm saying goodbye to my grandchild.'

'Mam, for God's sake, she'll only be down the road from you, so she will. It's me who needs to spend the afternoon with her.'

'Come on, son. We'll only be gone the hour. I could do with a pint and it's not often your mother's nagging us to go to *Mikey's*. In fact, it's definitely a first. Hurry up there before she changes her mind.'

Rory picked up his coat and headed after his dad who was nearly out the front gate. He looked back at his daughter in his mother's arms.

'She'll need her nappy changed, Mam. After her bottle. And she gets colicky so be sure to wind her for a good while.'

Éilis looked up at her son scornfully.

'I *have* managed to bring up two children you know, and one out of the two didn't turn out half bad. Get away out.'

Rory closed the door behind him and stood in the porch. He was twenty-one years old and six foot tall and he was going to cry. He took some huge gulps of breath and shook his head. Would his mam never let him alone about how his life had turned out? He had always been her golden boy. Now she couldn't bear to look at him. His father was gesturing to him from up the road so he hurried down the path and out the gate.

Sitting in *Mikey's* later, father and son nursed their pints of Guinness in silence. Usually they had plenty to say to each other, but not today. Rory knew that his dad wasn't angry with him. Not like his mam. He was disappointed with him and that was worse. He took a long slug of his pint and spoke.

'Dad, I'm twenty-one and I've my whole life to live. I know you never wanted me to marry Deirdre but I felt it was the right thing to do at the time. What happened to the baby was terrible and when Deirdre was pregnant again I still felt I wasn't ready. The last two years have been a total mess. First, losing my place on the teams and then my job at McFadden's Glass. But when Caitríona was born and I held her, I knew that it'd be alright in the end.'

Paddy lifted his glass in the same way, and fortified himself for speech.

'Son, how can your marriage work if you're down in Dublin and Deirdre is up here and living with her parents? That's not a normal marriage and I can't get shut of the feeling that it's what you and Deirdre both want. Living as far away from each other as you can. Am I right, son? Is there no love between you?'

Rory took another sip but it didn't work this time. He had nothing to say to that. He wasn't used to lying to his father. Best to skirt around it.

'Dad, I have to have a job to support Deirdre and Caitríona and this is the only way to sort it at the moment. I won't be away forever. When you married mam you were exactly the same age as me and the babies came within a couple of years then too. *And* you lived with granny and grandad for a few years until you had some money saved from McFadden's. There's not too much difference between your way and mine.'

'There's a world of difference, son. I would have moved mountains to be with your mam. I still would. She means the world to me. We overcame all our difficulties because nothing seemed too hard when we had each other. We were each other's strength. When you're lonely in Dublin and that gets too hard for you, what will you do for strength, son?'

Rory didn't need a sip of his pint to answer that one.

'I'll think of Caitríona, Dad. She's all the strength I need. Now I know it's my round and that but you'll have to wait for another time. I'm going back to spend an afternoon with my daughter; because no matter what my mother says, as long as Caitríona's part of my life then I must have done something right, somewhere.'

'Your mother loves you, Rory. She's worried about you and she wants you to be as happy as we are. She wants the best for you. She just thought you had it all and then you lost it. She blames Deirdre, not you, but she has to be all smiles to Deirdre and her family so she's taking it out on you. Go home to her, son and give her a hug and show her you're taking no nonsense away with you to Dublin.'

Rory expected to be in for an earbashing before he even opened the door. He had kept Caitríona out way after he was supposed to.

Deirdre insisted she had her in a routine already but from what Rory could tell, that routine seemed to change with Caitríona's moods. Deirdre found it difficult to accept that somebody new was in charge. He was hesitant to turn the key in the front door. Reluctant to relinquish his little charge.

There was no sound coming from the flat and all the lights were off.

'I'm in here!' Deirdre's voice sounded like an echo.

Rory turned on the light in the sitting room. It was stripped bare. It looked like they had been burgled. The kitchen was the same.

'Deirdre!'

'Come on in!'

Rory nearly ran down the hall with the baby still in his arms. The other rooms were almost the same.

'What's going on, Deirdre? Where is everything?'

'Mam and dad spent the afternoon helping me to move everything around to their house. We borrowed Gallagher's van. I've moved all your bits and pieces around there as well and I've packed everything that you'll need to take with you to Dublin. How was your afternoon?'

'Grand.' Rory would have liked to decide what he needed to take with him, himself, but he wasn't going to start a row right now. Deirdre seemed happy to let his lateness go as well. He might as well go with the flow.

'I thought Ger Collins said that there was no hurry moving out of the flat. He told us you could stay here until the end of the week.'

'You know once I make a decision I don't like to let it lie for too long. I didn't fancy being here on my own anyway and it was good to get it done. There's little left to move in the morning so you might come to mass with me before you go for your bus.'

That sounded more like an order than a request. Rory looked around for somewhere to put the sleeping baby.

'She'll have to sleep in here with us. Her cot's gone.'

'Us?'

'Eh, yeah. Dad moved the bed in your room back to their spare room. I suppose he presumed that we were sharing a bed... It's what normal married couples do. It won't kill you for one night. Anyway, when you come to visit from Dublin we'll have to sleep together in my parents' house. I'm not explaining any problems in that area to them.'

Rory sat down on the edge of the bed and cuddled Caitríona into him. He wanted to see lots of his daughter but it sounded like visits were going to be fraught with tension.

'I know it's only nine o'clock but I'm going to get an early night. Put her into the middle of the bed and move the pillows out of the way.' Deirdre started to get undressed. She pulled her nightdress out from under her pillow.

Her husband stood awkwardly by the bed.

'Deirdre... I, eh, don't know where you might have put my pyjamas? I don't even know if I still have any.'

'I haven't seen a pair of pyjamas in the wash for over a year, Rory. You'll not die in your sleep without them but we better get a pair sorted for when you're in my mother's. I've never in my life seen my father go to bed without his pyjamas. My mother would die of shock.'

Rory pulled his jumper over his head with a mental picture of Eiley walking in on him in his boxers and he couldn't help it. He burst out laughing. Deirdre was smiling up at him with a face that was asking him to share the joke. He told her and they laughed all the way into bed. They were still laughing when Deirdre switched off the light. They were both under the blankets turned towards their sleeping daughter.

'We did well in the end. Didn't we, Rory? I know we have our problems but Caitríona's our number one priority now and we have to sort life out for her. Isn't that right?'

'She's wonderful. Isn't she?' Rory wasn't answering the question properly but he was in total agreement that their daughter was the most exquisite creature that ever lived.

Deirdre reached over and held his hand. 'We'll be grand, won't we?'

Rory didn't answer that either but he nodded and smiled a smile that didn't make it all the way to his eyes. In the half-light Deirdre only saw the nod and the smile so she squeezed his hand and let go.

'Goodnight, then. Don't roll over on her now.'

'Yeah. Goodnight, Deirdre. I won't.'

Deirdre closed her eyes and settled down to sleep. Those long eyelashes were lovely. She was a gorgeous woman, was Deirdre. When she was asleep.

Rory thought that they'd be alright if he tried harder when he came back for the weekend in a fortnight's time. They could leave Eiley to babysit and he could take Deirdre out for a meal. She'd like that. Show the town that they were still a couple. It wouldn't take too much to make her happy. But would it make Rory happy?

His answer was there when he closed his eyes; the picture he saw every night before he went to sleep and in his head he said the word that kept him going through everything. She was out there somewhere. She had been sighted in Dublin.

Maria...

Chapter twenty

HE could order another pint of Guinness or he could go home to his empty bedsit. He didn't want another drink. He wanted some company but all the lads from work were gone home for the Halloween weekend. Dublin was one big fancy dress party and Rory felt like he had come as The Invisible Man. He shouldn't have told Deirdre he was playing a match and would come home on the Sunday, putting off the terrible few days he would have had to spend in her parents' house. He missed his little beauty of a daughter, but he couldn't bear to be around her grandmother and he wasn't too enamoured with having to spend a couple of nights sleeping with her mother either.

Going back and forth to Balcallan hadn't been too bad for the first year but lately it had become a real chore. His own mother had never completely forgiven him for the mess he had made of his life and his mother-in-law was a nightmare. It was getting harder to cope with Deirdre lately and her amorous approaches to him. Apparently Caitríona needed a sister or a brother. She was becoming too spoilt. And whose fault was that? Nobody was disciplining the child. She had no respect at all for the father she saw only once or twice a month, for a few days. When Rory brought her to his parents' house she would spend the day sitting on her grandfather's lap, eyeing Rory up suspiciously. She knew her grandad so much better than her own father.

'Will I fill that for you again?' The barman looked at him and stood waiting for an answer. Should he keep going? Sure what was there to stop for?

'Aye. Go on. Throw another one in.' If he was hungover tomorrow he could tell Deirdre that the team had won and he'd gone out for a few bevvies. He had kept up the pretence of being on the local team in Dublin, with Deirdre and with his boss at work who was Eiley's cousin. It gave him a bit of time out where no one needed to know where he'd been or where he was going. His boss, Brendan Mc Elhinney, was a lovely man but nosiness obviously ran in the family and everything was reported back to the Sharkeys as *news*. The truth was that he had been dropped from the team six months ago. Most games were played at the weekends and he had been summoned home too many times to make him reliable. His manager said he had only kept him on because he was such a star player but all the practice in the world was no use to him if Rory wasn't available to play.

His Guinness was propped in front of him.

'Great stuff.'

'A pound and ten.'

'There you go. Keep the change.'

'Thanks.'

Rory realised that that was the longest conversation he'd had with anyone since he had left work at four o'clock the day before. He should have gone home. Home? Where was that? He should let Deirdre have her evil way with him this weekend and have another child to try to cement his marriage. Give up his job in Dublin and take whatever was going in Donegal. Settle down.

He was twenty-two years old and he was going nowhere.

A group of seventeen-year-old girls poured themselves into the pub in a cackle of giggles. They were obviously coming from a party, but Rory wasn't sure if they were dressed in fancy dress or if that was what young ones were wearing these days. Listen to him. *Kids these days*. What age did he think he was for God's sake?

One of the girls reminded him of Maria. Lots of girls made him think of Maria. In all this time of walking the streets of Dublin, Rory had seen her in every dark-haired, green-eyed girl. It was still there. He was pathetic. Maria was gone. She was not interested in having anything to do with Rory McGee. He took a large sip of his pint and closed his eyes.

Six months before, Rory had walked passed a café and seen Maria sitting at a table, holding hands with a fella about the same age as her – maybe younger. He had stood there stunned at first; staring. Maria had been his life and he had been everything to her. How could she possibly be sitting there making eyes at another guy? When he had recovered himself enough to go into the café, the guy had been sitting by himself and Rory had gone over to him.

'I saw Maria here. Where's she gone?'

'I don't know anyone called Maria,' he had replied.

'Maria. She was here sitting with you. You were holding her hand.'

'Mary. My girlfriend's name is Mary Gogarty. You're mistaken.'

Maria had come out of the toilet, all smiles, and made for the table. When Rory had caught her eye she had let out a soft shriek.

'Jesus!' Her face had paled. 'What do you want? What are you doing here?' Then she had recovered her wits a little. 'Come on, Dónal. We're getting out of here.' She had grabbed his hand and pulled the confused man to standing. She then dragged him behind her, as he stumbled out of the restaurant looking back at Rory then back at his girlfriend who might have been Mary for some time now, but may have been Maria in a different life.

'Maria! No! Wait!' Rory had tried to go after her but he had tripped on a chair and when he righted himself she and her Dónal were gone out the door and had mingled with the Dublin spring shoppers.

'Do you know that couple?' A waitress had stopped him as he made his way towards the door.

'Yes. I do.' Rory had been hopeful that she would be able to tell him something about them. That they might be regulars there.

'Well they owe me for two pots of tea and as you seem to have scared them off, you can cough up.'

Rory had put his hand in his pocket and given the girl a pound note. She had smiled and turned on her heels.

'Wait. Do you know them? Do they come in here much?'

'You think I'm going to tell *you* after the fright you gave that poor girl? No chance. Now if you're not ordering anything for yourself then you can go. You're upsetting the other customers.' She had gestured towards the door and Rory had turned and left.

He searched up and down the streets for hours.

For weeks after that, Rory had spent every spare hour walking that same area but she was nowhere to be found. He had thought that it was best to tell Maria's family that he had seen her. At least they would know that she was okay. The Gardaí hadn't been interested. Maria wasn't in any danger and she was a nineteen-year-old adult who, for whatever reasons, had decided that she didn't want to see her family again.

Fiona and Gerry had come down to Dublin and, like himself, had scoured the area for a week. They had quizzed the waitress who told them that their Maria had been scared out of her mind when she saw Rory. They had asked him why. Why would she be so scared of someone she had only vaguely known from home?

'I don't know, Fiona. I can only presume that Maria didn't want to be seen by anyone who knew her. For whatever reasons, she had decided she didn't want to go back and had made a new life for herself in Dublin.' Rory hadn't looked them in the eye while he spoke. Once more he felt a bastard for lying to Fiona about why her adored sister had run away from home and why she was still running. He knew from the way that Maria had looked at him that she hated him and would always hate him. That nothing he could say or do could put matters right.

He downed his pint and got up to go. He had to get Maria out of his mind. He would go mad otherwise. He would head back to Balcallan first thing in the morning and surprise Deirdre and Caitríona coming out of mass.

'How was the match?' Deirdre didn't look overjoyed to see him. 'We weren't expecting you until much later this afternoon. Say hello to your daddy, Caitríona.'

132

Rory's daughter held on to her mother tighter and shoved her thumb further into her mouth.

'The match was fine, Deirdre. I eh, wasn't on the field at all myself. That's how I was up and out so early this morning. I'm thinking of quitting to be honest with you. I don't like not coming back to see Caitríona when I have a few days off, and it's not fair to the team that I'm not there every weekend to play. There's no continuity in that at all.' He put his arms out towards the toddler. 'Come and give daddy a hug, princess.'

Deirdre handed Caitríona over to him and the toddler wailed her response. Rory thought that she should be left with him a while and that she would eventually get used to him, but Deirdre took her back immediately and he didn't want to argue with so many people milling around outside the church. Eiley and Bart came out towards them.

'You're back early.' Eiley was obviously as glad to see him as her daughter.

'It's great to see you, Rory. How's life down there in the big smoke?'

Rory thanked God for Deirdre's dad once more. He didn't know what he'd do with these women if it weren't for his father-in-law.

'Grand thanks, Bart. It's good to get the few days off though, for the long weekend. How's yourself?'

'Ah, you know. Ticking along there.' And then quieter. 'We might have a pint a bit later if we can devise an escape route. What do you think?'

'Grand so, Bart.' Rory kept his voice down too. Bart seemed to enjoy his pints all the more if they were forbidden and therefore tasted all the better. 'We'll come up with something after lunch.'

The five of them then walked the few minutes back to the house in uncomfortable silence. Rory felt that he was an unwanted intruder. He would have broken the silence but he didn't want the snub that might follow anything he might have to say, so he left all his half-finished sentences stuck in his head.

That night, Rory lay in bed and watched the lightshade swim around and around the ceiling. If he didn't take his eyes off it soon, he knew that he might be sick but he felt kind of hypnotised. As long as he watched the bulb going around he didn't have to think about anything else.

He hadn't wanted to stay in the pub as long as he had but his dad and his uncle had come in as he was leaving; and his cousin was home from the States and buying everyone pints, so it had turned into a bit of a party. He had no idea what herself had said to him when he carried her father in the back door but there was probably no loss in that. He had a feeling he'd been sent to bed with no supper. The bedroom door opened and there she was. The woman of his bad dreams. Rory smiled at his own joke.

He closed his eyes and feigned sleep but missed the familiarity of the light going around. Now he had to listen to the real world. Deirdre was undressing. After a minute Rory chanced a quick peek. She was standing in the half-light with nothing on. He watched her fold her clothes onto a hanger and when she bent down to put her shoes in the bottom of the wardrobe, he felt himself being mysteriously turned on by her lovely figure and ample breasts. She came towards the bed and reached under her pillow for her nightdress.

'Deirdre...' Rory hoped he wasn't slurring his words too much. 'You're beaushiful.' He was sure that last word had been a bit dodgy. He should stick to simple words. 'Do you know that?'

'You're drunk, Rory. Go to sleep.' Deirdre went to drop the nightdress over her head.

'Don't do that. Come to bed as you are. You look lovely.'

Deirdre looked unsure but she put the garment down on the bed and slid in beside her husband. He opened his arms and she let herself be enfolded by them.

Rory felt his erection grow harder. He pushed Deirdre gently onto her back and reached down to kiss her nipples. He felt himself sober up. Was this happening? He actually *wanted* to have sex with his wife and judging by the hardness of her nipples, she wanted it too.

'You're gorgeous, Deirdre. Can we..?'

'So go on then, Rory, if you can remember how and if you're capable after all that drink.'

Rory wasn't sure if she was having him on by the sound of that remark, but he was too far gone in the nether regions to be able to pull back now. Somewhere in the back of his head a nicer, more sober, version of himself was telling him he needed to be more attentive to Deirdre's body than he *was* being but the pickled part of his brain won over and he climbed on board and relieved himself. When he was spent, he flumped on top of Deirdre and kissed her neck.

'You really are beaushiful you know.' Whoops. There was that word again. He'd have to find a better word.

'Are you finished?'

Was Deirdre angry? But surely she'd wanted that as much as he had. He rolled off her... or was she pushing him? Deirdre shot out of bed, put her nightdress over her head and when her face became visible again she looked furious.

'Are you alright? Deirdre?'

When Rory woke up the next morning the first thing he thought of was how much his head hurt. The second thing he thought of was the look on his wife's face when she had stormed off towards the bathroom the night before; and in response to both thoughts he groaned out loud.

Chapter twenty-one

RORY was feeling better. It was good to make a decision but now he had to stick to it. Deirdre was about to have another baby. He had spent nearly two years going back and forth from Dublin to Donegal and his daughter hardly knew him. He couldn't risk that happening again with his next child. He would give in his resignation at work and go home. They would have to get used to a huge cut in salary, if he managed a salary at all, but they would move out to their own place, no matter how small. There was no way he was going to live with his mother-in-law. He would tell Deirdre that it wouldn't be fair to her parents to have two babies around the place. He had learned to be diplomatic with his wife over time. Always tell her what she wanted to hear.

He tried to put the negative thoughts out of his head, and there were lots of them. The worst of it was that he would have to live with his wife, and sleep with his wife. Well one step at a time. He was doing this for his children and he wouldn't let complications get in his way.

He couldn't bear the loneliness in Dublin anymore. His romance with Maria was a distant memory. She had someone else in her life and didn't want to be found. Rory would always feel guilty that he had driven her away from her family. It would be hard to face them on a day-to-day basis in Balcallan. He was the reason they had lost Maria. But she could have come back by now if she'd wanted to. She could still come back.

Rory wondered, not for the first time, why Maria had never gone home. Surely the hurt had lessened by now. She had a new man in her life. She had moved on. So why the distance? He had stayed in Dublin because he could never face the fact that Maria was with someone else and she didn't want him. He had spent two years trying to find her. To explain. To work at winning her back. But Maria didn't want to be found. She had made a new life for herself and Rory would never be a part of it.

This was the last time he would pack his weekend bag or cuddle his toddler, while she wriggled away from him back to her mother. Somehow they would become a family.

Deirdre knocked on the door of their room, a courtesy they acknowledged each other during his visits. She looked radiant in her seventh month of pregnancy.

'Are you all packed? Dad says he'll give you a lift to the bus.'

'That's good of him... Deirdre... I want to talk to you for a few minutes before I go.'

'What about, Rory?' Deirdre's face took on a worried look. 'Shit, Rory. You're not seriously choosing this time to walk out on us, are you? Have you a girlfriend in Dublin? Is that it? I've often wondered, you know. You always seemed so eager to get back. This is a crap time to do this. I'm about to have another child.' Deirdre sat down on their bed and sighed.

Rory stared at his wife. This was certainly not the response he had expected from her and she didn't seem too put out about it either.

'Wait until after the baby's born, Rory. It'd be too difficult to sort everything out now. What do you say? Will you wait?' Deirdre looked up at her husband expectantly. There was no hurt in her expression. No accusation in her voice. Matter-of-factly, she would like him not to leave her for another woman until after she had given birth to their child.

Rory roared laughing. She was some woman. He had loved someone else for most of their marriage and now that he had decided to put all that behind him, she was asking him if he had someone.

'What's so funny?' Deirdre put on her *I'm very cross with you* face, which made him laugh all the more.

Rory sat on the edge of the bed away from his wife.

'Deirdre. I'm coming back. To Balcallan. The job is great in

Dublin and all that and I know the money is good but I'll not spend the rest of my days saying goodbye to children who don't know me. I'm packing this bag for the last time.'

If there was a joke, Deirdre still didn't get it.

'You're coming back? Back here?' She looked crestfallen.

'No, Deirdre. Not back to this house. I want you to start looking around for a place for us. It doesn't have to be in this village. Wherever you think best.' He knew that it would be a great idea to move a bit away if they were to try a new start.

'I'd better get a move on if I'm to make the bus.' Rory thought that he should at least give his wife a peck on the cheek if he was going away for a few weeks but she was looking at him as if she'd hate that more than anything he could try to do. So he picked up his bag and he walked downstairs. He wouldn't change his mind but it was going to be hard to live with Deirdre. She obviously thought so too.

On the road to the bus Rory put his idea to his father-in-law.

'Absolutely, Rory. I've never felt it natural the way that the three of you say hello and goodbye as often as you do. No. You're dead right. It's time to make a proper start. Especially with a new baby on the way. I'll keep the feelers out for a job for you, so I will. I'm delighted, lad, so I am. And Eiley will be too.'

Somehow Rory doubted that. Like mother like daughter. Would Deirdre end up like her mother? Would he end up like Bart? He shivered.

Chapter twenty-two

I LIE on my back on the newly-cut grass, looking up, my hand shielding my eyes from the May sunshine. An airplane is leaving its mark on the otherwise clear, blue sky. I prod Dónal as he lies across my lap and point upwards.

'I wonder where they're going, Dónal. Would you like to be on that plane?'

I don't have to ask that question. I know that he'd like to be anywhere other than Ireland right at this moment; away from trouble and fear. Far from O'Gorman and his Irish cause.

'You know I would, Mary. I wish we could get out of this country and get the hell out of this mess I'm in. Not for good but 'til the heat is off.'

'Where do you think they're going?' I watch the plane get smaller and smaller until it disappears.

'Africa, Mary. I'd love to go to Africa. See all those lions and tigers up close. Hear them roar in their natural environment.'

'Oh the terror of it all. No. None of that for me. Mind you, it was gas craic that day we climbed into the zoo over the back fence. The penguins were hysterical. Now me, I'd love to go to India. All that peace and quiet and meditating and all. A simple life. Now that's where the plane's gone to and I'm going to be on it someday.'

'India's a dangerous place, Mary. Hundreds of different casts with different dialects and religions all fighting with each other. Sure there's a war in nearly every country. Isn't it unbelievable how the English took over those colonies though, and even after all these years of so-called control they never managed to take away their language and their customs? Not like in Ireland where we ended up speaking a foreign language to this day.'

'Dónal, will you quit the *what the Brits did to us* for one day, for God's sake.'

'Ah, I'm only saying, Mary. It's a shame. That's all. We should be sitting here speaking to each other in our own language, in a country that's not split in two. That's all I'm saying.'

'Dónal. Didn't I say to you yesterday that we've enough problems of our own without trying to fix the world as well?'

He's been in a strange mood all day. There's something eating him. Something other than the usual shit we're going through. 'Concentrate on solving our own troubles and leave Ireland to solve itself for a while.'

That shuts him up. It shuts me up too. We lie in silence, each with our own thoughts for a few minutes. I'm thinking about what we're going to do when our baby is born. Where will we live? How will we feed it? What will we do for money? I hope that Dónal is thinking the same, but he has so much more on his plate besides domestic issues.

He must be reading my thoughts. In a nervous voice he breaks the quiet.

'Mary.' It's almost a whisper.

'What?'

'O'Gorman came to see me this morning.'

I squeeze my eyes shut. I can hear birds making various calls in the bushes and trees. Some children are squealing with delight, off to my right somewhere. Traffic outside the park is heavy and a siren announces somebody's crisis. My eyes open and his words echo. *He* came to see Dónal this morning. Our very own crisis. I feel a shiver down my back and along my arms at the sound of the name. I push Dónal off my lap and push myself up into a sitting position.

'What does he want?'

He doesn't look at me. 'A job. Driving. Tomorrow morning.'

'You'll not do it, Dónal. You promised.' I'm shaking him now. 'We won't wait until the baby's born. You can run now. Go anywhere you like. Africa if needs be. Anywhere as far away from O'Gorman as you can get. I'll follow after the baby's born. You can't do this, Dónal. You have to get away from them. You have to do it. For me.' I can't keep the panic from my voice. I reach out, my palms sweaty with fear, and hold his hand. 'For the baby.'

'I want to be there for you both and I will. But you didn't see him, Mary; the way he smiled at me. That horrible crooked smile he has. He didn't have to tell me what might happen if I didn't go along with what he said. His eyes spoke for him. O'Gorman doesn't request. He orders. If I go he'll look for me; or he'll send someone to find me. I'm in too deep. I know too much.'

'I don't understand how an intelligent fella like you, Dónal, found yourself wrapped up with this bunch.'

'Mary, I believe in what they want; that Ireland should be one island. Not split into two. When I was younger I thought that this was the only way. This was *my* war against England. I was doing *my* bit for my country. I still believe that but not with all this violence. But I'm in, Mary and there's no way out. I've seen others opt out, love, and it's not a pretty sight; believe me. Is that what you want for me, Mary? Is it? Because that's the alternative. But for fuck's sake, we've been down this road before, and all around the houses with it.'

'I'm about to have a baby, Dónal. What sort of a family could we be with this hanging over us all the time? They're murderers. You can tart them up any way you like but *The Cause* is for one thing only and that's to murder people; the innocent with the guilty; and your little bank raids funding them are as much to blame as the man pulling the trigger or pushing the switch.'

'I know you're right, Mary. There has to be a better way. Hundreds of years of this and we're getting nowhere, but... I don't know how.'

I look at my boyfriend and try to figure out how it all ended up like this. At first I had such a different opinion. Dónal was exciting. A guy who shared my idealistic opinions on a united Ireland. Parties always ended in a session where we outdid each other ballad for ballad. *A Nation Once Again. Kevin Barry. Come out you Black and Tans...* We knew all the words and after a few drinks we knew how to fix the world and everyone in it. I had unearthed my half-written novel and was writing again. Dónal was romantic and poetic and it was easy to fall in with him.

He didn't tell me of his real attachment to all this crap until I told him I was pregnant; but even still I hadn't realised to what extent he was connected – until recently.

A month ago Dónal came back to the squat in a state. He was shaking and his face was black and blue from a beating. He'd been ordered to rob a car and sit outside a post office to wait for the raiders to come out. But the night before he drank himself into a stupor worrying over me and the baby and how to get away from the devil and his cronies, and he never showed up. Later that day, a man came up to him in the road and asked him his name. He knew before he answered what was going to happen and that there was no way out but to tell him his name and to get the battering over with. When he came back to me he told me everything; why he couldn't be with me; why he couldn't look after me and our baby and why he was bad news and I should do my best to run from him and keep running.

But I was scared of being left alone to give birth again, so I nursed him and held him, told him what we would do and how we'd do it. We made plans for after the baby is born. We would start again, somewhere else, and keep running until we lost them. America. Australia. Anywhere.

Dónal looks over at me now, knowing what I'm thinking, then looks away. 'I wouldn't get far before tomorrow morning, Mary. And anyhow. There's something else. They've found out about you and the baby. I don't know how. I thought we were discreet enough but you can keep nothing from them. Nowhere is too far for them. It must've been the day I went to your place when I was hurt. I wasn't thinking straight. *He* told me not to let them down again and then he told me to give his regards to you and to wish you luck with the baby. I have to do this.'

Only then does he look me in the eye and I can see what he sees. There's only one thing scarier than the fear of the unknown.

The fear of the known. And me and my baby are a part of all this now. I should have left Dónal as soon as I heard what he was into but it's too late now. I can't leave him, and he can't leave those bastards. He'll steal a car in the early hours of tomorrow and he'll be waiting outside the bank or the shop. Afterwards, he'll take the car somewhere and he'll burn it out. There's no other way. This is the *safe* option.

Chapter twenty-three

I MOVE squat. Again. It's never too hard as I don't accumulate too much in the way of possessions but it's always difficult to lose the *friends* I've made and to try to make new ones. I never get too pally with someone; just close enough to be able to live around one another for a while, have a laugh. No one thinks too much about somebody being there one day and gone the next. This house seems worse than most. A lot of cannabis and too much heroin. It'll do for now and Mary Gregory, as I've introduced myself, isn't staying around here long. Another place to live. Another name. It has to stop. It's been nearly two years. Where did Maria go? She wants a place to call home.

Since Dónal told me that *he* was back, there have been several jobs. They're stepping up the campaign. While the rest of the country is negotiating peace talks, these guys are determined to show that there'll be no peace until there's unity. They need weapons and weapons cost money. Armed raid after armed raid is reported on the news. They know that they can use Dónal as much as they like. He's totally loyal now that a girlfriend and baby are in the picture.

Letting myself in the back door, I pull my coat around me to cover my bulk. I hadn't shown much with this baby until recently, and being so skinny otherwise I find it easy to hide my condition from the other members of the house. What they don't know about me is best for them and best for me. I tell them the same story that I've kept up for two years. I'm running from an abusive father. It has grains of truth. My father was a bastard when he had drink taken. Though Fiona says he was nicer when she was younger. That something went wrong between him and mammy.

I try to force any thoughts of my family out of my head. It's become easier over the years but now with the baby only a few weeks away, I'm thinking about my mam and my sister. I miss them.

Up until last month I thought that I might go home. I'd get over having Rory around somehow. I'd pretend that I don't care that Deirdre has had a baby and I *could* blame my father's treatment of me if they wanted to know why I left. Dónal has never brought up the subject of marriage but I've known that we could marry eventually. I wouldn't like to live in Balcallan but I would have contact with my mother and Fiona and they would get to know this baby. I'd never tell them about the first baby. Anna is safe and happy wherever she is. I've never told anyone. Not even Dónal. The grief of her loss hits me every now and then, but I deal with it myself. This time I'm keeping my baby. This baby has a father and mother. Grandparents.

But those are old thoughts that go back to that time before I realised that the only family we would ever have was fucking O'Gorman. Getting in touch with home is too risky. It isn't fair to drag them into this web. We're on our own. Dónal won't talk about the future. What does he expect me to do? Have the baby, come back to the squat and continue on in life as if nothing had happened?

One of my housemates is sprawled across the bottom of the stairs and I give him a shove to make sure he's alright before stepping over him and retreating to my own space. I've had a particularly difficult night *borrowing* money from the goodness of the capital. People are tightening their belts and becoming more wary. There are too many of us using ways to extort money from others and they're beginning to see right through me. I took money from Dónal now and then, before. I'm having his baby after all and we're very much a couple. But now that I know where all his money comes from it chokes me to rely on him for anything. Is my baby going to spend its childhood beholden to O'Gorman? I lie down on my mattress in the back bedroom and let the tears come. My past is a disaster and my present is even worse. No matter how hard I think about the future, I can't come up with any real solution. I can't leave Dónal. For the sake of this baby, I have to give it a father but how will we manage? *How*?

Then I start to shake and really cry.

***

I'm sitting on the park bench in the sunshine. I'm watching the children fly high on their swings and it makes me smile for the first time since I last saw Dónal. But then the terror seizes me again and the fear sits in my mouth. It's been days since I watched the news bulletin on the robbery of the bank. The one that went wrong, when the police arrested the driver of the getaway car.

'If I'm ever caught, Mary, don't try to come and see me. You don't know me. You never heard of me. Move away. Start again somewhere else. Go anywhere – but stay away.'

Dónal was adamant and I understood from the tone of his voice that he meant it. I haven't seen him since he left to do a job that morning, when a man *was held by Gardaí in connection with the robbery to help them with their enquiries.* I know that I have to wait for him to be released on bail and for him to find me. I think that this should have happened by now but I'm still waiting.

Looking at the mothers and their children, I wish for any one of their normal lives. I can't bear to watch anymore, so I get up and walk across the grass towards the park gate and home. Just as I am going through the gap between the trees I stop dead as a man steps out in front of me, pulling a balaclava over his face before I get a look at him. I've done everything that Dónal told me to, and they still found me. Will he harm my baby? I can't believe that I'm not screaming.

I stare hard at the eyes of the man in front of me. Glassy eyes. Unfeeling. Powerful. I realise now that Dónal never stood a chance against these men. He puts a hand out towards me and I flinch, but he touches me softly on the shoulder. His voice is low and almost kind. No threat in the tone he uses. Friendly. Is this how he was with Dónal?

'Mary. Hope you're keeping well and minding the baby. I've been keeping an eye on you. Dónal asked me to.'

I want to ask where he is but my voice freezes, deep down in the pit of my stomach.

'I followed him to your house. I knew he'd show up there eventually. Can you believe that he was negotiating with the police for a new life for yourselves in exchange for information? No. I couldn't believe that either. If he had stayed where the Gardaí told him to stay we might never have found him, but sure I knew he'd come to see you at some stage. Mad about you he was.'

Was...

He takes a deep breath and blows it out as if he's worn out from something.

'A bullet in the back of the head for his troubles, then buried in a place where no one will ever think to look.'

The feeling in my legs disappears and I'm kneeling on the ground; the balaclava hunches down beside me.

'Now what worries me, Mary darling, is what Dónal might have said to you before we silenced him. There are others who are all for sending you in the same direction as your boyfriend but I find that hard. A lovely girl like yourself with a baby on the way. I've never hurt a child before. But I'll be keeping an eye on you, so I will. Go home now and rest yourself, girl. Mind that little one. You look all worn out. Oh; and no need to keep moving house, Mary. It's exhausting and it's not worth it.'

He stands up but I don't watch him walk away. I lie down on the ground and stare into a grey sky. Another plane is weaving in and out through the clouds, carrying some lucky people to their destination. India? Africa? It doesn't matter. I'll never go anywhere with Dónal now. A bullet...

Two hours later, I'm still lying in the thicket. The world is a blur. I recognise the onset of familiar pains but I let them ride over me. I use them to try to obliterate the other pain but it isn't working. Nothing can cut deeper than that one. Nothing can hurt more. I'm still lying there in the afternoon when my waters break. I remember the last time that happened. Back then I had screamed out in fright but now I laugh. Then I cry. Softly at first, until the pain becomes too hard to bear and I scream at the mothers in the distant playground to come for me. I'm ready.

Twenty-four hours later, I walk out of The Coombe Women's Hospital without my baby. I'm dazed. This baby could have been loved. I want this little girl but I can't deal with her right now. I think of how much I've mourned Anna too. I've never stopped thinking of her. I'll come back for baby Shona when the danger's gone. When O'Gorman is no longer a threat.

I walk fast, ignoring the stitches where the baby has torn me. The nurses were shocked at my silence during the birth. They couldn't understand the pain that was inside me, that was hurting me far more than any physical pain ever would. I don't look back over my shoulder. Not this time. But I know that if *they* had their way, I would spend the rest of my life doing just that; with my beautiful baby girl who I've named after her grandmother. Shona would always be in danger as long as she's with me.

But away from me she'll be safe. I've taken her white baby blanket with me. I lift it to my face and inhale her smell, then let out an agonised cry.

I walk even faster towards the house in Crumlin. There's no point moving on somewhere else, he said. He'll find me. I clutch the bag to me. Another woman's belongings. Physically, it was so easy to do the second time. I've everything I need to get me through the next few days.

Except my baby. My babies. Shona... Anna... I can't go through all this again.

For three days I lie on the mattress in my room and let my delayed grief take hold, only moving to use the toilet. If anyone asks me what's wrong I tell them my boyfriend dumped me. It's something they're used to. If someone brings me something to eat or drink I take it but I never leave the room itself. This time I don't listen to the news or read the paper. I can't bear to hear about my abandoned baby or my missing, presumed dead, boyfriend.

On the evening of the third day, I stumble downstairs. Outside there's a man watching the house. Not O'Gorman, but I know he's watching for me.

I reach down and take the smouldering joint from the girl on the couch who has fallen into oblivion, after the first drag of yet another. I inhale deeply. It helps. I feel the pain recede a little and pull again. Nice. I finish to the end and the world looks better.

Then I go out to look for more.

Chapter twenty-four

RORY was still roaming the streets of Dublin. Grafton Street was awash with summer students enjoying a rare Irish heatwave. At ten on a Friday night he was leaving *Captain America's,* where he'd had dinner with a lady who was one in a string of women with whom he was trying to lose himself. This one had turned out to be particularly loud and obnoxious. She'd had too much to drink and was making a show of them in the restaurant. Rory excused himself to go to the gents, paid the bill quietly and ran down the stairs and out the door. He wasn't that hard up for a woman. Was he?

He had planned to be back in Balcallan by now but his boss had asked him to wait for a while until he found someone to replace him. Deirdre persuaded him to stay in Dublin until the baby was settled and that would be a good time to start again in Donegal. She said she couldn't possibly up sticks and move house so soon after having a baby anyway. He wondered what she would come up with next.

It suited him for the next month or two while the Gaelic football and hurling were reaching the end of their season. It was hotting up at the moment and looked like it might be a clash of the old enemies in the final, but as soon as that was all over he was leaving Dublin. He would have it out with Deirdre. If she didn't want to live with him she could come right out and say it, but he was going to live close to his daughters and that was that. He had only seen his baby girl briefly since she was born. He had been due to go back this weekend and he would, tomorrow.

At first Rory didn't pay much attention to the group of lads circled around a girl. They were only messing about. Doing no harm probably. There were a few Gardaí around anyway. If there was a problem then surely they would deal with it. He walked past, hands in his pockets and his face down. It was the girl's shouting that made him turn back.

'I'll take on the lot of you. Get losht. Go 'way.'

There was no mistaking the Donegal accent and even with the slur in the words, no mistaking the voice. Rory swung back and pushed through the group of boys that had been bothering her. They were only kids and they dispersed easily when the tall, well-built man walked among them.

'Clear off, all of you!' His voice was as strong as his stature and they scattered. One or two of them cowardly leaving taunts after them as they ran.

She looked blearily in his direction, nodded half-heartedly and turned to stumble away. Rory had seen her out of it a few times before and he knew that she wouldn't recognise him, but he walked alongside her anyway.

'Are you okay, Maria?' She looked up and eyed him suspiciously, as if she was wondering who this was who knew her name.

'Mary! I'm Mary!' she shouted.

'Of course you are.' Rory was sad that she didn't seem to recognise him but he wasn't walking away from her; not until he had at least found out how she had ended up like this and where she was living. But more questions brought no information. Either Maria was too far gone to know where she was or she wasn't saying.

Rory hailed a taxi and much to the driver's protests he shoved Maria into the back seat and gave the driver his address.

'If she damages my car it'll cost you.'

Rory ignored him. He sat and stared at Maria. It was hard to see past the mess but he knew what had been there and he knew what to look for. He could see it still. She was beautiful. She fell sideways and Rory caught her and wrapped her in his arms. He had missed her.

Later that night Rory lay in his single bed with his arms wrapped around Maria once more. He hadn't been able to get any sense out of her and had decided that the best thing was to let her sleep it off. He hoped that when she woke up she would be better. Whatever was going on between herself and that Dónal fella, he wasn't any good at looking after Maria, to leave her on her own and let her get into this state. Since the day that Rory had seen her with him in that café he had built up a deep hatred for the man that he didn't know, but whose name filled him with loathing.

Rory must have fallen asleep because when he woke Maria was lying, twitching beside him. He tried to wake her.

'Maria, it's me. Rory.'

'What the…' Maria pushed at him and tried to get out of the bed. Rory caught hold of her and tried to calm her.

'It's okay, Maria. It's okay. I was only looking after you. Making sure you were okay. Lie there, now. I'll make you a cup of sweet tea. You'll feel better then. We can talk.'

Maria wrapped her arms around herself, as if to stop the shaking. She looked at Rory with frightened eyes. He slid out of the bed and pulled the blankets back over her to keep her warm.

'I'll be two minutes, Maria,' he said and he went into the kitchen to make tea.

A few moments later, Rory heard the front door of his bedsit slam close.

'Damn!' He banged the two hot cups down on the table and ran towards the door. He opened it and called after her. But he was only wearing his boxers and Maria was gone.

Chapter twenty-five

A MONTH ago I was with Dónal; talking of plans for ourselves and our baby. I was a woman with a future. Somewhere out there Dónal and Mary would have found a haven for themselves. A man, a woman and a baby. A family. But now the family is scattered to the far ends of... well somewhere. Dónal is dead. Shona's in foster care. I'm... nowhere.

For three days now I've found myself getting a bus to Rathmines and getting off at the stop where Rory lives. I've stopped smoking weed. Just like that. The shaking and craving eventually gave way to anger. At least I'm feeling something. I hadn't touched drugs all the time that I was pregnant and I've never gone back to the crap I was at after I lost Anna. I don't need it.

I stand across from his flat and stare up at his bedroom window. He's probably at work in the middle of the day. I convince myself that that's the only reason I'm here. I've no intention of going to the flat and knocking at the door. I don't want to get in touch with the man who's been the cause of all the problems in my life. Well not all, but I'd never have left Balcallan the way I did if it wasn't for him. I'd be able to go back now. I'd have a safe place to run. With each day that I return to this street my fury grows. It's almost good to have a place to vent everything. Rory fucking McGee.

What's he doing here in Dublin? The flat I woke up in looked well lived in, as if he's been there for some time. Has he left Deirdre? And their baby? The child would be two now. The same age as Anna. *Our* baby... mine and Rory's. A toddler who looks like one of us... or both. Where's Anna? Shona? Two babies... No babies... No Rory... No Dónal...

My babies are safe but I can't go looking to take them back yet, in case danger follows. He would only harm them. They're safer without me, for now. So I let the tears fall and I lean against the bus stop and stare at Rory's window. I need somewhere to stay. I don't want to live in the squat anymore. I might as well stay here as anywhere. I don't care if I put *Rory* in danger. Good enough for him. I sit on the kerb and wait. I try to ignore the fact that I want to see him again. I put it down to being alone and afraid. But I know there's more to it. Feelings that never left.

Rory saw Maria from his window at the back of the bus. He was down the aisle and out the door as quick as he could push his way through the passengers.

'Maria!'

She didn't answer him but she looked up and made an attempt at a smile. She pulled her denim jacket close around her and folded her arms.

Rory moved slowly towards her. He wouldn't frighten her this time. He would take everything nice and slow. She had come to him though. This was a good start.

'Would you like to come in for something to eat, Maria?' He loved saying that name. It rolled off his tongue as if it belonged there. It would belong. Maria had come back to him. Rory had thought of nothing else since Saturday morning. Only where she might be. And here she was. Beautiful, beautiful Maria.

She shrugged her shoulders and nodded, then followed him into his flat.

'What can I get for you? I did a shop yesterday so there's a fair bit in the fridge and the presses. If you want to have a rummage you might see something that you fancy. And would you like a cup of tea... or is it coffee... or if you're thirsty there's some lemonade?' Rory was rambling; nervous that she might do a runner again. He made a play of putting the kettle on and gestured her towards the cupboards.

'Whatever you want. I don't mind.' Maria hadn't moved from

the kitchen door. She was darting her eyes around the place and looked like she might be about to scarper.

'Will we start with the tea, eh?' What was he going to say to her? She might not want to talk about where she had been over the past two years. Rory didn't want to talk about himself and his domestic affairs in case it sounded too cosy and scared her off before he had a chance to tell her straight. A newborn baby sounded far too family orientated.

Maria nodded. 'Tea. Okay.'

'With two sugars, yeah? Haven't I a great memory all the same? Do you remember the times we used to sit in that lovely café in Letterkenny for hours, drinking tea and talking about life? I loved those afternoons.' Rory stopped putting teabags in the cups and looked straight at Maria. For a moment she returned his smile, as if the memory made her happy too. But then she shook her head.

'No sugar, Rory. I kind of went off it as I got older.'

Rory continued with his tea making. What else had she gone off over time? Him? Sure what was he thinking? She was probably still with that fella Dónal he had met in the café. He desperately wanted to ask her about him but he was afraid of the answer.

'I'll make us some chops. And a few spuds?'

Maria laughed a little and her face relaxed. Away from the deer caught in the headlights look that she'd been wearing since she came in. 'I never thought I'd see the day that Rory McGee could make a dinner for himself. A right domesticated life you're leading these days. Are you here by yourself?'

There it was. Maria had thrown the dice for him and now he had to move his counter. Would he give her the whole story as it was or would he embellish it a bit to make himself look a little better? A little less married. He hadn't made a decision yet.

'Yeah. There's only me. I'm working here in Dublin. For a cousin of... well a cousin of Deirdre's.' There he'd messed up now and they'd have to talk about her. He'd mentioned her name but he could stall.

'So are you okay with the chops and spuds, then? I could throw a few tinned peas with it if you like?' Maria didn't answer but she put her bag down and she came and sat on the stool by the table.

'Grand so. There's the kettle ready now. And a drop o' milk. But no sugar. No, no sugar these days. Right.'

Tea on the table. Chops in the frying pan. Spuds boiling away on the cooker. Too early to open the tin of peas. He didn't know what else to say to her. Well he knew what he wanted to say to her but that would make her nervous and he was going out of his way to put her at ease.

'Maybe you'd like beans instead. I have those too. Or you might like them both together?'

Maria made a face.

'Well you know what I mean, not mixed up together obviously but on the same plate... or whatever...'

'Peas are grand, Rory.'

The noise of the boiling and the sizzling from the cooker was deafening.

'I better turn those chops over and check the spuds, then.' Rory walked the two steps to the cooker. The chops had been on low and weren't nearly ready. The potatoes would be hard for a while. He had to think of something to say. He stirred the pot a bit more. Come on. Come on.

'What did you call the baby then?'

Rory dropped the spoon and swung around. 'Eh, Clodagh.'

'Lovely. How old is she now?'

'Em, two weeks. She's a little dote.'

'Two *weeks*? Surely you mean two years? Oh my God. You've had another baby? You're still together? I'm sorry. I presumed... with you living here, and I thought you must be separated or something. But you're not.' Maria stood up.

'No, Maria. Don't go. We are. Separated I mean.'

'Some separation if she's still busy having your babies.'

'It was only the once, Maria. I was drunk. It meant nothing. Deirdre means nothing to me. My children do. Of course they do. But not Deirdre. Only you. Always you. I looked everywhere for you.' Rory went towards the door where Maria was and tried to hold her, but it was clumsy and it was like he was groping at her. She pushed him away.

'No, Rory. Stop it. Leave me alone.' She started to cry.

'Ah, Maria. I'm sorry. Sure I know. Everything's changed. I had no right to do that. I'm sorry. You're with someone else. I know. Don't cry, Maria. I'm sorry.'

Maria sat down on the ground and the crying became sobbing. She put her hands over her head as if she was trying to protect herself from being hit. Rory wondered if her boyfriend did that. Was he a bit easy with his hands? He hadn't seemed like a violent fella when Rory had met him that once. As always, the very thought of the man being with Maria filled him with anger but he knew he could say nothing bad about Dónal to Maria if he wanted her to open up to him.

He sat down on the ground beside her. 'Do you want me to get him? Dónal I mean. Will I ring him for you? Or do you want me to bring you back to him? What is it, Maria? What has you so upset? Have you broken up? Is that it? Or has he hurt you? So help me, I'll kill him if he's laid a hand on you, I will.'

Maria looked up at him and spoke through her sniffs. 'You're too late. That bastard has killed him already.'

'What, Maria? What do you mean?'

She looked down and wrapped her hands around herself. 'He shot him in the back of the head.' She was shouting but Rory looked at her as if he couldn't possibly have heard right.

'He's dead, Rory. They killed him. And I'm so frightened. They think I know something too.'

Maria had stopped shouting but she was still crying and it didn't sound like she would ever stop. Rory was staring at her, saying nothing. Had she said that Dónal was dead? Shot? By who?

'Know *what*, Maria? About Dónal?' But she didn't answer and this time, when Rory put his arms around her, she didn't fight him. She nestled into him and the tears came and came. 'Cry away, Maria love. Cry away.'

Chapter twenty-six

THE girl on the bed was a different girl than the one that Rory had loved before. Even as she slept she looked troubled. Her eyes blinked, as if disturbed by dreams that they couldn't block out. Maria had been talking in her sleep. *'Take the babies away. Don't let him have the babies. Mind the babies.'* Was she talking about *his* babies? His and Deirdre's? So many questions and Maria wasn't ready to answer. Did she think that his children would be in danger if he helped her? That his being with her was putting his own children at risk. *Was* it? Would these people know so much? He shivered. He had promised Maria that he wouldn't leave her. That he would keep her safe. He wouldn't break that promise. He had hurt her once and nothing would make him hurt her again. He leaned over her sleeping frame and whispered.

'I love you, Maria. I've always loved you. I'll never hurt you again. I'll never leave you.' And he kissed her forehead.

Maria woke and cried out. 'No! Get off! Go away! Leave me alone!' And she jumped up from the bed and ran from him.

Rory followed her.

'Okay, Maria... It's okay. I was only minding you. I won't hurt you.'

But she was crying again. Slumped on the couch. Would she ever be able to stop? Rory went over to her and crouched down beside her.

'I know you loved him. I'm not trying to take his place. But I'm staying with you for now. You need me to help you. There's too much danger. You have to get away from here. Don't you understand?'

Maria sobbed louder and he raised his voice.

'We'll go to England. I have friends in London. They're not from Donegal. They'll not recognise you or know anybody that you know. We'll be safer there. No need to make any decisions about the future yet, Maria. We need to get away from here.'

Maria sat up slowly. Her face was pale and drawn. She had always been a slim girl but now she had lost too much weight. Her clothes hung on her. Her hair fell around her face and shoulders in a thin cloak. Her eyes were hollowed out from crying and drugs. But somewhere in there, Rory could see the old Maria. He knew that it would take time but that if he kept chipping away he would eventually come to that place where he had left her. Two years of building a wall around it; Rory didn't care if it took another two, to break it down again. Maria was the only girl he had ever loved.

He would leave Deirdre. She would be happy to be left. They would come to an arrangement about the girls. They had managed without him all this time. Eventually he would persuade Maria to go home. Back to her family. They would have the life they should have had before the nightmare. He took Maria's hand gently and smiled softly at her.

'The only thing that is important right now is for you to get out of Ireland as quickly as possible. That's the thing you have to do. Whatever comes later can be decided at another time.'

Maria nodded and took a deep breath to shake away the latest fit of crying.

'Where's the house that you're living in?' asked Rory. Maria gave him the bones of her address.

'Grand. Go back there. Pack a bag. Only what you *have* to bring. If they're still watching your house then you don't want to make them suspicious. I'll meet you tomorrow.' He scribbled on a piece of paper. 'Here's my number. Ring me at work and I'll tell you where.'

'You can't walk away from everything, Rory. You have a job. A wife. Two babies. I'll go myself. I've managed to mind myself in Dublin for years on my own, I'm sure London can't be too different.'

'No, Maria. You haven't managed. You shacked up with danger and you put yourself at great risk. There's no way you're going to London on your own. I don't have a wife. I hate my job. And my children will still be here for me when I get back. I'll be back to them when you're safe. Whatever happens I'm coming with you.'

Rory moved a little closer to her and rubbed the back of his fingers along her cheeks, to wipe away the tears. 'I know you don't want to hear this, Maria, but I love you. I always have. And I know that you don't love me. Dónal has died. You loved him but he's not here now and you told me yourself that he said to run if anything happened to him. So run. We'll go tomorrow. You have to trust me Maria. You're not thinking straight at the moment so you have to let me do your thinking for you. Let every day happen.

'I'd never forgive myself if anything happened to you, Maria. You're all that matters.'

***

I walk towards the squat in Crumlin, dragging my feet behind me. It's all well for Rory to be so decisive and masterful but it's hard to go along with it. Dónal is dead. I gave birth to two babies and they're gone. What if O'Gorman knows where my babies are and harms them, to teach me a lesson for running away? I don't know what to do. It would be easier to let Rory make the decisions; to go along with everything he tells me to do. But he doesn't know about the babies and I haven't been able to tell him. The fewer people who know they exist, the safer they are.

I don't know where Anna is. I lost track of her whereabouts after she was fostered out a few times. But I know where Shona is. I've been desperate to go there to see her. So many times I was so close to getting on a bus to the home where she is and walking in and claiming my baby. But some kind of self-preservation kept me away. Shona's safe but only without me. I sent a note to them to say that I'd be coming for her. When I can. And I will.

Passing Crumlin hospital, deep in thought, I don't see a man come walking straight into me. He runs off without even saying sorry but when he's gone I realise that on his way past he's put a piece of paper into my hand. I rub my arm where he walloped into me and stare at the crisp paper.

I unravel it. There's a handwritten message on it but it's not signed. A summons to a meeting. It must be from O'Gorman. My legs give way and I find myself sitting on the side of the street. It's too much. I can't live this life. I want my babies, and to be left in peace to go home to my mother and my sister.

It says to meet him outside the Abbey Theatre at 8pm. That's a strange place to ask to meet if he means me harm. There'll be lots of people there. It'll be safe. Perhaps if I plead with him, swear that I know nothing about him and promise that I will never tell what I know of Dónal's death... Then I remember the eyes in the balaclava, in the park, the day that Shona was born. The voice that told me that Dónal was shot in the back of the head. There's no way that man will accept anything I say.

Reaching for the top of a wall, I haul myself back up and start to walk again. I have to get away. I'll tell Rory. He'll know what to do. I cross the road to the phone box and dial his number. I blubber the details of the note.

'Okay, Maria. I'm walking out of work right now and I'm going home to pack some clothes. Only the bare essentials. I need to go to the bank as well; get some sterling. Forget what I said earlier, Maria. Don't go home. You need nothing. Meet me in town, outside *Clerys* at 4pm. We'll be on the boat tonight. By the time he's standing at the Abbey, we'll be gone. Be careful, love. We're nearly there. Stick with me. It'll be okay. See you outside *Clerys*.'

I'm not sure how long I stand in the phone box. I know that Rory's right. I've no option but to run. They've decided to get rid of me the same way they murdered Dónal. But if I go to England I might never be able to get back. I might never get to see Shona again. Or Anna.

Thinking of my babies makes me think of the baby blanket I have in my bag in the squat. I walked away from Anna without having anything to remind me of her. I knew that the separation from Shona wasn't long-term but I still made sure to bring the baby's blanket. At night, I sleep with it wrapped in my arms as if I still have my baby there.

I'm going nowhere without that blanket.

I'll go there quickly, take my bag and jump on a bus into town immediately. I quicken my step. It'll be okay. Rory's right. I'll go to England for now. I'll write another letter to the home and tell them I'm coming back for my baby. I'll wait until O'Gorman's bastards have forgotten about me. Rory said that we would go back to Donegal eventually. O'Gorman doesn't know of my link to my family. I severed it myself. It's all going to work out fine. I run up the path and into the house.

Nobody's home. I'll see if there's something to eat and drink and go straight back out. I'm moving in a haze. I want something to take the fear away. I can't think clearly. Walking around the kitchen, I try to ignore the stash of smack and crack that I saw Mark hide in the skirting boards when he thought I wasn't looking. I fiddle about with the kettle. I don't need it. I've never touched that heavy stuff and I hate what I see happens to others after they've taken it. I'm not even smoking weed. I'm doing fine. My hands are less shaky. I need to hurry. Rory'll be waiting.

But if I do take a little of Mark's stash, it would be the last time I would take anything. I could never take drugs with Rory around. I know he'd be totally pissed off with me. Mark would kill me but that doesn't matter because I won't see anyone in the house ever again. I'll be on the boat before Mark even notices it's gone.

The tea is made and it's hard to see where I'm spreading the jam on the crackers through the tears. I don't have to have a full dose. I could half-fill the syringe. I've seen others do it enough times. Enough to calm me; to make the leaving bearable. My babies. I want to see them again. I want to hold them and to care for them. And it will happen. But first I have to go away for a while and this will make it a little easier. It's only to get me through today and then no more. Rory's right. It's a fool's game.

So this is the last time. Ever. It isn't going to happen again.

The euphoria begins as I lift the skirting board; the anticipation of floating away from O'Gorman and all my pain, wrapping around me already. I collect what I need. I copy what I've seen Mark and his friends do, their ritual is still engrained in my head. Once I begin the preparation, I know that there's no pulling away now. I have to do this.

Getting my bag together in the sitting room, I love the feel of the white as it sails through my veins and into my bloodstream. My mind sharpens, my energy rises and I feel a surge of pleasure. I know I shouldn't have had the whole lot. It was madness. It'll be hell to try and make it into town on my own. But the further in the heroin goes the more I know I can take on the world. Then the brown kicks in and softens the razor edges of the white. Everything stops hurting and I know I'm going to be alright. In fact, I could probably go to the home first and collect Shona before I go on the boat. Why did I not think of that before? It's clearer now. I should've taken this earlier. I understand why Mark does this. It's easier to make plans now that my head's free of all the pain of the last few weeks.

I'll leave my sleeping bag here. I won't need to bring that. Only the bare essentials Rory said. Or was that before? Today did he say bring nothing? But Shona's blanket. I need that. I'll go nowhere without that. And anyhow I'll need it to wrap Shona in when I collect her from the home. I wrap it around and around. I'm wrapping my baby up tight, keeping her warm. I hold the baby and rock her back and forth, humming softly. My head's so sharp. It feels good to know where I'm going; great to make plans. I lie down on the couch and caress the blanket that's wrapping my baby. I smile at her. Goodnight, little Shona. Sleep well. Soon we'll go to get your sister. We'll all be together with your granny and your aunty. And Rory has come back to me. We'll have a perfect life. Sleep well babies.

Chapter twenty-seven

'SHIT! Wake up, Maria.' Rory shook her to get a response. She managed to open her eyes to slits and smiled a mad, wild smile, mumbling something incoherent before slipping away again.

He had waited under *Clerys*' clock for almost an hour, until he realised that she wasn't coming. The address she had given him in Crumlin was etched in his memory though, so he'd headed straight there – but he wasn't prepared for what he found.

'Where's the note they gave you, Maria?' He looked through her pockets and around the sitting room of the squat, but gave up once he'd taken in the mess of the place. Torn, dirty clothes were discarded on the floor, with some hanging from string along the flaking walls, in an effort to air or dry them. The couch she lay on was covered in burns and rips.

'Fuck this anyway. I'll go next door to the chipper and get some tea with lots of sugar and I'll try to get it into you.'

He walked towards the kitchen and, picking up her jacket from the sticky linoleum floor, Rory smelt the freshness of it; the hope that was there this morning when she was going to put her life right. But that was before she had bumped into that lot again. He felt in her jacket pockets now. Pretty, flowery fabric to hide something so sinister. Sure enough there was a rolled up piece of paper; written, unsigned.

Meet me outside the abbey theatre tonight at 8. It's for your own good. Bring no one.

If only she had done as Rory had told her. Panic must have driven her to take something very strong and then she had come back to throw herself into the mess that she was in now. Maria's answer to every problem in her life.

He needed to get her the fuck out of this cesspit and out of Ireland. He looked around the disgusting kitchen that must have once served a family with children, judging by the pictures still hanging crooked on the walls. The smell of filthy dishes with rotting food was overpowering and he rushed towards the back door that had been left open, breathing in the fresh air outside. He was worried about leaving her again but it didn't take long to pick up a couple of teas and he was back in the house within minutes.

As he made for the sitting room the sound of movement stopped him. Was she up or was it another squatter? She'd be well ready for something to revive her. He smiled, determined now. He'd get her going and they'd be out of here soon. Walking down the hall and into the sitting room he stopped dead when he saw a well-built man hovering over Maria, the needle of the syringe in his hand plunged into her arm. A roar came from somewhere deep down inside Rory, and as the man extracted the syringe and stood up; he rushed forward and threw the scalding tea in the intruder's face.

'Aaagghh! Fuck you!' The man screamed in pain and grabbed a blanket from Maria's arms to wipe his face. Rory flung his large frame on top of him and pinned him to the ground while wrestling the syringe from his fingers.

'You're too late,' the man laughed. 'I was finished. She's as good as dead. That stuff'll not take long in her system.'

This news sapped Rory's strength temporarily, and he loosened his hold as he looked back over at Maria. She was hardly moving. Only her eyes were rolling. The man who was trying to kill her used Rory's distraction to force him off and push him aside. Realising his mistake, Rory flung himself back on his attacker. Pushing the man face down on top of the blanket, he plunged the syringe with the full force of his anger into the struggling man's cheek, ripping skin and flesh. Yelling out in pain again, the man used all of his strength to heave Rory off his back.

Rory landed in a corner and froze as he watched the animal pull the syringe out with a stifled roar, his green eyes wild and trained on Rory. He swiped up the blanket that had already taken all the splattered blood and used it to hold the rest of the flow. He stumbled in Rory's direction and, with his free hand, he held the syringe towards his prey in a knife grip; the needle only centimetres away.

'You'll not get rid of me that easily, you interfering bastard you,' he said.

Rory willed himself to attack again but the image of what the man had been able to do was all he could see. He had killed Dónal and Maria and now it was Rory's turn. The man came in closer and touched Rory's neck with the tip of the needle. Rory stood completely still, paralysed. The wound on the face in front of him leant an added malice to the now warped speech.

Then his attacker relaxed his grip. 'I'll not do away with you just yet, shithead. A murder here, with one overdosed corpse already, would raise far too many questions. I'll wait. Some day or night when you're least expecting it though, I'll have you. I'll enjoy the planning. I'm leaving you with your good-as-dead friend but I have your number, Donegal boy.'

Rory's eyes widened at the realisation that the man knew exactly who he was.

'Yes, and your family. You'll want them protected. And the baby too.' He nodded his head in Maria's direction. 'She died easy. I'll not make it so relaxing for *you*. In the meantime go home to Donegal and shut your mouth.' He lowered the blanket from his cheek and the syringe from Rory's neck and he smiled through the pain in his face. The result turned Rory's stomach.

The animal's glassy eyes held a smug, satisfied look. Suddenly, the note that Rory had dropped during the fight caught his eye and he reached down and picked it up. Reading it, he smiled an angry smile and looked up at Rory. He then stood back and flung the bloodied, white blanket in Rory's face. He began to walk away, turning back briefly at the door to blow a kiss in Maria's direction. 'Night, night, little girl. Sleep well.' And he was gone.

Maria wasn't moving.

Rory wanted to run after the man and kill him with his bare hands but he knew he had to tend to Maria. There would be a way to save her yet. He staggered over and fell on his knees beside her. He took her limp hand but despaired as her eyes began to relax. She was lying lifeless on the couch.

'Oh, Jesus, Maria! No... I'll get help... You'll be okay.'

Rory took his hand away. She was looking too weird. He'd phone an ambulance and tell them that she'd overdosed. They'd bring her to hospital and make her better. He'd take her away afterwards and hide her from these mad people. He kissed her forehead and sobbed. Her lips were turning blue.

'Back in a minute, Maria. I love you. Hang in there.' It was so hard to leave her and he shook her one more time in desperation. 'For fuck's sake, Maria, *please* wake up!' He clutched at her hands again and ran his thumb along the tips of her already blue fingers. He swallowed the bile rising into his mouth. He pushed himself up on all fours and then onto his feet. At last that survival instinct kicked in and he staggered out of the house and ran to the phone box at the bottom of the road.

Standing on the street later, Rory watched them carry Maria out on a stretcher; her beautiful face covered. He had known she was gone but this confirmation made the truth unbearable. He put one foot forward to move towards the ambulance, to tell them what had happened; that Maria had been murdered. He had to let them know that he had seen who had done this terrible thing, and how. But he shrank back when he saw that the animal was on the other side of the street, half hidden in a porch; watching; his hands in his pockets, casually staring at the ambulance, waiting to see what Rory might do.

He wouldn't do anything yet to satisfy him. But first thing in the morning he would go to the police. Let him think that Rory had run for now. This hard man had taken Maria and had taken Dónal before that. The pain of the cut to his face had meant little to him. He and others like him would do away with Rory without blinking. Maria was gone. Running to the ambulance

167

now wouldn't bring her back.

Rory sank further into the laneway where he was hiding and watched the ambulance take her. No sirens. No need. The man looked around once more, the fresh cut vivid on the side of his face. Rory put his hand inside his jacket and felt for the little, white blanket that Maria had wrapped around herself before she died. Now it was seeped in that animal's blood. Tomorrow Rory would give it to the police. He had all the evidence he needed.

For now though, he was going to slink away like a coward and say nothing. If he did nothing and the police enquired later, they would hear from her friends that she was a drug user. He had told them on the phone that his friend had overdosed. That's what they would believe. That she had taken contaminated drugs. The only evidence of his scuffle with the killer was the blood-stained blanket. There would be no murder hunt until he handed that over. He walked back to his own flat looking over his shoulder, waiting.

***

Fear kept Rory from the police. He never went back to his job in Dublin. He stayed inside his flat and cried for three days, then went home to Deirdre. He hid the blanket in a box of school books in the attic in Deirdre's father's house. He would decide what to do with it in a few days… but then he fled to London. He had to keep away from his family; lie to them to keep them safe. He would go back to get the blanket in a few weeks…

But the years disappeared. The loss of Maria and his own terror never left him. He waited for that man to do him harm, and he was sure he would. It was only a matter of time.

Chapter twenty-eight

THE seagulls screeched in the winter sky as Rory made his way along Brighton Pier to meet with Gerry and Fiona. He shivered with the cold and the anticipation he always felt whenever his friends from Balcallan came to the UK for a visit. He could see the café in the distance and breathed in the sea air to steady himself, before walking fast towards the entrance and greeting the couple who had been his only link to his home and family for the last sixteen years.

'Sit down there, Rory. You're looking great altogether.' Gerry always opened with a line about how well Rory looked and Rory always laughed it off; knowing full well the years were disappearing fast on his looks and his hairline was definitely receding.

'Ah, but it's good to see the pair of you. I've been looking forward to this weekend for weeks, so I have. Have you the pictures and stuff?' Rory could never wait to feast his eyes on photos of his growing daughters and to hear other news about how they were doing at school and so on.

Deirdre had been using Fiona as her go-between all these years, allowing her husband pictorial access to their girls in his absence. She had accepted Rory's story, that he had mistakenly got in with a bad crowd in Dublin who suspected him of grassing on one of their friends after a robbery. He had convinced them all that these people had vowed to make him and his family pay in the worst way possible, and that he was keeping away from them for their own safety. He had never given anyone from home his address, only a mobile number which they used to make plans to get together in a different place outside London every time that the Martins travelled over to see him.

'Wait now, Rory until we get a cup of tea into us. It's freezing out there. I can't understand why you choose such wild places to meet us all the time. Brighton Pier for God's sake. There isn't another mad person out there this afternoon.' Fiona rubbed her hands together to try to get warm. Rory was never sure why she always came over with Gerry for the twice-yearly visits but she was always there and he had grown as fond of her as he was of the man he called his best and only friend.

'Grand, Fiona. We'll get the tea into us with a bit of grub. I'm starving after the train ride down from London. But listen, you *know* why it's best to meet in remote places. And somewhere different each time. Haven't I made it clear enough?' Rory watched Fiona and Gerry share a look and he knew from their faces they had come over, this time, with something more to talk to him about than just the usual news. He beckoned to the waitress and soon they were digging into a full English fry-up and a pot of tea.

Afterwards, when they had finished with the photos and the general updates from home, and Rory had quietly shed the usual tears, seeing how his daughters were growing into beautiful young women, and marvelled at how much they were achieving in everything they did; he put the large envelope to the side and folded his arms. 'So what is it you both are itching to tell me? You have something to say, so you might as well spit it out. Is it bad news? Has something happened to someone?'

'No, Rory. Nothing like that.' Fiona stood up from the table. 'But I'm going to hit the shops in the lanes for a while and let yourself and Gerry talk. He *has* something to say to you. Listen well and heed what he says.' She squeezed Gerry's shoulder encouragingly and she was gone out the door, leaving the two men to sit and contemplate things in silence for a while.

'Will we go for a pint?' Gerry sounded like he wanted some familiar ground under him to get this thing off his chest.

'A bar stool it is then, but only the one. I've a new job starting tomorrow and I want to be in the full of my health hanging out of that scaffolding.'

Ten minutes later, the two were sitting up holding their pints of Guinness and sighing contentedly after the first sip; and Gerry had texted Fiona with their whereabouts.

'It doesn't taste the same over here,' said Gerry. 'It doesn't travel well.'

'Don't be ridiculous, Gerry. This is brewed in the UK. It hasn't travelled anywhere.'

'I don't know how you stick it at all. I know I couldn't hack it long-term.'

'Ah, it's alright. You get used to it.'

'Is that good enough for you though, Rory? To get used to it. To have a life that's just alright.'

'I thought we were talking about the Guinness.'

Gerry pulled his stool nearer to the bar and shook his head. 'No, Rory. I don't suppose I'm talking about the pint. It's the life you lead here. It's been such a long time. You change jobs. You change flats. You move around London and you make no real friends. Sure that's no life. In the meantime your parents, your sister and your daughters are all living their lives without you in them, and you've missed out on so much.'

'What would you have me do, Gerry? It's not safe to live in Balcallan. You know that.'

'Rory, it's been sixteen years. Whoever was after you has lost interest. They've never found you. That fella who threatened you way back then is probably grown up now, married with a family and getting on with his own life; while you hide away here and vegetate in a half-life.'

'What are you saying, Gerry? That I should go home now and pretend that none of it happened? Go home to my wife and daughters who would welcome me back with open arms and forgive and forget the years of absence? Even if that fella is off my back now, I couldn't face Balcallan. My parents have never spoken to me since I left. I only get snippets of news that Rita sends through you. Deirdre has managed to do a fabulous job bringing up the girls on her own. She's happy enough with the cash that I send to her account every month. She certainly doesn't want me shaking up her hard won easy life.'

'You've let the best years slip by Rory. But in two years' time you'll be forty and what have you done with your adult life? When you were twenty you had it all. The hurling, the great job, family and friends. Somehow you've ended up, still a young man might I add, but with nothing. With nobody. I never hear you mention a woman on the scene when I come over so I'm presuming there isn't a long-term relationship on the go. What have you got, Rory? Admit it. There's nothing to keep you here anymore... Come home.'

'What would you know of my life here, Gerry or how it would feel to turn up back in Balcallan as a complete failure and have to start from scratch? You with your lovely wife and daughter and the community you've built around you. You have it all. I have nothing. I couldn't face everyone the way I am now.' Rory's tone was angry but Gerry felt the anger was directed inwards.

Both men picked up their glasses and drank quietly, thinking their own thoughts. Eventually Rory let out a sound like he was clearing his throat violently and it was only when Gerry saw him race towards the *Gents*, he realised how upset his friend was. He wouldn't go after him. Let him have a bit of dignity and they'd take up the conversation when he returned. He could see how going back would be hard for Rory but he was going to tell him when he came out, that this would be the last time he would come over with Fiona to see him. Rory could come home or stay here. Let him make his own decisions. He suspected that it wouldn't take too much to make the man who lived in a miserable bedsit, in a lonely city, come back to the place where he belonged.

Fiona came up behind him. 'Did he do a runner?'

Gerry reached over and gave his wife a hug and sat back on his stool.

'Only to the loo. He'll be back. He's in a bit of a state. Will you have a glass of wine?'

'This place is a kip. I'd rather not. Did you tell him you're not coming back?'

'I didn't get that far. But I'd say if he's any doubts about what to do for the best, telling him *that* will turn him in the direction of home. I hope so. Because he's a good man. And he doesn't deserve to rot away here, into old age, with nobody.'

Part three

Chapter twenty-nine

FIONA knocked lightly on her daughter's bedroom door.

'Fuck off and leave me alone.'

'Come out and talk to me.'

'*Fuck* off and *leave* me alone.'

Fiona pushed down the handle and walked in. Anna was curled up in a ball on her side, her back to her mother. Fiona walked around, sat on the bed beside her and took her hand.

'It's too much for me to take in. I can't even think what it must be like for you.' She squeezed her daughter's hand and Anna squeezed back, weakly, but it was recognition of sorts.

'Sit up, love. Let's get this out in the open before it festers.'

Anna sat up and put her arms around her mother. They sat like that, in silence, for a while.

'I told him to come to see us in the morning, Anna. To give us time to talk it out and try to make sense of the whole thing. For what it's worth, Rory is equally upset with everything that's happening at the moment. We've spoken on the phone for a long time. He told me that he never suspected for a moment that Maria had been pregnant when she left.'

'It's no use, Mam. I'm not talking to him. Not now. Not ever. I'm so fucking angry with him. It's all well for you to side with him and go off into battle with this bloody politician. Rory hasn't told you that he's your bloody father.'

'No Anna, he's told me that my sister was murdered. And not only that but that he was the original reason for her to run to Dublin and get herself into all that trouble. You're so right. It's all well for me.'

'She was my *mother*, even if I never knew her. I can't believe that I've been living around the corner from my natural father for the past two years. He's one of Dad's best friends.'

'Anna, he wants to talk to you. The man is having it rough at the moment. His other daughters won't speak to him since their grandmother told them that he was having an affair with me. *Their* mother won't speak to him when she finds out that he was having babies with *your* mother while he was married to *her* and having babies with *her*. Your dad won't speak to him when he hears that *he's* your birth father and he was carrying on with Maria when he was newly-wed and having babies and never told him and... Jesus, Mary and Joseph, but it's bloody complicated.'

Despite the seriousness of the whole thing, or perhaps because of it, the two women burst into hysterical laughter and sat back into the pillows.

When they had pushed the laughter as far as it would go, Fiona tried again.

'So will you talk to him?'

'No.'

'Okay. For now. Change of subject. Will I go back to your father do you think?'

'Oh, that bit's easy. I don't know what the fuck the two of you were sparring about anyway. Yes. I think my poor eejit of a father has suffered enough.'

'It doesn't suit you, Anna. The F word.'

Anna burst into tears again. 'Oh, Mam... I'm so angry.'

Fiona put her arm around her daughter. 'Me too, Anna. Me too.'

They sat quietly like that until Anna finished her crying.

'Listen,' said Fiona. 'We're not going to agree on this but I don't want to fall out over it either. I do actually agree with you that what Rory did by not telling us about his past with Maria was shit. But that aside, I want to go ahead with him and get at this guy. I know you don't want me to but I have to. He killed my sister. He murdered your mother. A man can't murder people and walk away from it. He can't change his mind and decide, *well I didn't like being Mr Bad Guy, I think I'll do a turnaround and become Mr Nice Guy instead.* If O'Gorman's a killer, I want him behind bars. It's as simple as that.

'And something else you won't like. I think Rory McGee's a good man. He loved Maria and he's had a hard life because of that. He needs to move on and he can't do that with O'Gorman still on the loose. I still want to shake him half to death but I also want to help.'

Anna looked over at her mam and nodded. 'What about the girl in the papers and on the news? Shona Moran? What do we do about her? Do we go up and knock on her door and say *hey, I think you might be my sister?*'

'I don't know, Anna. I'm not entirely sure that Maria *did* have another baby. I have no idea if this girl *is* her daughter. She looks like her and the date she was born on coincides. Then there's her name... I think the best thing to do, is for me to delve around a bit more on that one. Leave it with me.

'But first I'm going to ring your dad and you and me will go home. Take a few days off from college. Okay? We need to talk this out with Gerry. It's his birthday on Friday. Sure we could all do with a bit of a celebration to take our minds off things.'

'Okay. But Mam, I'm not ready to talk to Rory yet. I need some time to get used to all this and you better get used to my new-found use for the F word. I'm going to need it for a while to help me get my head together. I must say it's useful enough when it's needed. I mean for God's sake, Mam. A week ago Rory McGee was not my father. Maria wasn't murdered. And Shona Moran was an interesting story in the news. Not a possible sibling.'

They reached out, held hands and smiled.

'Fuck!' they said together.

Chapter thirty

ANNA cheered with her family and friends, filled with love and pride, as her dad blew out the candles.

'Happy birthday, old man! We'll be doing the big five-oh soon enough.' She was first in with the hugs and kisses.

'Less of the *old* young lady!' Anna stood back as her dad was hugged by friends and family in their sitting room.

The beauty of the Donegal summer's evening caught her as she passed the window. As a child she had taken it all for granted, but each time she returned from Dublin it was like seeing it for the first time. Muckish Mountain standing majestically to one side and Tory Island lifting itself importantly out of the sea to the other. On this beautiful evening it warmed her heart. Balcallan. Her home. Looking around at the people she loved, she wanted never to leave it again.

'Anna, help me with the champagne in the kitchen.' Anna looked over to where her mother was calling her and followed her mam out of the room. Fiona was looking tired but still beautiful tonight; her love for her husband, radiating from every part of her lovely face.

The television was a constant companion in the Martin kitchen. 'You have that thing on 24/7, Mam,' said Anna, smiling and reaching forward to turn off *The Late Late Show*. Then the face flashed up before her again. They were talking about *her*. She pressed the volume switch.

'Jesus, Mam. Will they ever leave her alone? Do they not think she's been through enough?'

Fiona smiled at her daughter. 'You've become fierce protective all of a sudden. It's hard to believe that she was involved with that guy.'

'Mmm. It's mad in Dublin at the moment. Every Arab you pass on the street is stared at as if he's Jameel Al Manhal. But do you know what's weird, Mam? Didn't Rory tell you about the guy, Dónal, that he thought might be Shona's father? Wasn't he involved somehow in the IRA?'

Anna looked over at her mother. She had a strange look on her face. She walked over and put her hand on Fiona's shoulder.

'Mammy... Are you okay?' Anna was worried about her now. She looked like she was in pain. Her touch seemed to pull her mam together. Fiona smiled a false smile at her daughter and spoke in a high-pitched, nervous voice.

'Sorry, love. Ah, I don't know what to do about it all. If anything.'

'I can't believe you haven't told dad about her yet, Mam. You can't keep secrets from him. Look what happened before. We should have opened up about everything. Not let it out in stages. It would have been easier.'

'Give it time, Anna. He has enough to be getting his head around at the moment. We all do. Come on! Get out there to the party and hand out these glasses to the thirsty hordes. I don't know why you ever insisted on champagne. Nobody ever drinks it. Go on with you. You and your Dublin sophistication.'

Anna carried the tray of glasses to the sitting room. Her mother had changed the subject too quickly. She knew her mam. Fiona Martin was up to something. She had been tired and snappy all week.

***

Ever since she had seen the girl's face splashed across the newspaper pages and the television screen, realising her birth date and her name, Fiona had been obsessed. Shona Moran was eighteen. Anna was twenty now but that picture looked like Anna had looked aged eighteen or so, give or take a few blemishes and different haircuts. Though many people in Donegal had been talking about the woman who was wanted for questioning in connection with the would-be bomber, no one else had taken in the likeness of the girl to Anna. To the people of Balcallan, Anna's adoption by the Martins eighteen years ago was well forgotten. A blessing in disguise since Fiona and Gerry had produced no children of their own. To her friends and family, she was *one* of the Martins.

As a teenager, Anna had confided in Fiona that she sometimes saw other people who she thought resembled her. She had discussed what it would be like to find herself a member of a totally different family. Occasionally, when problems were teenage-rough, she had even been horrible enough to scream obscenities at Fiona.

'You're not my mother. What right have you to tell me what to do?'

For such behaviour she was punished in exactly the same way any child would have been. As Anna matured into adulthood, Fiona almost forgot *herself,* most of the time, that Anna hadn't always been hers.

Since Fiona had first realised the possible relationship between Maria and Shona, she had been consumed. The newspapers that had delved into every part of Shona's life had reported that, she too, was adopted. The preparations for the party hadn't been enough to take Fiona's mind off the girl that she was sure was Anna's sister. She had cried herself to sleep the previous night, thinking of what Shona was going through. She knew that it was unreasonable to feel such hurt for someone that she had never met. She had spoken to no one else about it. She knew that talking about this would be opening another Pandora's Box in the family. Gerry had lived by the saying, *if it's not broken, don't fix it.* But Fiona had begun to delve through the internet on back stories to do with this girl.

She thought about her daughter, who had followed her mother's thoughts on the relationship without running off immediately to meet her possible sibling. But Anna *had* acknowledged the likeness. They hadn't mentioned Anna's adoption for years.

There was no need. Anna was their daughter. Having failed to get pregnant after years of trying, Anna had made their family complete.

It never *seemed* to bother her, but was she as blasé about it as she let on? Fiona liked to think that she was good friends with her only child and that she would tell her if she had problems. Was there ever an adopted person who *never* thought about their blood family? She had thought Anna to be that person because she was actually related to them, but it could be something that Anna thought about a lot.

She and Anna had sat down with Gerry when they came back from Dublin and told him what they had found out about Rory being her birth father. He had gone very quiet and had asked them to explain in detail exactly how the story came together. He had asked if Anna was going to build more of a relationship with Rory and he had seemed happy that she was adamant that nothing like that would ever happen. To his daughter he had been all smiles and encouragement. Later, when Anna was out, he had calmly told his wife that he would never speak to Rory again and he never wanted his name mentioned in the house.

Fiona had asked Anna not to mention the arrival of a possible sibling as she felt that she needed a lot more proof before she could acknowledge that the girl might actually be part of their family.

She let go of the table that had been holding her up since Anna had left the kitchen. Thank God for the party. It gave her thinking time. But she would have to come up with answers. Gerry was going to be too full of a hangover tomorrow to be able to talk about it with her. She was on her own for now. The only thing she *could* do was to talk to her daughter. Could Anna take all this in? Of course not. Her whole world was coming tumbling down as it was. But Anna was right. Fiona *had* to tell Gerry. She couldn't keep this all to herself for much longer.

That beautiful face. It was *so* familiar to her.

***

Anna noticed her mam come back into the sitting room to get ready to toast her dad; looking like she'd seen a ghost. She considered how unsteady she was at taking the champagne glass that was offered to her. Fiona took her place beside her husband and he put his arm around her. Anna watched Fiona's face relax and smile; their differences of late put aside and thrown away, to let twenty-five years of love and friendship have its lead.

I wonder will I ever meet someone who can do that for me, she thought. *Imagine having a man who can make everything a little better with a touch.*

Her dad was making a speech. Everyone was in stitches. Nobody knew that her world was tilting.

***

Fiona lay in bed, listening to Gerry's drink-induced snoring. God but it was hard to think with that racket. She folded back the duvet, eased into her slippers, wrapped herself in her dressing gown and shuffled downstairs. The still and silent aftermath of the party was everywhere. The conservatory was a peaceful place to escape to, as always. Fiona sat down in an easy chair and thought about tomorrow.

Anna, how do we deal with all of this without wrecking your life?

A photograph on the windowsill mocked her from where she sat. *Happy families.* Since Anna was little she had gone through each person in the photo with her time and time again.

'There's Granny Sonia and Grandad Manus. There's you, Mammy... and that's Maria, isn't it, Mammy?'

'Yes love, that's Maria.'

'And she was my mam that had me in her tummy?'

'Yes, she was your mam.'

'You must have missed her when she died, Mammy.'

'I did, Anna love. I missed her.'

'Why did she die, Mammy?'

'She was sick, love. So she died.'

184

'What was she like, Mammy? Tell me about her again.'

And Fiona would tell Anna all about Maria. How Maria had been born when Fiona was growing out of dolls and how Fiona had felt like Maria was her baby. How they had spent so much time together. How Maria had missed her when Fiona married Gerry. How Maria had seemed so wild and free. Until she was sick.

'But she's always with me inside, Anna. I'm sure she looks out for me, and for you too, love.'

Chapter thirty-one

FIONA was walking away from the door, having waited ages for it to be opened, when she heard him call her back.

'Tommy Farrell? Sorry. I'd forgotten you were… that it would take time for you to…' She came back towards him.

'Yeah. Eighteen years old and crippled. I'll never get used to walking with a cane. Are you Fiona?'

She nodded.

'Before you come in, I want to ask you one thing.'

Fiona was taken aback by his aggressive tone of voice.

'Are you a journalist?'

'No. I told you on the phone. I'm…'

'Okay, okay. I know what you told me on the phone. You want to talk to me about Shona. You have some information on her background. If we had hot dinners for the amount of chancers we get ringing us… but come on in.'

He sounded as nervous as she was herself.

'We'll sit in the kitchen. It's handy. I can't believe I've agreed to something so completely ludicrous.' Tommy caught his foot up in a baby walker on the way down the hall and fell forward. A sticky mess of crumbs fell out over the floor and he reached over for his walking stick and straightened himself up again.

Fiona reached out to help him but he shrugged her off. They sat in the kitchen and Fiona wondered where she should start with Shona's story. She smiled over at him to try to put them both at ease.

'You're from Donegal?' he asked; a little gentler now.

'Yes. That's right.'

'Can I get you a cup of coffee?'

'Ah, no. You're fine. Don't go to any trouble now.'

'Right. So what is it you want to tell me about Shona?'

'You're Shona's boyfriend? Ruby's dad?'

Tommy's face fell again. 'I'm Ruby's dad. Shona and me… we're not together… haven't been for a long time. Can we keep this about Shona? You said on the phone that you wanted to talk about her.'

Fiona didn't answer. She was staring at a photo of Ruby on the kitchen wall and realised that her face was screwed up as if she was about to cry. Then she looked at Tommy staring at her and tried to pull herself together.

'Are you alright?'

'Yes. Sorry… I'm fine… She's gorgeous… your little girl… She looks like her mother. And her… my…'

Tommy slid his fingers up and down the side of the table as if he was rubbing at an imaginary stain. This awkward silence wasn't what she'd anticipated at all. She had come to Tommy, thinking he would be easier to talk to, less involved than Shona or her adopted parents. But she hadn't expected him to be so agitated. It was best to come right out with what she had come to say.

So she told him her story, hers and Shona's. She left nothing out; and as she spoke Tommy sat back in awe, listening to the wretched tale of what may have brought Shona to *who* and *what* she was.

'The time since I met Shona has been hell,' Tommy whispered. 'The only good part was having Ruby. I hated Shona. I wished she were dead.'

'Go on Tommy. Tell me what it was like. I'm listening. I'll not judge you on what you say but I want to know what happened to her.'

Tommy took a deep breath. In and out as if trying to get the words right. But he couldn't do it and shook his head. 'It's Des you need to talk to. He's Shona's dad. He's the only person who could do her story justice. He loves her, and although I've come to forgive her for some of the wrongs, I'm not the right person to sell her virtues.'

'Would he see me do you think?'

'I'll ask him. Don't be surprised if he says no though. He's fiercely protective of Shona since she came back to us and all that. Now that the charges have all been dropped against her, he won't let her near the press and he's made her close down all her social media pages. We both have. She's even thinking of changing her name.'

'I'm not the media. I'm her birth mother's sister.'

'I'd say to Des that's even worse. But I'll try. Only because I think that meeting you and your family might be good for Shona. She's been in pieces for too long and I've grown fond enough of her to want to put her back together again.'

Chapter thirty-two

FIONA wished she had brought a book with her to read, to take her mind off meeting Des. Life was so bloody complicated right now and she'd like to be anywhere else but in the café of this hotel near Dundrum. She should have left things the way they were and not shaken up this particular storm. Getting used to Rory's news about Maria's murder was hard enough without finding that her sister gave birth to another daughter before she died.

Too late. There was Des Moran now. Fiona recognised him from his television interviews, appealing for news of Shona when she disappeared. Tommy had told her that Shona's parents were both fifty, but this man looked a lot older than his years. She sat up in her chair and painted on her most charming of faces.

'Lovely to meet you at last, Mr Moran.'

'It's Des.' He held out his hand to shake hers.

'Of course and I'm Fiona. Sure we're almost family'. His hand went limp and fell away slowly.

Total silence. It was far too soon for such familiarity. Des and Fiona sat opposite each other and fiddled with their breakfast menus. A waitress came to take their order.

'I don't think I could manage more than toast and tea, Fiona.'

'Make that two rounds of toast and a pot of tea, please.' Fiona was heartened to hear that Des was obviously as nervous as her.

A stillness, charged with expectation, sat between them. Fiona knew that it was up to her to speak. It was her, after all, that had asked for this meeting.

'You must be worried, Des. But you know... I'm not trying to pull your daughter and grandchild away from you. I'm so glad that you let Tommy persuade you to meet me. I spoke to him first because I thought that he would be a little more removed from the situation than you or your wife. I didn't want to go straight to Shona in case you thought that she'd been through enough and should be left for a while; and I had to make sure that she was who I thought she was before I took the plunge...'

Fiona had practiced this conversation so many times in her head. She knew exactly what she was going to say. She had a tough battle ahead of her and diplomacy was to be her most powerful weapon. Honesty and integrity would win out with Des Moran. Starting here.

But she'd only just begun and she'd frozen.

'You know it's crazy, Des; I knew exactly what I wanted to say to you this morning. But having spent weeks trying to work out how to get to meet Shona, without actually going straight to her; then eventually finding my way to you; I can't think of anything else to say to you now. I don't know how to continue.'

Des smiled a small smile. It was something.

'Same here,' he said. 'Why don't you start by telling me all about a subject that's obviously dear to you? Your sister. You said on the phone that she looked like Shona.'

Fiona nodded enthusiastically. 'Shona is the living image of my sister. When I focussed properly on her picture on the television, I was sure that she had to be Maria's daughter.' Fiona reached into her handbag and pulled out a photo of her sister when she was eighteen. 'This is her,' she said and handed it to Des.

He was quiet for a moment while he studied the picture. Fiona could see from his face that he could recognise the similarity.

'When my mother first told us that she was having another baby I was delighted. My mother was older than most mothers of my friends so I think it came as a shock to her to find herself pregnant. When Maria arrived in our house she was treated like royalty from day one. As for me, she was my princess. Maria took over the role of my baby doll.

'As she grew up, she ruled the roost. My father tried to get us to stop spoiling her but we completely ignored him. He was the only one who tried to impose any discipline on her but it was the wrong kind of discipline. Dad had become a drinker and that fuelled her lack of respect for him. I loved my father for who he had been before but Maria never saw that side of him and they rubbed each other up the wrong way, always. For the rest of us she had charm in abundance. She would cock her head to one side with her little thumb stuck in her mouth and tell us she was sorry. She was never going to do that again. Ever. We forgave her everything.'

The tea arrived and Des went to pour for them.

'Go on. I'm with you so far.' He nodded for her to continue.

Fiona swallowed a sip of tea. It was good to talk about her sister. 'She was often in trouble at school but one of us, usually me, would cover up for her. I suppose, as she got older, someone or other always shouldered her responsibilities. She could never commit to anything, little Maria. She'd spend five minutes learning piano, dancing, riding – all the usual little girl pursuits. She'd stick at nothing. She always wanted life to be different but as soon as it was, she wanted to change it again. At home, myself and my mother would be left walking the stray dog she insisted on keeping, feeding the rabbits that she had promised would make her a more reliable person.

'She changed her friends with alarming regularity. Once she became a teenager we could never keep track of her. She was always out with someone new. By the time she was fifteen my poor mother and Maria were barely on speaking terms. I was the only one she confided in, if she did at all.'

Des nodded again as if he knew where she was coming from.

'I know I sound like I'm describing all her bad points, Des. She wasn't a bad child. If she'd been handled differently, she might've stood more of a chance. She was obsessive and she always had an addictive personality. The sad part of it was that she was actually clever. According to her teachers, she was a gifted writer. Unfortunately, she used her quick brain to hoodwink others into doing whatever she wanted. She could lie convincingly at the drop of a hat. She was witty but often she used her wit as sarcasm. She was a little fighter, Des, but I loved her so much I turned a blind eye to all of her antics.

'When she was about sixteen, she changed. She became quiet. She was sullen all the time. Even I began to resent how she messed up the family; and I didn't realise that she'd started to dabble in drugs until it was too late.

'Then in her last year of school she seemed to grow up overnight. She worked as a receptionist in the glass factory in the summer and kept clear of the drugs. She had a smile for everyone and we were sure that she had pulled herself together. I realise now that it was because she was pregnant with Anna and she had told nobody.

'She disappeared on her nineteenth birthday. Mam woke up and she was gone. I'll never forget the sight of her birthday cake sitting in the kitchen, going mouldy, for a month. No one was allowed to throw it out. Then one day I came in and it was gone. None of us knew that Maria was pregnant. We searched everywhere but I suppose she didn't want to be found. I never set eyes on her again – until two years later in the hospital morgue. I've never stopped missing her. I still feel guilty that I could've done more to save her... To stop her from... dying...'

Fiona stopped when she realised that she was crying in public and that Des' face was stricken.

'I'm so sorry, Des. I don't know what came over me. I never talk about Maria like that. I always try to keep her memory alive as someone who was kind and beautiful. Loving and intelligent. And she was wonderful. Here, have you a tissue? What do I look like?'

Des fumbled with his napkin and handed it to her. After mopping her eyes and taking a few deep breaths, Fiona sat back; deep in her own thoughts about Maria and Shona.

'What about Shona, Des? Bet you can talk about her without making a show of yourself?'

They both laughed nervously and looked around at the other diners, who had decided that the worst was over and had gone back to their full Irish breakfasts.

'Actually, Fiona, before I say anything else I have to tell you that I went into an absolute rage when Tommy first told me who you were. We've all the crap of the world on our doorstep right now and the last thing we need is for Shona's birth family to come out of the woodwork and stir things even further.'

Fiona looked down at her lap, embarrassed by Des' words. She knew from the beginning that she was being insensitive and intrusive. But as the weeks went on and she couldn't tell Gerry or speak about it to Anna, she had to go and find out more.

'But I imagine, Fiona, that you didn't have any choice about going to find Shona once you realised that she existed.'

Fiona smiled and sniffed again.

'I don't need to tell you much about Shona. You described her well when you talked about Maria. Like mother, like daughter -- if that's what they are. And like you with Maria, I love Shona. I've mostly turned a blind eye to her drinking and her lies. I always thought she'd come around; that she'd grow up or something. With everything that's happened lately I was beginning to believe that it was too late now anyway...

'Getting involved with Jameel Al Manhal and running off to Wales with him. Running away from her own baby. I thought she had more sense than that. More empathy. But it was finding out about being adopted after she gave birth to Ruby that put her over the edge. It was partly our own fault. Hiding her background from her. I firmly believe that she knew nothing of what Al Manhal was up to. She was drifting and lost and she fell for the wrong fella. That's all. And she's paid for her wrongdoings. We all have.

'But since this latest chaos has gone on in her life, Shona is beginning to show a different side of herself. Since she came back from Wales she's been a model daughter and mother. She and Tommy won't get together, I'm sure. They should never have moved in with each other in the first place. But she has thrown herself into life with her daughter and she's staying off the booze for now. The one thing I do believe is that Shona was not involved in all this rubbish with that Al Manhal bloke. I know that she knew him... and in her naivety she may have thought herself in love with him, but that was all. Wouldn't you agree with me on that?' He sat back in his chair, his face showing a desire to be believed.

'Yes of course... only...'

'What? Only what?' Des' tone was accusing. His look was defying her to contradict him.

'I know that Shona couldn't be involved in all this. But... Her mother... Maria... Well I found out that she was involved with a guy who was wanted by the police at the time that she died. She seemed to be drawn to all the wrong sort of people. And I think that... I'm not sure... but if he was Maria's boyfriend at the time, then there's a possibility that he was Shona's birth father and...' Fiona stopped and changed tack. Des was looking distressed. She would have to leave all that alone for now.

'Look, Des. I didn't save Maria and then it was too late. But it's not too late for Shona. If Maria hadn't died when she did I'm sure that she would have turned her life around for the sake of her child, as Shona is doing now. She may have been attracted to this terrorist guy, as her mother was to her father, but that's all. She did nothing wrong. She can't have.' Fiona realised that she was reaching across the table and holding hands with this complete stranger. When did that happen? She pulled away gently and made a play of folding her napkin and clearing her throat.

'I know that. When Tommy told me about you and Anna, Fiona, I did some digging. Shona is over eighteen so the children's home where we adopted her from were reluctant to give me any information without her knowledge. But seventeen years ago, when we adopted her, they did give me the date that she came to the home, and they showed me a note from her mother. It was unsigned, but it said that she was coming back for her soon. I think if Maria is Shona's mother, then you're right in saying that she wanted to do right in the end by her children. If she hadn't died...

'The thing is, Fiona, and you're going to think I'm horrible when I tell you this, I haven't told my wife that I was meeting you or anything about you and Anna. Shona and her mother had such a difficult relationship with each other as Shona grew older. But lately they're both trying so hard to change. Norah will go berserk when she finds out what I've been up to behind her back. And I need to talk to her before I start to discuss it with Shona. That is if I decide to go ahead with this right now. It's all come at such a bad time...'

Fiona was thinking the same herself. With everything that was going on in their lives at the moment, this was the last thing that Anna needed and she knew that she should have talked it over with Gerry first. Too late. But she would go straight home and explain what was happening now.

'Tell me about that beautiful baby of Shona's. I saw a photo in Tommy's house but I didn't like to ask for one. Have you any?'

Fiona stared at the pictures that Des produced from his wallet. Her great-niece. Maria's grandchild. She felt the love she had for Maria reach out into the pictures of this baby. She was desperate to get to Shona.

Chapter thirty-three

HEADING back to her car, she waved goodbye once more to Des and pulled her buzzing phone out of her bag. It would be Gerry ringing again. She had ignored his calls so far and was going to tell him that she'd left her phone somewhere else. More lies but that was all coming to an end now. She was dismayed to see Rory's number instead but answered it anyway with the new-found aloofness she reserved for any of her discussions with him of late.

'Rory.'

'Hiya. I eh, was wondering whether there was any give with Anna yet?'

Fiona had to think twice about what he meant. Her mind was full of Shona, and the Rory and Anna problem had been left behind for a while.

'Sorry? Oh, no. She still thinks you're a no good, lying piece of...'

'Fiona, for God's sake...'

'Ah look, I'm on my way back to Donegal now and I'll talk to her again. Rory, let her go for a while. Let her come to you in her own time.'

'Yeah. I know. I hate the idea of her being so angry with me though, you know?'

'She's every bloody right to be angry with you. I'm angry with you. Gerry's furious with you. You sat with him in our house recently, drinking away, and *forgot* to give him the monumental bit of news that you were actually *with* Maria before she left Donegal. That *you* were the fucking reason that she left her family. You were so busy telling us that Maria was murdered that you forgot to mention, until now, that you were the original cause of her leaving us and ending up on a slab in the morgue at the age of twenty.' Fiona was crying again. The morning with Des, and now listening to Rory, was all too much. She sat into her car and turned on the engine.

'I'm sorry, Fiona. There is no amount of apologies I could dish out to you and your family to make things right. Nobody is speaking to me right now and that's the way it should be. I know that I should run back to London and hide away for another sixteen years. I should tell my daughters that I've fucked up again and that they're better off without me. And they are. But I can't do that. I've spent the last two years trying to build bridges and I don't want to lose that bond now. I never expected to revisit what happened to Maria but I have. *We* have. All of us. And in doing so I found out that I have a daughter by the one woman I loved more than anyone in the world. I can't walk away from that either.'

'Yeah. Father Of The Year and Mr Popular all rolled into one. So where are you?'

'In Dublin. Staying in a hostel for a bit. You?'

Fiona looked up to find that Des was still in his car looking at her on the phone. He probably thought that she was talking to Gerry or Anna already. 'I'm in Dublin too. Listen, I'll call you back in a minute.' She was furious with Rory and there were times that she wished that she and Gerry had left him to his misery in London; but she was going to tell Gerry all about meeting Des so she might as well try the words out on Rory first. She drove down the road and pulled into a layby.

'Fiona?' Rory answered before her phone registered the rings. 'You never went to find her did you? Did you see her?' Rory's voice went up a few notches in his excitement.

'Look. I saw her dad. And a few days ago I saw her boyfriend.'

'Fucking hell, Fiona. Is it her? Is it Maria's baby?'

Fiona took a deep breath. She wanted time to digest all of this. She knew she should be talking to Gerry first and then to Anna. Suddenly, she was realising her mistake in ringing Rory back.

'Rory. I haven't met her and I haven't spoken to Gerry or Anna yet. Can we leave it for now? This doesn't involve you. Stay out of it.'

He went quiet for a minute and Fiona wondered if he'd been cut off.

'Rory?'

'Yeah. I'm still here.' He sounded very cut up. 'If Shona is Maria's daughter then it does involve me. And that makes her Anna's sister. Shona is another person whose life has been torn apart by that politician. If Maria had lived, Shona would have been brought up by her mother and most probably by me too.'

'But she didn't live and Shona is nothing to do with you. Leave it, Rory. I mean it. We're in it up to our necks at the moment. Sit back for a while. Wait for Anna to come around. Give us some time to get to know Shona if we can. We need to get DNA proof that they're definitely sisters yet. There's no point in ploughing into this without thinking it all through. So back off, Rory. Yeah?'

'Okay. I hear you. Fiona, listen. I've news too on O'Gorman. He's got a big press conference coming up next week. I'm thinking of going along and making an announcement about what he did. In front of all the photographers and that. Speed things along, like. If we give it to the Gardaí and they can't prove anything, or worse if he pays someone to hush it up, then we'll be bound by law to do nothing about it because he'll be deemed innocent. But this way, at least we'd have exposed him before the Gardaí get involved. And well, I thought it would make it so much better if you and Anna were there too. Maria's own family. And if Shona was around it would be perfect.'

'Rory.'

'Yeah?'

'Go away and leave me alone. Leave us all alone. Do what you like with your fucking politician but do it on your own.' Fiona cut him off and took a deep breath. 'Will he ever learn?'

She pulled her car out of the layby and headed for the motorway. It was time to head back to Gerry and Anna with her news, and put all thoughts of Rory and that horrible O'Gorman out of her mind for now.

The journey back up to Donegal flew by. Fiona could hardly remember passing places she knew that she must have passed, but she was almost home. The meeting with Des had gone better than she had hoped. He had made her feel that she had reached the right decision in looking for Shona. It was so difficult for him to be caught in the middle of what was best for his daughter and what was best for his wife. Now he had to go back to Norah and tell her what he had done. From what he said about his wife's thoughts on the matter, she didn't envy him.

And she had to go and do exactly the same, only it was worse for her. She had told Anna before her husband. Gerry knew nothing about this whole affair. She would have to start from the beginning.

She pulled into her driveway.

She had hoped that she would have hours before he came home but his car was parked there already. Anna was due back today too. She would have to be told about how the wheels had moved on. Fiona swallowed and turned the key in the door.

'Hi, Gerry. You're home early.'

An uncharacteristically belligerent-looking Gerry greeted her from the door of the sitting room.

'Where've you *been*?'

'Sorry?'

'Where have you been? I'm not home early. I'm home since this morning. You haven't been here and you haven't answered your mobile. I've been worried sick, Fiona. Where have you been?'

Fiona looked over at her husband and knew exactly what he was thinking. Up until recently they'd had an honest marriage. They never kept secrets and here she was for the second time, of late, doing exactly that. When he heard what she had been up to behind his back this time he was going to flip. Gerry was the easiest going person in the world but this would push him to his very limit.

'My mobile's out of battery. Sorry. Sit down, Gerry.'

'Don't tell me to sit down. Tell me where you've been and that there's nothing wrong, Fiona. Tell me that the reason you've been running around behind my back and throwing lies at me *again*, is totally innocent.'

'I'm sorry, Gerry.' Fiona reached out to hold his hand but he snatched it away.

'So you're sorry. Now tell me what you're sorry for. I'm worried Fiona. I'm not going to fly off the handle after the way I messed up the last time. But for God's sake, I thought we had both learned some lessons from all that. Now has this something to do with that gobshite McGee?'

Fiona knew that she had no choice but to tell it as it came.

'Well I need to sit down even if you don't...' She sat with her hands in her lap, not knowing what to say to her husband. There was no easy way... 'Gerry, eighteen years ago Maria had a baby called Shona.'

He looked confused.

'Fiona, eighteen years ago, Maria died. What are you talking about?'

'Four weeks before she died she gave birth to a baby girl. She called her Shona, after our mam. She left her the same way as she did Anna. Shona was adopted after a year when they gave up looking for her mother. Don't you remember at the time, Gerry, the others in Maria's house said that they thought that she might have been pregnant? Well they were right. God, she must have been so miserable then, to have given up two babies. No wonder she...'

'How do you know all this?' Gerry walked over and this time he did reach unsteadily for her hand.

Fiona knew that her husband had reacted badly to his lack of an easy life recently, so she looked for the right words to soften the story – but there were none. She explained to him how she had seen a picture of Shona on the television screen and had been amazed at the resemblance to Maria. She ignored Gerry's look of incredulity as she recounted the rest of her suspicions and her follow up.

'And you know what? Shona's adoptive father said that she was an alcoholic, Gerry. Imagine the poor girl has inherited Maria's addiction problems, God love her, and...'

'Will you slow down, Fiona? I can't keep up with this at all. When were you talking to her father? Why was this girl on the news anyway? What had happened?'

'The bomb, Gerry. Do you remember the bomb that was planted in Dublin? She was involved with the guy who was responsible for it, but she had nothing to do with the bomb.'

Gerry dropped Fiona's hand as this little gem of information sank in.

'That girl from the Luas? The one that...'

'Yes. Yes I know, but the reports about her are rubbish, Gerry and the charges were dropped. You know, I met with her adoptive father today, in Dublin, and he said that she was...'

'You did *what*? Oh and I suppose he wasn't a bit biased of course!' Gerry was getting very upset now but Fiona ploughed on regardless.

'Anna's due home soon, Gerry. We have to talk about what we're going to say to her. She already knows of my suspicions, but she has no idea that it's even more likely that she actually *has* a sister...'

'What we're going to say to her? We're going to say nothing to her! In fact, Fiona Martin, you're going to put this whole business out of your head from this minute. I can't believe you went behind my back with this crazy quest of yours, as if it had nothing to do with me; as if Anna wasn't my daughter as much as yours. You fed her this nonsense without talking to me? Her own father? Or did you tell that bastard who's telling everyone now that he's Anna's father? Does *he* know?'

'She has a right to know that she has a sister. I was wrong, Gerry. I made a mistake. I know that. But with the news of Maria's killing and all, I don't think I was thinking properly. It's out now though, and I'd rather we told her than she heard from someone else.'

'She wouldn't hear from someone else if you hadn't opened up this mess! You want to upset her perfect life for what? You *have* one of Maria's daughters. Now you want to have the other? Did you mess up *their* lives too? Is some poor mother in Dublin distraught because you turned up and threatened to muscle in on her fragile world? As if they haven't enough to deal with at the moment. As if *we* haven't.'

'It's not like that.'

Fiona thought of Norah, and how Des had told her that his wife would be adamant that Fiona would have nothing to do with her family. Was Gerry making sense? Should she have left well alone? Easy for him to say. Maria wasn't *his* sister. He could think with his head all he liked but she didn't have that luxury. This was Maria's daughter; Maria's grandchild.

'Gerry, I saw photos of Maria's granddaughter. The girl is the spit of her mother and of Maria as a child. She's...'

'Maria's!' Gerry was shouting now. 'Maria's family. Not yours. Maria's mess. Not ours. Maria was a troublemaker when she was alive and eighteen years after her death she's still causing trouble. And you want Anna to be associated with all this?

'*...Look Anna darling. Your mother was a drug addict. Murdered by the IRA. She abandoned two babies in a hospital. Your sister is an alcoholic. She also abandoned a baby if I remember from the newspapers. And the icing on the cake? She was arrested by the police for terrorist activities, no less...*

'You want our daughter to know all this crap, do you? You think she has a right to know all this. Well you're wrong! Maria Dooley was a drug addict and she whored around from the age of eighteen with Rory and then with a terrorist. And now you're telling me she had another daughter who went exactly the same way as her mother? Thank God Anna doesn't take after Maria. She'll never know any more of this. She has a right to be protected, so she does, and I'm going to make sure she stays that way. Anna's had a good life up until now. She liked her life as it was. As it *is*, Fiona and it's staying that way.'

'I think *I'll* make that decision, if you don't mind...'

Fiona and Gerry turned abruptly to face their daughter standing in the hallway.

Twenty minutes later, after a lot of expletive-laden screaming, Anna had locked herself in her room, refusing to speak to her parents. Gerry was locked in the study refusing to talk to Fiona. And Fiona was hiding in her bedroom, staring at the photo of her sister.

Beautiful Maria. Troublesome Maria. Still inflicting pain and chaos after all this time.

Chapter thirty-four

ON the drive down to Dublin the next morning, Anna had to pull in twice to wipe away the tears. Her anger had turned to confusion and as she neared her destination, that was turning to fear.

The address that her mother had given her was where Shona's boyfriend and their daughter lived. According to her mother, Shona didn't live there anymore. She hoped to get some information from Tommy about Shona *before* she met her. Her mam had told her that Tommy was approachable, but that no one had told Shona about Anna yet. At the very least, Anna might meet her niece.

She threw the word around in her head for a moment. Niece. Her name, Ruby, made her shiver in anticipation. Would she look like her mother? Or her grandmother? She might look like Anna herself.

She thought about her family; all those people who she had grown up around. Now she had a sister. How bloody dare her father say such words about her family? Because that's what these people were. *Her* family. To him they were people who were muscling in on his peace and quiet.

Twenty years old and she felt like a hurt child. She was angry and she wanted to lash out. She needed someone to talk to. Her two best friends were scattered between London and New York. Her boyfriend of two years had left her *to find himself* and she hadn't had more than a postcard in six months.

Anna felt that the body that had been her life had cut her off like an unwanted limb. She had to find Shona. Her gut told her that Shona was feeling the same sense of not belonging. Both sisters going through the most traumatic period in their lives at the same time. They could help each other.

She picked up the piece of paper her mother had written the address on. She wasn't far now. 60, Glen Alla Avenue. She followed Fiona's hastily drawn map. Turn right after Dundrum Town Centre. Anna thought about how many times she had shopped there. She went to the cinema there. She ate at the trendy restaurants, and all the time she could have passed by her sister and not known.

Turning into Glen Alla estate, she drove towards the Avenue. Number 60 was in the middle of the road, on the left and she pulled up outside, slowly, and took a deep breath. She sat in the car for a few minutes looking through the front window of the house. A baby girl was in a man's arms in the front room.

The man walking out of the room was much older than Anna had expected. Older than her father. This wasn't Tommy. Her mother had told her that Tommy walked with a stick, after that horrendous crash caused by the terrorists. Anna had expected someone her own age. She wasn't sure that she could convince this older man to tell her Shona's whereabouts, if he knew them. She put her head down on the steering wheel and closed her eyes.

She was feeling scared now. She knew that it was the anticipation of meeting this whole new family but deep down she was scared of seeing Shona herself. The information her mother had given her about her sister; her alcoholism and her abandoning her child when she had run away from the police; were alien to the quiet, happy lifestyle that Anna had been leading until now. And then there was this question of Shona's connection to that terrorist. What if it turned out to be true? She wouldn't want anything to do with a person like that.

She jumped when her car door opened.

'Anna? Why don't you come on in? Your mother rang and said you were on your way.'

She looked up, happy to see such a kind face looking at her.

'You're not Tommy.'

'No, love. I'm Des Moran. Shona's... Shona's father. Tommy's at college. He won't be back for a while yet. Come in and sure we'll have a chat. Come on and meet the baby.'

She opened the car door and eased herself out, following Des into the house. When she walked into the sitting room to where the baby was sleeping in her buggy, Anna didn't trust herself to speak. This was her sister's child. This time yesterday she wasn't convinced she had a sister.

'Hi... I'm Anna.' She reached down and touched Ruby on the cheek.

'Come into the kitchen when you're ready, Anna. I'll put the kettle on and we'll sit down. Would you like a sandwich after your long drive?' Des sounded as nervous as she felt.

Half an hour later, when the teacups were empty and the small talk was done, Des brought the chat around to the real reason for Anna's visit.

'Your mother tells me you want to meet Shona.'

Anna started at the mention of her sister's name.

'Yes. I want... I mean I... Yes, I need to meet her. I had a long think all the way here about whether it's the best thing to do and all that but I believe it is. We need each other right now. Well I know that I need Shona and I hope that when she finds out who I am that she'll be pleased.'

'You know, I think she will, Anna. I've mulled it over myself today as well, since your mother rang this morning. I was thinking about ringing Shona to ask her what *she* wanted to do but I couldn't figure out how to give her such monumental news without being face to face. I worry if I did, Shona might do another runner. She's good at hiding away from the real world. So I think that the best thing to do is for me to speak to her first and let her make her own decisions about everything. I've suffered from losing Shona's faith in me once before and I don't want to break it this time. I've kept all this from her mother too, even though she's worried sick about her. I've rowed with Tommy over it because I am afraid he will fall out with Shona

206

again. He's had to put up with an awful lot of crap in his life lately. Shona has treated him abysmally and now, with trying to overcome his injuries, his life is a bit of a mess.

'They're getting their act together now. They're living separately, which is a good thing. Mostly Shona comes over here to mind Ruby while Tommy is at college but she's out helping her mother with some shopping today.'

'Do you mind me asking how you lost her trust in you before?'

'No, I don't mind. You see... We didn't tell Shona that she was adopted. She overheard an argumentative conversation between her mother and Tommy when Ruby was born. That was when Shona went completely off the rails and this mess she's coming out of now is a continuation of all that.'

'I don't blame her!' Anna couldn't believe that this had happened to her sister. Growing up with a cloud of lies around her.

'You should never lie to your children about something as important as that. My parents have lied about my mother as well. And as for my *birth* father. He's made a whole life out of lying. It makes you feel almost... abused in some way.' She felt the need to find Shona even stronger now that she'd heard about what she'd been through.

'Anna. Whatever about this man Rory McGee, don't be too hard on your parents. It's always so difficult to decide the right thing to do. We've muddled along with Shona since the day we brought her home. We bought all the best books on how to bring up kids, but Shona never seemed to play by the same rules as anyone else. She's still dancing freestyle to this day.

'Yes, we made a mistake not telling her that she was adopted but we had this notion that we would adopt a few children and tell them altogether when they were a bit older. Then we kept putting off the other children until Shona had settled down, but she never did. In the end, we just couldn't face having any more. Then we put off telling Shona that she was adopted until she was mature enough to deal with it and that never happened; and then she was pregnant with Ruby and that wasn't the right time either.

'We *were* wrong. *We've* suffered because of it, as well as Shona. Especially Norah. She always felt that every wrong turn that Shona ever took was because of something wrong that *she* did. The more she felt that she'd messed up, the more she *did* get it wrong and eventually they ended up living their lives sliding around each other, trying to avoid contact.

'Now, from what I gather from your mother on the phone today, she's heartbroken over what happened to you last night. Your father shouldn't have said what he said, but he's going through an awful lot of heartbreak himself at the moment. They wanted you to grow up knowing that they had chosen to have you as their daughter; not that they kept you out of obligation to your mother.

'I suppose they were wrong too. Two sets of crap parents who screwed up big time... out of love. Because that's what it all boils down to in the end.'

Anna answered with her silence.

'Maybe it's something that you and Shona need to talk about together. I'll talk to her soon and I'll ring you and let you know how it went.'

'I'd like to see her as soon as possible, Des.'

'Of course you would, love, but you can't rush something that hopefully will have a whole lifetime to work itself out.' Des handed her a piece of paper and asked her to scribble her number down on it.

He looked thoughtful while Anna wrote.

'Before I speak to Shona, I need to speak to her mother first. You might not like this but I think it would be a good idea to have... well, a DNA test first. To be honest I don't doubt that the two of you are related. You're the spit of each other. But it would be heart-breaking to go down this road only to find that we were all wrong. And these things can be sorted very quickly. Then, if Shona agrees, I'll ask her to meet with you. Okay?' Des smiled. 'What do you think?'

Anna took a deep breath and nodded her head. Butterflies gathered inside her.

'Have you a hairbrush or something in your handbag that I could have, to use for a test? And I'll get something from Shona too. It'll be done quickly and we'll know for sure then.'

Anna reached into her bag, pulled out her brush and handed it over. 'It's strange to think that something as simple as this could connect us. My apartment's not too far away, Des. I can get back here as quickly as you want. I'll be waiting for your call.'

Anna was looking forward to being on her own for a while, to get her thoughts together on all that had happened. She might ring home tonight. Let her parents know what she was doing. Des' little lecture was having the desired effect.

'Anna. When you see Shona, she might be a little off with you at first. She doesn't make friends easily. She's going through so much at the moment and, as well as everything else, she has a drink problem... She hasn't touched the stuff for a while and I'd say that's fairly hard on her too. She's... well... look, tread carefully. Okay?'

Anna looked worried. Her mother had told her about Maria's addiction problems a few years before and she knew about her grandfather's drinking. What if it ran in the family?

'Don't worry, Des. We'll be fine.'

'Of course you will. Now I better do something about the dinner. Tommy's always starving when he comes in from college.'

'What's he like, Des? Tommy I mean.' Anna was curious about the man that had stood by Shona through all that had happened.

'Well, if you'd asked me that question when I first met him, I would have said he was a young wimp of a fella, but he's growing up into a lovely young man and I'm fond of him. He's had to be mother and father to that baby a lot of the time and he's done a great job. Since he was injured, he's had to deal with some horrific pain and rehabilitation but he's coping amazingly well. There's nothing perfect about this little family but sure show me one that is.

Then he paused for a second and added, 'I don't know about him and Shona though. I'm not sure why he's stuck by her all this time but I can't see the two of them ever being together as a couple. Apart from the obvious, I doubt that they ever *were* properly together. I think he's given up on playing happy families. Given up on Shona that is, not Ruby. He loves that baby more than life itself. Sure you couldn't say a word against her when he's around. I have to remind myself that he's only eighteen. He seems so much older. But they've developed some sort of a relationship. Friendship I think though, more than love.'

There was the sound of a key in the door and Ruby woke with a gurgle, as if she knew who it was.

Anna watched as Ruby's daddy went straight to the sitting room and picked her up and cuddled her to him.

'How's daddy's beautiful princess? And look who I found on my way home. Here's your mammy and your granny. Were you a good little girl for..?' Tommy stopped short and stared at the mirror image of Shona, standing in the kitchen doorway. It only took him a moment to realise who it was.

'Anna..? Oh my God.'

'Hello, Tommy,' Anna said. Her heart was racing as she stared past him out into the hall. She wasn't ready and this would be too much for her sister to take.

Shona and Norah walked in and Shona immediately went to take her daughter from Tommy. The huge smile on her face faded fast, however, as she looked around the room.

'What's going on?' she asked, looking at the stranger.

Norah stared at Anna too but her face showed that she knew exactly what it was.

Chapter thirty-five

ANNA and Shona sat in the sitting room, one staring at the wall and the other at the coffee table. Shona had stopped crying but she was still looking dazed. Des had been wonderful throughout. He had taken Norah in hand when she looked like she might faint. He had sat her down with Shona and had explained Anna. He had kept it simple; had said it was a shock to them all. Anna, of course, was aware that he and Tommy had known for a few days but she said nothing. Shona had sat with her hand in her father's, crying.

'Are you sure? Are you absolutely sure?' Norah kept asking; as if their likeness could have another reason.

Des had briefly talked about Maria. Anna had managed to say a few words but the shock of seeing her sister so close up was taking its toll. Then Des had suggested that Shona and Anna come back to their house for a while, to talk it out. It was up to them if they wanted to get to know each other now or to wait until they had it all verified. Only they could make that decision.

'If it's okay with Anna, I'd like to talk to her now,' said Shona.

Anna nodded and Des turned to his wife.

'It's all turned out for the best, Norah. I didn't know how I was going to bring up such a thing, the way our lives have been, or even whether to acknowledge it right now.' Then he turned to the two sisters. 'Don't feel you have to thrash everything out with each other right now. Get a feel for it all. I'm going to take Norah out for a while. We need to talk ourselves. Text me, Shona, when you're ready for us to come back.'

When they had left, Shona and Anna sat without knowing what to say.

Eventually Anna spoke. 'I like your dad.'

More silence. So she tried again. 'It's a pity he didn't stay. He was doing a great job.'

'Do you know who he is? My dad?'

'Sorry?' Anna was confused.

'You said our mother was called Maria. Your adopted mother's sister. And you said that she's dead. So who was our dad? Is he alive?'

'Shona... I don't want to take away from the wonderful family that you already have. Neither of us wants, for one minute, to replace our parents...'

'Is he alive?'

Anna shook her head. 'No. I believe he's dead. I only found out recently about our fathers...'

'Our fathers? What do you mean?'

'We're only half-sisters. Maria left Donegal when she had barely turned nineteen; pregnant by a man called Rory McGee. Rory has been a friend of my adopted parents all my life and he's only recently decided to do some maths and realise that he's my father.'

'So how did you find out about *my* father? How do you know that he's dead?'

'From Rory. He's been hiding secrets about our mother most of his life. He didn't know about you... that Maria had had a second baby.'

'So how did they die?'

Anna hadn't wanted to get into all this so early. She wanted to chat about being sisters. But she could understand Shona's hunger to find out about her parents. Anna had known who her mother was all her life and why she hadn't been there for her. But Shona had no idea. She hadn't even known she was adopted until less than a year ago. She must be desperate to piece the jigsaw together.

'Shona; I grew up thinking that Maria had died of a drug overdose. She took drugs. But I found out recently that...' It was hard to voice the truth.

'What? Don't pussyfoot around with it, Anna. I've had a lot to deal with lately and I'm not easily shocked anymore. I've had to put up with too many lies as well and I've come to prefer the truth. No matter what.'

'Rory was with our mother when she died. He's saying now that she didn't overdose; that she was murdered. He says that your father, the man we think was your father, was killed about a month before Maria. He was involved with the IRA. He wanted out. He was shot and soon after that our mother was killed because they presumed she knew too much about him. But Rory said she had known nothing. She was about to leave with Rory and go into hiding, when they caught up with her. Rory was in the house with her when they used a syringe to inject her with bad heroin or something and make it look like she'd overdosed. He was there when it happened and afterwards he ran from them, terrified for himself and his own family. He knew that Dónal, *your* father, had been killed. And then Maria. Rory said he was sure that these guys would do the same to him if they even *thought* he posed a threat.'

Shona looked wide-eyed at Anna and then burst into hysterical laughter. 'You're joking. My mother was an addict and she fell for a terrorist? For fuck's sake. Your father, this Rory guy, he made this up. He's been reading the papers about what happened to me and he concocted the story. It couldn't be true...' And then she looked at the way Anna was biting her lip, her eyes full of tears, and they both cried again.

Anna came to sit beside her. 'I'm sorry, Shona. I'm sorry it's all so difficult. I think we should stop there; ring your dad and ask him to come back.'

Shona stood up and walked to the window.

'No,' she said. 'I want you to ring *your* dad. Rory. I want to talk to him. I want to hear straight from him what happened.'

'I can't do that, Shona. You said yourself that you couldn't live with any more lies. Well that bastard knew all about my mother's past and never said a word all these years. He was the reason she left home and got herself killed. He watched our mother being murdered and ran away. He could have brought her killer to justice; your father's killer too; but he sat around for eighteen years and lived a make-up life. He has two other daughters at home who I grew up with, went to school with, never knowing that they were my half-sisters. He lied to them and to his wife. My adoptive father was Rory's best friend. For eighteen years he said nothing to him, like it didn't matter. He used him. I'll never speak to him again, Shona.'

'At least you have the choice to speak to him or not. You *have* a father.'

'I've always had a father and so have you. Don't lose sight of who you are, Shona. Your parents are the people who brought you up.'

'Anna, I've no idea who I am. I feel different. Until I had Ruby I felt that I had no one in the world who I was related too. It's going to take a long time to get used to, but I know that meeting you is the best thing that could possibly happen to me. Right now I need to make sense of my life and only you can help me do that. And Rory too.'

Anna stood up and went to her sister saying, 'we'll help each other, Shona.'

Then they held each other close, crying for all the wasted years.

Chapter thirty-six

THE noise in the children's play centre was deafening. Rory wasn't sure how Shona thought that they could have a conversation here. Ruby was crawling and climbing her way around the baby gym and waving at her mammy. Rory thought about his own beautiful daughters and sighed. How long would they block him out because of his *treatment of their mother,* among other things? He was sure Deirdre was enjoying all the attention she was getting as a result of all her *suffering.*

'Do you want a coffee?' he raised his voice to Shona.

'No. You're grand.' She shook her head and moved her chair closer to Rory's. He had filled her in on a lot of her background on the phone but she had a whole new line of questioning. It was nearly lunchtime and maybe it would quieten down then.

'So if you were in love with my mother, you must have hated my father? Are you the wrong person for me to ask about him?'

'I only met him the once, Shona, and then I didn't see your mother for a long time after. By that time, your father was dead and your mother was in danger. But yes, I hated the idea of him. Maria was the only woman that I ever loved, Shona. I know you probably think I'm a little shite to be getting your mother pregnant at the same time as my wife, but at that time Deirdre and I only... well, you know... just the once after a friend's wedding when we were both drunk, and then Deirdre ended up pregnant. We married in the first place because of Deirdre's first pregnancy and then she lost the baby soon after. We hardly knew each other before that. I never loved her in the same way that I loved Maria. I thought that your mother ran away to Dublin because she heard that Deirdre was having a baby and I presumed she was seething with me, and rightly so. I only found out recently that it was because she was pregnant with Anna. At the time that your mother was killed I had two choices. I could stand up and point the finger, therefore putting myself and the rest of my family at risk, or I could slink off to London when no one was looking and stay well clear until I was absolutely sure that they were all safe from harm. Deirdre had had our second baby by then.

'I decided the safest thing to do for them was to sever my link to Maria and therefore to Dónal. I was shit scared. The bastards had already associated me with Maria by then. As it was, it took me years to stop looking over my shoulder. I ran from Maria's murder and kept quiet because two people had been killed and I had no wish to be next.'

'And if Maria had given birth to me four weeks before she was killed, how come you never knew until recently that she'd had a baby?'

'After two years of searching, I only found your mother a few days before she was killed. She never mentioned you. I've thought about it a good bit since and have come to the conclusion that she gave you up for your own safety. She knew that your father had been murdered at that stage and that she was in danger. So leaving you, no matter how difficult it would have been for her, was probably done out of absolute necessity. When I found her first, I remember her talking in her sleep. She said *don't hurt the babies... please don't hurt the babies...* At the time I thought, for some reason, that she was talking about *my* babies but I realise now that she must have been talking about you and Anna.

'Fiona told me that the children's home where Anna lived had received an anonymous letter begging them not to have her adopted out. That her mother desperately wanted her back but wasn't in a position to look after her yet. They received another letter a few months before Maria died, telling them that she would come soon, that she was getting herself sorted. I'm not sure how she figured that out but I can only presume that she didn't know at the time of Dónal's involvement with those monsters, and was hoping to set up home with the four of you. That's why I'm sure that leaving you was done out of fear. And you say that she sent a letter to the home about you too, saying she was coming for you. But Maria had no idea that she would be following Dónal so soon after.'

'You haven't answered my question from earlier. Did you hate Dónal?'

'Yes. I hated him then and I hate him now. I suppose he loved Maria and I presume she loved him, so my hatred is unfounded. But if it weren't for your father and his involvement with that bloody crowd of murderers, Maria would still be here. I was making arrangements for us to run to the UK. We were leaving that night. I was going to get in touch with Deirdre when we were settled, about getting access to my girls. I had it all made up in my head. Maria would forget your father eventually and I was going to make a life with the girl I loved, instead of sitting out a life with a woman who drove me to tears. I suppose I was probably naïve enough not to think that Maria was only going along with it because she knew I was her ticket out. I imagine Maria also presumed that I would go along with her wish to go back and get her daughters, but I had no idea at the time that either of you even existed.

'Maria went to her squat to get her bag. And if you look at it differently, then yes she did die of a drug overdose... Because when she went back she obviously decided to go too far with something strong. It was the one that killed her because if she hadn't done that she would have been long gone before that bastard O'Gorman came and shot her full of a huge dose of bad heroin.'

'What did you say?'

'What do you mean?'

'You said that bastard O'Gorman...'

Rory sat back in his chair. He was exhausted after all his telling. He hadn't meant to mention O'Gorman to Shona, yet. Too many people already knew about him and he hadn't a shred of proper evidence against the guy.

217

'Rory... Did you actually *know* the guy who you saw injecting Maria?'

He guessed he'd have to keep going with it. Shona would find everything out eventually. He might as well tell her now.

'Yeah. I didn't know his name at the time. But... well I saw him again recently... and I know it was him. He has a defining scar on his face. I put it there myself when I tried to save your mother. It's faded over the years but it's still there. And his eyes... I would never forget those eyes.'

'So who is he? Have you approached him? You know the identity of the man who killed Dónal and Maria; I presume you're doing something about it.'

Rory stared at the little girl who came crawling over to her mammy at that moment. She looked up at him with her grandmother's eyes. Maria's daughter looked at him, ignoring her own daughter for now, waiting for his answer. Shona had told him that they were waiting on DNA results to prove that she was Maria's daughter but he knew Maria and he knew without testing that Shona was her daughter.

'Yeah, I am, Shona. I loved your mother. I know that she possibly didn't love me in the same way, because of my treatment of her, but I don't care.' Rory spent a few minutes explaining to Shona over the loud music about O'Gorman and how he'd recognised him again. 'Fergal O'Gorman murdered Maria and I have no way of proving it yet; but I'm going to make him pay, somehow.'

Shona reached over and took his hand. He was shaking, Shona was crying and little Ruby was whimpering. 'Can I help, Rory? There must be some way I can help you.'

'Actually there is something, Shona. I was hoping that Fiona and Anna would come with me but that's looking less likely now. I have something planned. I could do it on my own but I know it would work better if I had someone related to Maria.' The music in the play centre stopped for a minute and Rory was able to stop shouting. 'I've been planning a way to oust O'Gorman in front of as many people as possible. To get it on the news, as far reaching as we can. I think I have something big but I know that it will work better with you on board. I want us to turn up at his press conference tomorrow and tell the cameras exactly what he did. I've already written to all the media to get a hype going.'

'Whatever it is, Rory, it had better be good. I don't need all this on my plate at the moment. Do you have any evidence of what he did? Apart from the scar that you say is still on his face. Only *you* saw him there.'

'I'm waiting to hear back from a company of private forensics. If they say there's a match to O'Gorman's DNA then I'll be able to go to the Gardaí with my head held high and we have him.'

'What did you give them of O'Gorman's, Rory?'

'A cigarette butt that I retrieved from outside his offices when he stepped outside for a smoke. And a baby blanket, Shona. Your mother was hugging it to her when she died. I didn't realise then but it must have been yours, as it was so soon after she gave birth to you. When I was wrestling with O'Gorman, after he killed Maria, I stuck the syringe in his cheek and cut him badly. He used the blanket to mop up his own blood. If there's a match then we have him.'

Shona reached down and picked up her own baby, wrapping her arms around her protectively and shaking her head.

'No, Rory. I can't. I understand why you want to do this but I also realise now why you ran from them the first time around. I'm too steeped in crap already. I'm only beginning to settle down after the fear of being hunted by crazy people, intent on doing me or my family harm. I've no choice but to choose Ruby over bringing him to justice.'

Chapter thirty-seven

FERGAL O'Gorman's face was on every post and his eyes stared at Rory from surrounding railings. Every available space held photos of politicians. *Your life in our hands* his caption read; smiling at the world; no shame. There were dozens of faces of different men and women but Rory saw only one. He drove along the street towards the hotel, his mind a mess.

He knew what he had to do though. His beautiful Maria had been murdered; and that bastard couldn't be allowed to walk away from it. O'Gorman had committed a terrible crime. More than once, as it was probable that he had murdered Shona's father as well. Rory put his foot down on the accelerator and let the car take him there faster. He ripped past the pictures of all the candidates until they were blurs around him. All but that face. The smug smile of O'Gorman bore into him.

Anna should be here beside him. She was *his* daughter and Maria was *her* mother. She should want revenge as much as he did – but Anna wasn't speaking to him. Nor was Fiona, or Deirdre, or his other daughters. Not even his best friend, Gerry. Everyone had decided that he was mad to pursue this and he wasn't even sure if they believed him. He had lost their trust as he had allowed everything in his life to topple before him, all because he wanted to put the past to rights. He had stood by once before and allowed Fergal O'Gorman to wreck his life and now here he was helping him to do it again.

But there was something inside him pushing him on and he had to go with it. He had nothing else. He knew he would never rid himself of the regret he felt over not doing anything the first time around, but he couldn't go to his grave having never put it right. It was never too late.

'We're nearly there. Another couple of minutes.' Nothing words. But something to break his train of thought. 'Are you sure you want to go ahead with this?'

Shona nodded, leaned her head back and closed her eyes. 'I can't believe I've given in to this after all,' she said. 'But something is telling me it's the right thing to do – and, for once, not just for myself.'

More silence gave rein to his thoughts. How would he do it? What would bring the man down fastest? Should he do it alone or should he let Shona be an accomplice? If the media found out who she was they'd have a field day with her recent experiences but it was probably best to do it together. Between them they could tear him apart. Strike where it would hurt most and when he was down and vulnerable they would keep at him until he was begging for them to stop. Then they would walk away. Leave him for the journalists and the media. Vultures to the smell of blood.

He swerved the car into the entrance to the hotel and was waved down by an attendant. Rory wound the window down.

'The car park's full. You'll have to swing around and find something down the road. The place is throbbing with press. I gave the last place to someone from *RTE* and I had to turn a fella from the *Herald* away before you. If you're going in you'd better hurry or you'll never fit into the place. I don't know what has the world so excited.'

So it had worked! Rory allowed himself a small smile. They had all taken the bait and they were all here. Waiting. Wondering.

'Well we've promised them a performance, Shona, so we better perform. Are you right?' He turned the car around and headed for a space down a side road.

'I feel a bit sick, Rory but I'll be okay I suppose. I was doing a bit of research on the web last night. It's tough trying to associate this man you've told me about, with the man who's supposedly done so much good in recent years. Are you absolutely sure that this is the same person? He looks... I don't know... almost cuddly.

Like somebody's daddy or something.'

Once he'd reversed the silver Mazda into the tight parking spot, Rory removed his seatbelt and opened the door to go. He turned back to Shona.

'Oh he's cuddly alright. He's not someone's daddy or someone's husband as it turns out, Shona. All that he denied your own father, he denied himself. Too difficult to live his lie close to others, I expect, so he chose to live it alone. Good enough for him. There's no doubt that this man killed your mother, and if he didn't kill your father he was certainly in on it. Look, I know it's hard for you to associate now with then. You didn't even know them. O'Gorman took that away from you. The right to know your parents. The right to grow up with them. I never knew your father and I resented his existence but he didn't deserve to die.' Rory let the door close again and sighed.

'I loved your mother more than I've ever loved another woman. She was beautiful and intelligent. Loving and caring. I know now that she loved you and she cared about you. I need to do this to this man because I loved her and I watched her die at his hands; and though I fought him then, it was too late. I ran away. Well I'll not run away today. I'll not let him live his wonderful, cuddly life so easily, when he denied me and your mother the life we would have had together.'

Rory looked hard at Shona and tried to gauge her feelings. Was she tough enough for this? Did she *feel* enough? He could do this without her but it would serve him better to have her at his side. Maria was *her* mother.

'I'll do this alone if I have to, Shona but it would mean everything to me if you came along. I wish Anna was here too but she'll not speak to me after this. I'll have to live with that because I can't live with the alternative; with doing nothing. I'm going in there to rip him to shreds. Follow me or stay here. I'll completely understand either way.' Rory climbed out of the car and closed the door hard. He took a deep breath to calm himself and walked down towards the hotel on his own.

The function room was thronged and he began to feel sick too. He didn't blame Shona for not wanting to come in. He wanted to run away himself. There was a buzz all around him. One that he had created. His letter to the newsrooms had let them know that Fergal O'Gorman was not the teddy bear that he let on to be. He had promised a story to fill their papers on Sunday and throughout the following weeks, if they turned up here today. It could have backfired on him. It could have been discredited as a load of nonsense and nobody would have showed up. But it only took one big guy to think something of it and the rest would follow like sheep. Baaaaaaa....

He allowed himself a second congratulatory smile.

It disappeared though, when he saw Fergal O'Gorman heading towards the top step to face his fans. His eyes looked determined with the challenge of success as he shook hands with those around him. The scar on the side of his face had faded considerably over the years and either he'd had some work done to it recently or he had used special make up to cover it up.

He'd had years of experience in cover up. He was the master.

Rory pushed forward to stand close to a cameraman from the *Independent*.

'I hope this is worth our while.' Rory overheard him say to his colleague. 'It's a hard job to pour so many of us into a function room for nothing.'

'You heard what the boss said, Martin. If it's decent, everyone will go with this story and we can't miss out. But you're right – it had better be big. Here we go. He's on his way to the stand.'

Looking closer at Fergal O'Gorman, Rory thought that he looked tired. He was dragging himself a little. Three days before the elections and he was probably all talked out. Well he wouldn't give him time to say much. He would go in there quickly and let him have it.

'Ladies and gentlemen...' The politician cleared his throat and started to speak but Rory was so engrossed in deciding what he would say himself that he wasn't listening. Now that he was here he was ready for anything. He couldn't stomach that voice for one more minute.

'Mr O'Gorman...' Rory called out, interrupting the speaker. The buzz in the room was hushed and everyone looked back to the man who had spoken. Go on, Rory. You have their interest now. You have the man exactly where you want him.

'Mr O'Gorman, before you go any further I have a question I need an answer to...' O'Gorman looked down at Rory, his eyes narrowed.

'It's usual to let the speaker *speak* before you start asking questions. What exactly is it that you need an answer to, Mr eh..?'

'McGee. Rory McGee's my name.' Microphones were set for recording as the journalists recognised the name at the end of the letter. Cameras were being checked. Rory paused before speaking again. 'Why did you murder Maria Dooley, in a squat in Crumlin, in 1997?'

Journalists jumped into action all around him. The buzz picked up momentum as people repeated the question around the room to those down the back who hadn't heard what Rory had said.

O'Gorman leaned into the microphone and grabbed it with both hands. By the look on his face Rory thought he was about to pick it up and fling it in his direction. But he spoke again.

'I'm not sure what asylum you've escaped from Mr McGee but you'd better turn around and leave before you say one more word of your lying crap.' He nodded towards the security man at the door and indicated to him that he should lead this mad person out of the building.

'I *saw* you, O'Gorman. I was there; watching. You've forgotten that it was me who gave you that scar on your face that you're always trying to hide. Maria knew all about your armed bank raids so you silenced her. Did you silence Dónal O'Grady too? He disappeared about a month before you killed Maria.' Rory turned towards the crowd. 'This man was different back then. Anyone who knew him was terrified of him. I've been afraid of him for half of my life but I'll not stand and let it go for one more minute.'

'What proof do you have of these allegations?' A shout from the other side of the room. Cameras were flashing wildly. There was so much talk that Rory could hardly be heard.

He turned back towards the man whose scar suddenly seemed to be jutting out from the side of his purple face. 'I have a blanket that Maria was holding at the time. O'Gorman left traces of his own blood on it. I kept it all these years, in the hope that I would have the courage to do this. It's with the laboratory now, undergoing DNA tests. The girl he murdered, Maria; her daughter is outside here waiting for me to come out. That girl grew up adopted by another family because this man took away her own mother. I wish she was here now, to see this man who has the look of guilt written all over him. *Your life in our hands* your caption reads. Her life was in your hands then, O'Gorman, and you just took it away.'

O'Gorman's face was distraught. Suddenly, a voice shouting from the back of the room made everyone turn.

'I'm not outside, Rory and I've seen and heard everything.' Shona began to walk forward and the sea of journalists parted to allow her get to the target. She kept walking until she was standing in front of O'Gorman. Her short hair was tucked under a cap she'd found in Rory's car with his local GAA club logo emblazoned across the front. No doubt she was trying to disguise herself and her background from the media.

'So what answer have you? Why did you murder my mother?'

'I never… I… Jesus Christ!' O'Gorman handed the microphone to a colleague and shook his head from side to side. He reached his hands out to Shona. He was shaking. Rory hadn't expected him to give in so readily. But his whole body language seemed to be admitting that everything Rory had said was true. A stifled sound then came from his mouth and he fell on the ground at Shona's feet.

Someone ran to his side and shouted for an ambulance. Rory was surrounded by journalists asking him questions. He was sure the same thing was happening to Shona at the top of the room. Flashes blinded him and the whole thing took on a surreal edge that he wasn't sure he could cope with. Had O'Gorman had a heart attack? Was he dead? He tried to push people out of his way so he could get to Shona and O'Gorman and see for himself what was going on.

It couldn't be all over. In all the time he had imagined what today might be like he had never envisaged this. Somebody had the microphone in his hand and was beseeching everyone to leave the room and give the ambulance crew space to move when they arrived. But nobody was going anywhere. This was where it was at. They had been right to come here today. Rory had promised them a show but they were given a little bit more than they had bargained for.

He pushed his way up the room to get to Shona and, thankfully, his new-found celebrity status meant that people were moving out of his way. O'Gorman was beginning to come around. Had he only fainted? Was he overtired as Rory had thought earlier? A man beside him was helping him up and telling him there was an ambulance on the way. He looked haggard. He stumbled as he tried to move forward.

'I want to get out of here. Help me out of here.'

'Go to the hospital, Fergal,' the man was saying. 'We should get you checked out.'

Rory stared as the politician shook his head and waved his arms as if he was trying to swat a fly.

'No. Leave me be. Get me out of here. Let me out.'

'Come on, Fergal,' another colleague was telling him. 'Go to the hospital and get looked at.' Then in a lower voice. 'It might be the only way you can get out past all these cameras anyway. Go on, Fergal. It'll give us a bit of time to look at all this and sort it out. For the sake of the party, would you go with them when they get here?'

Rory looked over at Shona who was shaking her head and making signs to him that she wanted to get out of there herself. O'Gorman sat down on a lower step. He put his head in his hands.

'I've come straight from the hospital this morning,' he said. 'A few weeks ago I thought I was suffering from exhaustion... from all the canvassing. But it's...' It was barely audible to those immediately surrounding him. He looked up. He caught Shona's eyes and locked with her for a moment.

'I came here today to pull out of the elections. Something... has happened. I had written my speech. Here, Miley', he called, 'have a look at this.' He handed a piece of paper to a familiar journalist near him.

Miley scanned the page and his face became paler as he read on. 'Jesus, Fergal. I'm so sorry.'

'Take the microphone, Miley. Tell them what it says.'

Rory and Shona stood motionless as the journalist haltingly spoke into the microphone to tell the assembly that Fergal wanted to thank everybody for all their support over the years but he had some bad news. He was dying. He wouldn't live for much longer. Cancer of the oesophagus. There was little that doctors could do.

Those around him were hushed, but as the news began to sink in, noises filled the room until there was an ecstasy of flashing and reporting.

Fergal folded his arms across his chest as if he was in pain and he gestured to his colleague to help him to standing again. He then turned towards Shona and Rory.

'I don't know what you intend doing about the slanderous allegations that you made today, Mr McGee. You can bring it to court but you'll find you're mistaken. I never killed that woman. By the time you find that out through the legal system though... I'll be long dead.'

Chapter thirty-eight

FERGAL O'Gorman listened to the long bleeps as his friend Danny's mobile rang in the south of Spain. The sound of the foreign ringtone made him long to be there in the sun, instead of stuck in Ireland in the total mess that he found himself in. Somehow, blue skies always made everything seem easier.

But even sunshine and lapping waves wouldn't make these problems go away. He was dying and he hoped it would be quick as he was already in a lot of pain. And to make matters worse, the past had caught up with him in the guise of Rory McGee.

'*Si*?' Danny answered eventually.

'Danny. How's it going?' Fergal wanted to dispense with the small talk but he was having a problem with articulating his words.

'Eh, fine, Fergal. I wasn't expecting to hear from you so soon.'

'You mean you haven't heard? I thought you always listened to the Irish news there.'

'I was working. So, is the media in a frenzy about you resigning? I told you you'd be missed. You've done wonders for that party and for Irish politics in general...'

'No, Danny! Listen! We're in big shit here. There's a fella called Rory McGee causing mayhem. Have you ever heard of him?'

Danny went quiet on the other end of the line.

'Well *have* you?' Fergal knew that the name must mean something to him. Danny wasn't just his caretaker in Spain. He was a friend from way back and these new developments would affect him too.

'It was a long time ago, Fergal. Mary had a friend from Donegal called Rory McGee. He was more than a friend before she met me. He was the reason she left Donegal but I never found out exactly why she was so angry with him. She never wanted to talk about him. I can't believe you've forgotten the name though. He was the reason you were scarred for life.'

'Him?' He thought about it for a moment and shivered. 'Danny... he was there. He's announced to the media that he witnessed *me* murdering Mary. He called her Maria; and he says he ran away at the time because he was scared of what might happen to him. He has a girl in tow; says she's Mary's daughter.'

'No way, Fergal. Mary was still pregnant when she died.'

'Maybe not. The girl's name is Shona. She's eighteen. And Danny... she's the spit of Mary.'

Fergal gave his friend some time to let this sink in before he spoke again.

'Danny, I'm coming to Spain. I can't stay here and let the press drag me over the coals because of what happened. I'm going through enough shite without McGee and his poorly-timed revelations. I'll text you with my flight details and you can pick me up. And, Danny, I'm staying in the villa, okay? I'm not going to hospital. I found out today that everything has spread and it's a matter of a very short time. Morphine me up and let me get on with it.'

'Fergal, there must be something...'

'I mean it, Danny. Leave it!'

'Jesus, Fergal... Okay. We'll talk more when you get here. But listen, before you leave, find out where they live. I want to find out more about them.'

'After all this time, Danny? Let it lie.'

'No, Fergal. I most certainly fucking won't. I'll pick you up at the airport.' Danny disconnected and Fergal was left staring at the mobile.

Going to Spain was the only thing he could do. Over the years Danny had become the family he would have liked to have but never wanted to risk. Sure, there had been plenty of women; but Fergal was never going to risk his old life taking him, and any new family he might have cultivated along the way. His parents were long gone, as was his only brother. Fergal had swept the past away and knuckled down to the politics of Irish life. He had put Mary's murder behind him. He had been a part of the beginning of the ceasefire and he had never let go. Most of his ideals had come to fruition. He had fought his heart out to win his battles, one at a time; but not through violence. That was for the past. This was a new Ireland and he and Danny were of one opinion. This was the right way; the only way. Danny had come up with all the ideas from his home in Spain, while Fergal put them to the powers that be in Ireland. Danny did all the groundwork, although he hadn't set foot in Ireland for almost two decades.

Fergal stepped out of his office and surveyed all the goings on around him. His Dublin party headquarters was the hub of where it was at. For all these years, Fergal and his party had taken every idea, every problem, bit by bit, voice by voice and made life better. He was surrounded by paperwork that was the beginning, middle or end of so many people's stories. Because that was what it boiled down to. People. Fergal O'Gorman had worked his arse off for years to make *their* lives better. To make Ireland a better place for them all. Now he was leaving and he wondered who would miss him. Would he be renowned for all the hard work he had done over the time he had served, or would he be remembered for the day that a man had stood up at a press conference, pointed the finger at him and called him a murderer? He didn't need to ask. To hell with this.

'There's a huge crowd here this afternoon for the weekly advice clinic, Fergal.' His secretary brought him back with a bang. 'What do you want to do? Are you taking it yourself or do you want me to get someone else in? I'd recommend you don't go down there. That crowd is not made up of people wanting their local TD to get a few jobs done for them.'

'No, more like people wanting to have a gawk at a dying man, who apparently murdered a woman. But I *am* going down there, Trish. This will be my last clinic as their TD, my resignation is official from the end of today. Let them say what they like. This weekly clinic has helped so many of them to air, and ultimately solve, their problems over the years. *This* will be my last day in the office, not that surreal morning in the hotel.'

'I knew you'd say that. You're a stubborn shit, Fergal O'Gorman but I'm going to miss you.'

Chapter thirty-nine

IT was a small gathering of immediate family and close friends, to celebrate her birthday. Deirdre didn't want to make a fuss, considering that everyone in the village... for God's sake the whole country... was talking about them. She had spent her life wishing that it was different. That she had married a wonderful man and had gone on to have her two daughters alongside the friendship that other couples came to expect. She loved her girls, but it had been lonely. Two years ago, when Rory had first come back to Donegal, she had tried to bear it. She had to see it from the girls' point of view. Their father wanted to be a part of their lives and it was their decision to let him or not. Typical of that lazy shit to turn up when all the tough work of rearing was done.

It was hard for her to let them go to him but she had allowed it to happen and now he had fucked up their lives again. And in the middle of it all, it was her birthday and she felt it would be good for all of them to have something to take their minds off the crap going on around them. So here they were. A select few. Mostly family. And everyone had been warned that they weren't to talk about the elephant in the room for one afternoon.

'Would you like a top-up there, Gerry?' She was still begging the Martins to forgive her and her mad mother's accusations and had been delighted when they had turned up today.

'Lovely, Deirdre. Thanks.' He was obviously doing his best. As he said himself, she'd been through enough.

'Are you okay there for more dessert, Mam?' Eiley was looking very subdued.

'Ah, I'm not hungry, love. The cake was gorgeous. Absolutely perfect. I couldn't have done better myself.'

Deirdre stared at her mam. Eiley *had* made the birthday cake herself. Sure Deirdre couldn't bake a cake to save her life. Her mother was worse than she had thought. Eiley had seemed very relieved that Rory had left when the shit first hit the fan. But now with all the latest news, she couldn't cope with the fallout. Eiley had been best friends with Fiona and Maria's mother, Sonia. Perhaps hearing that Sonia's daughter had been murdered had brought all the suffering back to her. She was certainly avoiding Fiona.

Rory was a bastard to do all this to them. If he needed to put the past to rights he should have gone to have counselling like most normal people; not gone on live television to tell his woes to the world.

The papers were full of pictures of him, pointing the finger at O'Gorman. Some of them took Rory's side. Others were more sympathetic to the poor, dying politician who couldn't possibly have done what Rory had accused him of. But all of them ran the back story. The one where Rory McGee had been having an affair with Maria Dooley, all the time he was married to Deirdre. That they were simultaneously having babies. Deirdre in Donegal, Maria in Dublin. That he had apparently watched Maria being murdered and run for his life, all the way back to Donegal and on to London; eventually returning to his family two years ago when they were fool enough to take him back. Deirdre thought back to that time so many times this week. She had no idea that she had been giving birth to Caitríona while Maria was giving birth to a half-sister in Dublin. She would talk to her mother more about Maria, but not yet. There was no point asking Eiley in her present state of mind.

'Hi, Caitríona. It was good of you to invite us.' Anna had just arrived.

Deirdre watched for her daughters' reaction to seeing their half-sister for the first time since she had come back from Dublin after all the commotion. Caitríona and Clodagh had thought it was a good idea to ask her over today. They had known Anna all their lives and had agreed that they shouldn't change the way they were with each other. Best to settle things before too much awkwardness set in. But now Anna was standing here in front of Caitríona, smiling at her and expecting her to greet her as if everything were normal – and Caitríona couldn't do it. She couldn't ignore the elephant. She nodded and said, 'Hello, Anna,' and then she burst into tears.

'Oh Caitríona, I'm so sorry. Don't...' And then Anna was off too.

'This is all crazy. I never wanted any of this. I'm only getting my head around the new facts about my mother and now I have to figure out how your father is my father too.'

Deirdre couldn't stand and listen anymore.

'Come on now girls. We decided we would leave it all for today, didn't we? It's better this way. You all need a break. Take it easy. Come on and have a glass of wine and relax a bit. I'm telling you, if I had that man here beside me I'd give him a piece of my mind. He has us all in bits over the whole affair.'

'You won't have to wait long then.'

Deirdre turned around to face Rory who had let himself in the back door. She stared, unbelieving, that he would have the audacity to show his face.

'Hello, Deirdre.'

Complete silence. Gerry came over and put his arm protectively around his daughter and Clodagh put her arm around Caitríona. Heads turned and faced Rory.

'I'm sorry to burst in on you all like this, but I'm going away to Spain for a couple of days and I wanted to tell you myself how sorry I am about everything that's happened. I'm glad you're all here.'

'Going to give another little speech are you, Rory? You like an audience, don't you?' Fiona came up beside him. 'I think you'll find that everyone here has heard as much as we want to. Or was there something about your sordid past that you neglected to tell us? And to drag poor Shona into it now. As if her family haven't been through enough.' Fiona sounded like she'd had enough herself.

'Fiona...' Rory's face crumpled at her tone of voice. 'You of all people must understand how important this is. Your sister was murdered by that man.' He turned around. 'Anna, Maria was your mother. I have no choice but to do this. I've been living with these demons for the last eighteen years and I have to get it sorted. I have to oust this fella.'

'Well, bully for you, you dirty, great louse!' shouted Deirdre. 'Go off now and oust the man who robbed you of your girlfriend and leave the rest of us in peace. I've been holding my tongue with *you* for the last eighteen years and more and I reckon I've done my time.'

'Deirdre, please... Can we talk?'

'Nothing you have to say that I would want to hear. God help me, but I've been defending your crap to your daughters for far too many years – I could do with a break. You couldn't even let me celebrate my birthday in peace. So why don't you do me a favour and get the hell out of here?'

The assembly stared hard at Rory.

'Anna, please. You're right to feel the way you do. I had no choice but to keep it from them over the years, though. I worried for their safety. Those men killed your mother and Shona's father. I had to make sure that they didn't know about my family. I had to protect them.' He turned back to Fiona.

'He's in Spain, you know. O'Gorman. Gone running off to hide away from the Irish press. I'm going after him, Fiona. I'm going to get that shit and finish his chameleon days.' Rory took an envelope from his pocket and handed it to Fiona. 'This is a copy of the DNA results concerning O'Gorman's connection to Maria. This is yours to use, as much as mine.'

Fiona took a step forward to take the letter and began to say something. Her face had softened a little and Rory looked hopefully at her, but Gerry grabbed her arm and spoke.

'Rory McGee. You and I have been friends for most of our lives. Best friends. I know you thought you were keeping your family from harm but you were wrong. What you did, knowing Maria was murdered and saying nothing; then being part of our lives on the outskirts, was a dreadful thing to do. Fiona'll not forget that and neither will I. And now you've dragged Anna's other sister into this. It won't be long before the media realise that it was Shona Moran hiding under that cap at the press conference. Hasn't her family been through enough?' Gerry was clenching his fists trying to keep calm.

'It was Shona's choice to go…' Rory knew he was clutching at straws.

'Enough,' said Gerry. 'You've said your piece and you've broken up Deirdre's party; like you've broken up your family and friendships in this town. I suggest that you about turn and head back to Dublin and stay there. There's no welcome for you here. You're an uninvited, unwanted guest. Goodbye, Rory.'

Gerry then took Fiona gently by the elbow and led her away from the room, along with the weeping Anna. Clodagh burst into tears and Rory moved towards her but Caitríona stood in his path and glared at him; then whacked him across the face with the back of her hand; her ring deeply scratching the side of his cheek for good measure. He yelled out in pain and grabbed his face.

'Caitríona, for Jesus' sake! As if your mother didn't do enough damage with her broken glass.'

'Don't bring Jesus into it, you! That was for nobody's sake but your own. As far as I'm concerned, Mammy didn't hit hard enough that day and I hope the scars never heal on your ugly mug. Get the fuck out of here before I do worse to you and don't let me see you near me or mine again.'

Caitríona then turned to her, now sobbing, sister and wrapped her in her arms.

Chapter forty

THE small crowd around the table was beginning to struggle with conversation. Norah had been welcoming to her daughter's new family at the beginning of lunch; but Shona could tell that she was now finding it hard to keep up the banter with these people, who were responsible for another upheaval in their lives. She put Norah's best silver knife and fork down, having been ordered earlier to polish them up for the occasion, and dredged up some more chatter.

'So, how long have you lived in Dublin, Anna? We've probably passed you lots of times locally, without knowing.'

'About a year.' Anna spoke through her food as she struggled to empty her mouth to answer the question. She swallowed hard and continued. 'I started college in Belfast first, to be nearer to home, but I transferred to Dublin then. I love it and I can't see myself going back to Donegal any time soon.'

'Your mum and dad must miss you though.' Norah smiled an understanding smile at Fiona. 'It's a shame your father couldn't get here today.'

Shona shot her mum a look to shut her up, realising that Norah was opening a worm can. They were probably wondering which father she meant.

'Well I, for one, am over the moon that you're living near,' said Shona. 'I can't believe we'll be seeing so much of each other. I woke up this morning and had to pinch myself to believe that this is all happening. When the results of the DNA came through I was thrilled. I knew that it was true before, but to have the proof was the icing on the cake. I have a sister! You've no idea how much I've always wanted one of those.' Shona smiled over at

Anna and the tension around the table lifted.

'Me too, Shona. And I knew as soon as we met that there was no doubt that we were sisters.' Anna reached over and squeezed Shona's hand. 'We've a lot of catching up to do.'

'Why don't the two of you go away together, for a weekend?' Margaret, Shona's Godmother, was doing what she did best – getting the ball rolling in other people's relationships. Such a shame that she doesn't have someone of her own, Shona thought. Margaret had been the gel that had kept Shona together when she had run to Wales with Jameel. It was Margaret who had brought her home, and she had been like her guardian angel since Jameel was killed; even cutting her holiday short as soon as she had heard that Shona's birth family had been in contact.

'That's a brilliant idea. We might even make it more than a weekend. Do you fancy a bit of a sun holiday, Anna?' Shona's eyes were sparkling.

'Where were you thinking of?' Fiona had a bit of an edge to her voice.

'Well, I was hoping to go to Spain actually. I loved learning Spanish at school and our teacher spent a lot of time telling us all about Spanish culture and people and that. I'd love to try it out.'

'Is that the only reason?' asked Fiona. 'You're not planning on going along with someone else or meeting up with anyone while you're there?'

Anna looked over at her mother and stood up with a jerk, sending her glass of coke flying across the table; seeping into the white linen tablecloth that Norah had spent an hour ironing that morning. There would never be a mention of wine in the house when Shona was around. Norah had said that she wanted everything to be perfect, and for Shona's new family to know that she had grown up part of a loving, caring environment. Anna grabbed her napkin and started to mop but gave up and began to walk away from the table. 'Excuse me,' she whispered, 'I need the bathroom.'

Norah looked suspiciously at her daughter as Shona's eyes pleaded with Margaret to try to retrieve the situation.

'What is it? What's all this about Spain?' Margaret wore her *I'm taking no nonsense* expression. 'You're up to something. Don't you think you've had enough excitement in your life lately, to do you a hundred years?'

Shona met her question with silence but her face said she knew she was beaten and she'd have to share her secret.

'I know where she's thinking of going...' Fiona looked murderous. '...and who's behind her madness too. This reeks of Rory bloody McGee's plans for getting to that politician.'

'What plans?' Norah shook her head. 'No more, Shona. Leave life alone for God's sake, will you? Whatever it is, let it go. It was bad enough you running off to that press conference with that fella. At least you weren't recognised.' She looked around the table at everyone, still wondering what it was that could have them all so angry with Shona.

Anna was back and standing in the doorframe. 'She wants to go to Spain with that imbecile who's telling everyone that he's my father. No doubt he's filled your head full of crap about his past and buttered you up to help him in his quest. But I, for one, will not be going with you, to help fulfil that man's wish to *have closure*. I can't believe you fell for his rubbish and I certainly can't believe that you thought that I would go along with it.' Anna came back into the room and took her seat. She swept up her soggy napkin and settled it on her lap as the tension reached bursting point.

Shona could see her father getting ready to speak. The quiet man could only put up with so much. Des knew when to intervene in a crisis and now was that moment. 'Shona. Everyone around this table deserves a full account of what you're getting yourself into, so out with it lady.'

Shona thought it was all best out in the open anyway. No more secrets.

'Fergal O'Gorman sent me a letter. It came to Tommy's house and I picked up the post when I was there with Ruby. He says he's in Spain and he wants me to go and see him. He gave me the address. The letter says he'll tell me about my birth mother, and he says that… well he says he has a gift for me.' Shona wore her most persuasive look. She desperately wanted them to understand.

'A gift? What sort of gift?' Des' tone was uncompromising.

'He didn't say, Dad. But this man knew something about Maria, Anna. And he knew my father too, He's dying, and I want some answers from him before it's too late. If he was going to be around for a while I would leave it. But if Fergal O'Gorman dies before I have a chance to confront him, then I've lost my chance to get to the bottom of all this.' Shona looked around the table to see how she was being perceived and decided it was worth continuing. 'I know the timing stinks but I want to go to Spain and hear him out, collect my information, and then I promise to leave well enough alone; for a while anyway.' She sat back, slumped in her chair. The exhilaration of this get-together had left her and she felt exhausted.

'Shona's right.' All eyes turned to Norah, the most unlikely person to have agreed with her daughter up until now. 'This year has been the worst time in both Shona's and Anna's lives and for that reason it was probably the best time for them to meet. To be there for one another. I'm delighted that you got in contact, Fiona and I think that meeting you and Anna was a tonic for Shona.

'But it also brought Rory McGee, and all his revelations. It's Shona I'm looking after here and I think that finding out all she can about her birth family is important to her. As she says, if this man dies then his secrets go with him.'

'Thanks, Mum. I'm glad you understand. I only want information.' Shona was sitting up again, hopeful that the situation was gearing up in her favour.

'Wait one minute!' Des hit his hand on the table. 'There's no way you're heading off to Spain with a man you don't even know. Is there any sense in your head whatsoever? You're only getting to know your baby after all your shenanigans running away from her and now you're planning another separation? Have you discussed this with Tommy? No? You may be eighteen and a

240

mother but I'm still your father and I say no bloody way! Okay?'
Des was red in the face now and his fists were clenched.

Shona swallowed as the gathering of *family* around the table
squared up to each other. Margaret was the only one who hadn't
had words with anyone yet. Shona knew she had put the cat
among the pigeons and ruined everyone's appetite again, but
she felt that the circumstances were out of her control this time.
Norah and Des must have known that their daughter would try
to find her birth family someday. But this was turning into such
a mess.

Margaret stood up and began to collect the plates. The scraping
of leftovers, of which there were many, shook everyone from
their silent state.

'That was lovely, Norah. Thank you.' Anna had been brought
up well. Even in the circumstances, she'd remembered her
manners.

'I've made a cake for you all,' said Margaret quietly. 'You're
going to absolutely *love* what I wrote on the top of it.' She carried
the plates to the kitchen and came back moments later, carrying
a large chocolate cake and placing it centre stage on the table.

'Ta, daaaaaah...!' Margaret looked around the table to see
what the reaction would be. It had seemed like such a wonderful
idea last night. A celebratory cake with the words *Anna, Shona,
Sisters in Training* decorated around the top, in the shape of a
heart.

Shona was the first to start laughing; followed by Anna who
caught her sister's mirth and, trying to stifle her giggles, ended
up spluttering over the cake.

'Oh, sorry,' she snorted. 'I think your cake is gas, Margaret.
Jesus, Shona, I'm so annoyed with you, but I think I'm going to
go with Margaret's suggestion that we're only *in training* and
we've plenty of time left to work out our differences.'

Shona watched as Margaret breathed a sigh of relief. The
laughter spread and Des was beginning to smile. The only
person she didn't seem to win over was Fiona. Her face still held
its stony expression.

'Do you want a proper knife, Margaret?' Shona asked. 'That cake looks much too nice to attack it with any old cutter. I'll get a better one now if you hang on there for a moment.' Shona fled to the kitchen as quickly as possible before the situation went belly-up again. She was beginning to count the minutes until they would all go away. She needed to have a good talk with her mum to work on all the ins and outs of this trip she was planning. She lifted the silver cake knife from her mother's good cutlery box and immediately remembered the last time she had seen it used, for Ruby's Christening cake. What a disaster of a day that had been, the poor baby. The vague memory of getting plastered and screaming abuse at all the guests made her shiver. She never wanted to go back to that time in their lives but if she wasn't careful now she would wreck everyone's head all over again.

Before she even opened the door of the dining room, she could hear Fiona's sobbing. She rushed in and handed the cake knife to Des. 'Cut that quickly and we'll have a slice to cheer us all up. Fiona, are you okay? I'm so sorry. This meal was supposed to be the start of something happy and it's turned into... I didn't mean to, but I know my timing on this is terrible.'

'I'm sorry, Shona.' Fiona tried to speak through her tears. 'I've been trying to get through all this. First, finding out that my sister may have been murdered, then hearing that Rory was Anna's real father...'

'Birth father!' Anna interrupted.

'Yes, birth father.' Fiona continued, sniffing loudly to gather herself. 'I've been keeping it all together but something snapped here with Shona's talk of going to Spain... I've been so angry with Rory... keeping those secrets all these years, and though I realise why he had to do it, to keep everyone else safe, it doesn't mean I can look at him yet without fuming...'

Norah reached for the lace-trimmed napkin that Fiona hadn't bothered using and handed it to her. Shona then watched her mother cringe as Fiona blew her nose long and hard and stuffed it up her sleeve.

'I *do* understand your need, Shona,' Fiona continued, 'but it's too hard to manage it all. The man murdered Maria and now he's dying and I want an end to it.'

'I can't do this either, Shona.' All eyes turned to Anna. 'If this man *has* murdered Maria then I understand why you want me to be there when you confront him. And I would, but there's no way I could travel with Rory or stay in the same hotel as him, pretending to be all happy families. I *won't* say one word to McGee. Not one fucking word. I'm sorry.'

Shona cringed as her mother pursed her lips at Anna's use of bad language.

'Anna, you should keep that word in check, you know.' Fiona shook her head.

'Yeah, Mam. I will. As soon as I've put all the monsters back in their box.'

Chapter forty-one

RORY could see his oldest friend through the window, settling down to an evening in front of the football. He rang the doorbell. Gerry ignored the sound and continued to watch the television, so Rory opened the letterbox and called out.

'Please! Let me in or talk to me at the door. You can even listen to me through the letterbox if you want, but I can't stand what's going on with us all.'

Gerry got up and closed the curtains.

'Please!' Rory shouted.

Gerry turned up the volume, so Rory shouted louder.

'I *have* to speak to you, Gerry. There is so much you don't know that I want to explain. Especially about Anna. I need you to understand *why* I had to keep it a secret. It was for everyone's safety. After what happened to her mother; I couldn't put anyone else at risk with those mad feckers.'

He waited for a response that wasn't coming but he needed this man on his side. Gerry had always been there for him, had been the only person to forgive him his abandonment of Deirdre and the girls. He wasn't giving up on the man that was so familiar to him after a lifetime of chats and friendly banter.

'Let me in, Gerry. For all our sakes. Hear me out and it'll be over with. If you want, after that, I'll never darken your door again.'

The two stayed silent for a moment; one crouched in the cold, the other now turning off the television; both men desperately needing to talk to each other, while wanting to run a mile in the opposite direction at the same time. Rory closed the letterbox and stood up. He knew he should walk away but if he did there would be no coming back. He wanted to give it one more go. He banged his fists on the window of the sitting room and shook the house with his roars.

'Shit, Gerry! Open the fucking door, would you? I'm going nowhere 'til you let me in.' Thirty seconds later, the front door was thrown open.

'Get your arse in here then and let's see what you have to say for yourself.'

Gerry stared at Rory and his face relaxed its fury.

'You look like death, McGee. I can't believe I'm allowing you the time of day. He left the door ajar and walked back into the sitting room. Rory followed slowly, closing the door behind him.

Standing with his back to the fire, Gerry didn't invite Rory to move from the doorframe.

'So? Spit it out.'

'Can I sit down, Gerry?'

'No. Get on with it and get out of here.'

Rory was shaking. He yearned for a whisky in their hands as they sat by the fire, to make this easier, but he wasn't going to be let away with that. The fire was dimming and Rory knew that Gerry wouldn't be throwing a few welcoming logs on it and encouraging him to stay, so he took the hint and dived in.

'I married Deirdre because she was pregnant, Gerry. Then she had the miscarriage and we should have called it a day. But twenty years ago, here in Balcallan, that wasn't done. When you married you were together for life. Deirdre was suffering in the aftermath of losing the baby but all I knew, at my young age, was that her demands on me cost me dearly; first my place on the county team and then on the local team. I met Maria. As you so rightly said she was a lost cause and at first I only wanted to help her. But I fell for her. It was easy. I wasn't in love with anyone else. Especially Deirdre. You can't understand that, I know. You loved Fiona from the start and always have.' Rory coughed and paused for a moment.

'Get on with it, McGee. So you were a young fella and you fell for a child who should've been at school.'

245

'Maria Dooley was more grown up and sensible than any girl I'd known.'

'So grown up that she ran away on her nineteenth birthday, with a baby on the way, and spent the next two years getting stoned in between pregnancies.'

'Ah, Gerry. She fell for the wrong man.'

'What? And you were the right one? Give me a break.'

'I loved her, Gerry. When she left for Dublin I was heartbroken. It wasn't my decision to go there when I lost my job. It was Deirdre sent me there without a thought for what I wanted. But when I was there I spent all my free time trying to find Maria. When I did she was with *him*.'

'Fickle, wasn't she?'

'Maria thought that I had knocked her up at the same time as Deirdre. God knows what was going through her poor head when she left here but you can rest assured that I wasn't her favourite person.'

'Thought? You *had* been bonking the pair of them. Proper little stud you were. Makes a different meaning of the expression *Irish twins*.'

'I had no idea that Anna was mine, Ger…'

'Convenient that.'

'I know. I was an awful eejit, but…'

'But nothing, Rory. You were a dirty little liar back then and nothing's changed.'

Rory's face darkened and he marched across the sitting room. 'I'm no fucking liar now,' he hissed into Gerry's face. 'I'm trying desperately to tell the truth here and get a murderer to face his just desserts. Have you no compassion left in you, Gerry? Have you not been listening to me? I had no choice but to tell the lies I told. Maria's family and my own were in danger and I…'

Gerry shoved his fist up into Rory's jaw and sent him sprawling to the floor. Pain shot through his hand and he yelled.

'You deserved that you fucking toerag. You're a piece of shit after what you've put my family through…' But he stopped short as he watched Rory curled up on the floor and sobbing like a baby.

'What am I supposed to do now, Rory? I've known you all my life and I've never seen you like this.' Gerry looked down at the beaten man on the floor and the years of friendship took hold of him as he leaned down and held his hand out to help Rory off the ground. He immediately sat him down on the chair beside the fire and threw a few logs on it. Rory had given him little choice but he sighed his shame on giving in so easily. He handed a whisky to the crumpled heap on the chair and sat down to hear the whys and the hows.

Chapter forty-two

ANNA pulled into her parents' driveway slowly. She hadn't yet spoken to her dad, of Shona's plans for going to Spain. Her crazy nut of a sister. She had wondered all these years about who she might be connected to out there and then ended up with *loop the loops* for her birth family. She was still clinging onto the hope that she wasn't actually related to Rory but she could see the resemblance between herself and Caitríona and she knew that this was all true. And what was it that Norah had said the other day about herself and Shona? Having them both in front of her was like looking at the same landscape but in different seasons.

A head to head with her dad about the whole situation was exactly what she needed. She lifted the off-licence bag from the passenger seat and swept out of her car. A vintage bottle of Jameson was just the ticket for getting her dad relaxed enough to tell him all she wanted to get off her chest about her new *madzer* family. It was getting to the stage now where she wished she could turn the clock back permanently. This was not where she wanted to be. Sometimes it was safer to be ignorant than to know the truth. She knew more than she wanted to now and she thought that Shona was shaking up a bed of cockroaches.

Turning her key in the door and walking into the hallway, Anna stopped to listen, confused at the male laughter coming from the sitting room. Her dad and… no way. It couldn't be. She was used to seeing those two friends together of an evening, when her mam was out at one of her classes, but she must be hearing things. There it was again. That laugh. Jesus. It *was* him. It was bloody McGee and her dad, laughing together.

Bursting through the sitting room door, she let a roar at the

248

pair of them in their easy chairs by the fire. 'What the hell are you doing? What is this? A *who's Anna's father* meeting? How dare you let that toad back into our house?' She spoke to Gerry but glared at Rory.

Both had jumped up at her explosive entry, with Rory sloshing his tumbler of whisky over his sleeve in fright. He stood speechless but Gerry recovered himself quickly.

'Anna, you need to hear what Rory has to say before you throw him out. He was threatened, in a squat in Dublin, by that murderer.' Gerry was trying not to slur his words.

Rory went with Gerry's flow but was weak in his approach, having explained himself previously. 'I had no idea that you were mine.' he started. 'I had no idea that Maria had gone on to have a second child either…'

'Thank God Maria abandoned me, Rory,' Anna interrupted angrily. 'If it meant that I could grow up with decent, loving parents instead of a man who dumped his wife and children at the first sign of a bit of trouble.'

'A *bit* of trouble? The man who murdered your mother, Anna, was more than a bit of trouble. He was a menacing bastard who would have stopped at nothing to make sure that he got away with what he did.

'I thought back then, that when O'Gorman said, *you'll want to protect the baby,* that it was mine and Deirdre's girl he was referring to; but he must have been talking about you or Shona. You were brought up by Gerry and Fiona and they were better parents than I could have ever been without Maria. But I can tell you this. If she had lived and she had told me about you and Shona, nothing would have stopped me from marrying her and being with you both. Deirdre and I would have worked things out. We all would have been happier than we were.

'They're all *what ifs* now, Rory.' Gerry interrupted the conversation that was going nowhere. 'I'm beginning to understand why you couldn't take any chances. If that lot had known that Anna was yours and Maria's, then she would have been more at risk than anyone.'

'If you'd seen what they did to your mother, Anna; how she died; you'd understand why I had to live that lie.' Rory was clutching at Gerry's turn of heart. 'I wanted to come home and be a father to my girls and a friend to their mother. But I couldn't and I've had to live with that all these years.'

Anna could only stare at the two fathers who were eating away at her heart. Eventually, she spoke softly.

'I wish I'd never set eyes on you, Rory. You're breaking me into pieces with all this talk of Maria and how she was killed. Could you not have kept it all to yourself for the rest of your life? Look what you've achieved with your meddling. Can you not see all the people you've knocked over in your hurry to nail your murderer? Your actions threatened my parents' concrete marriage. Deirdre is suffering the whole mess again and your daughters are lost since your revelations. Then, as if that's not enough, you go to find Shona and drag her into all your crazy planning. That girl was beginning to find her feet after falling off the side of the world last year. Her family deserve to have her back to themselves again.

'And what good can all this possibly do now? The man is dying of cancer. If he murdered my mother, he's getting what he deserves anyway.' Anna couldn't get any more words out. She leaned against the doorframe and brought her hands to cover her face as she wept. Both fathers put down their drinks quickly and raced to her side.

'Anna, sweetheart, I'm so sorry all this has happened.' Gerry knew his daughter better than Rory and had the right words ready. 'Come and sit by the fire. I'll get you a drink and we can talk about this some more. A good chat is all this needs, you know. I'm always telling you that talking a problem out is half the problem sorted.'

Anna allowed her dad to steer her towards the chair that Rory had vacated and she fell into the cushions. She accepted the whisky that Gerry was holding out to her, without a word. Rory was hovering by the door, looking unsure as to what to do. Anna wanted to scream at him again, to get him the hell out of her house, but she had spent her life listening to Gerry's wise words and she had to admit that there was an element of wisdom in what he was trying to tell her now. She knew how angry her father had been at the recent happenings in their lives and, like Anna, he had blamed McGee. Everything that was going wrong had started with him. But had he a choice? If he was telling the truth now about being threatened back then; if he had been protecting his family; then she might have to go along with all this. And even if she was still so damned angry with all that had happened; she couldn't take it *all* out on Rory.

He was turning around at the door now. 'Will I go?' Three words, full of pleading. Her birth father was asking for her forgiveness. For understanding.

Will I walk away from your life and leave you to get on without me or do you think you could ever find a place for me?

There were so many bridges to build. Too many problems that needed straightening. But in the end she knew that the power to salvage this lay with her. Gerry was looking at her now, over the rim of a whisky tumbler, waiting for her verdict. She downed her foul drink in one go, then shook her head.

'That's so disgusting,' she said. 'I don't know how you drink it. But I suppose it'll hit the spot quicker.' She sniffed loudly. Rory picked up a box of tissues near him and walking slowly over to her, offered it out. She took one, blew her nose and found herself laughing at the absurdity of it. 'Oh, that'll diffuse the whole situation so it will, Rory. A box of tissues.'

'Ridiculous. I know,' he ventured. 'I'll go now. You have to talk your problems out with your... dad.' But he didn't move. He stood there with the box of tissues still held out and Anna looked up into the eyes that were uncannily like her own. How had she never seen that before?

Because this man would have been the last man on earth that she would have thought was her birth father.

'Sit down, Rory. Have another drink. I'll have a red wine though, Dad. That stuff's horrible.' She held her empty glass out to Gerry. 'Let's do what dad says, Rory. Let's thrash this out over a few glasses and see what we can come up with.'

Chapter forty-three

FIONA was on her way back from her yoga class when she saw Eiley Sharkey on the footpath ahead of her and wondered if it was too late to cross over to avoid her. She may have been trying to let go of Deirdre's part in her row with Gerry, but there was going to be no such leniency with that interfering old bat. Eiley waved to her and hastened her footsteps to get to her.

'Fiona, love. How are you?'

Fiona stared hard at the older woman who had somehow been her mother's closest friend.

'Fiona, *love*? How *dare* you, Eiley Sharkey, after the hassle you've caused my family with your stupid accusations.'

'I know, Fiona. I'm so sorry about all that. I've been wanting to talk to you ever since but every time I knocked on your door there was no answer. I never meant to cause all that harm. I was looking out for Deirdre like any mother would. And I thought I was doing it for your sake too. If your mother was alive she would have been able to tell me I was wrong. I still can't believe I was sucked into the whole affair.'

'You mean lack of affair. Try to get your facts together next time you're playing Sherlock Holmes.' Fiona tried to pass by but Eiley reached out and held her arm.

'Please, Fiona. Try to put it behind us. For the sake of what your mother and I were to each other.'

'My mother? Don't you bring that beautiful woman into this. I can't believe that the two of you were even friends. When I think of the lovely way mammy used to talk about you and her when you were young. Well either she was wrong or you've become a bitter old woman, Eiley because there's nobody in my family wants to pass the time of day with you now. So if you'll excuse me I have better things to do than speak to the likes of you.'

'Okay. I know. And you have every right not to look in my direction again. But I was thinking of Deirdre, Fiona and I'm so sorry that you were caught up with all that. At the end of the day it was Rory's treatment of my daughter and granddaughters, that had us all tied up in this mess.

'That pair should never have married. If ever a couple weren't suited to each other...'

Fiona had had enough now. 'Eiley you don't know the full facts of what went on in Rory's life. Neither of us know what might have happened if Maria had lived. He would probably have left Deirdre properly way back then and she would have met someone she loved, instead of them making each other miserable.'

'I know, you're absolutely right, Fiona. But they're both still young enough to find someone else. I certainly hope Deirdre does because it's lonely living by yourself when you're my age. Or any age I suppose.'

Fiona's face showed no sympathy.

'Before you go, Fiona. Can I ask you something?'

Fiona didn't answer so Eiley ploughed on. 'Has Rory's going to Spain with Maria's daughter, anything to do with finding your mother's Spanish family?'

Fiona was incredulous. 'How did *you* know that they were going, Eiley? Through Caitríona and Clodagh? Are they your new detectives now? Of course they're not going looking for a family that my mother left behind a long time ago. Not that it's any bit of your business.'

'Wasn't I at Deirdre's birthday drinks when that eejit came looking to tell us where he was off to? Then yes; Caitríona told me that your niece Shona was going with him. Well I thought that with Sonia being from Spain and the girl being Sonia's granddaughter and called after her, that she might want to find more of her family. And well, I have some old addresses of Sonia's...'

254

'No, Eiley. She has enough to be troubling her with all that's going on in her life at the moment, without going off looking for distant relatives as well.'

'You're right, Fiona. She's been through a lot in the last year with the Gardaí and all, without making life more complicated for her. There's no doubt but she's Maria Dooley's daughter, though. She was a wild one too, your sister.'

Fiona couldn't believe the woman. 'Go home, Eiley. You're a bad gossip and a pain in the arse, so you are. I have nothing more to say to you. I don't accept your apology and I don't want to have anything more to do with you. Now go to hell.' She pushed the older woman out of her path and stormed off towards home.

'For God's sake, Fiona I was only saying what's true.' Eiley shouted after her. 'And just so you know, Rory McGee's been away up in your house the whole time that you were at your yoga.'

Fiona didn't give Eiley the satisfaction of looking back at her after this statement. But *Rory* in their house? Gerry would have sent him packing, surely. And Anna was due home this evening. She'd go wild if she saw the man anywhere near her parents' house. She hastened her step towards home and hoped she was in time to sort it out before anything else went wrong.

She turned her key in the door and pushed it open. Anna and Rory were standing in the hallway and he was laughing. Anna was smiling but it faded quickly when she saw her mother.

'Hello, Fiona,' said Rory. 'Anna and me were getting to know each other over a jar. I'm away to Spain tomorrow and I'll be a happier man going there, now that I've a few problems solved here.'

'Where's Gerry?' Fiona noticed how flushed Anna's cheeks were. She must have been on the wine. Gerry came out of the sitting room still clutching his drink. They'd been having a bloody reunion party.

'I'm here, love. The football's over and you're too late to play referee. But I think it was a one all draw.'

Chapter forty-four

SHONA watched Tommy hobble into the chaos of the kitchen; rubbing his shins after the pain of travelling on public transport to college and back, using a walking stick for support. No matter how great she was now with looking after and feeding Ruby, she would never be good at the tidying up after. Sometimes her mother came over before Tommy arrived home and she would leave her pristine mark on the place; but today there was no sign that anyone except Shona and a baby had been there all day.

'Looks like Croke Park after an All-Ireland match,' said Tommy.

'Hiya. Eh, sorry about the mess. You're early.' Shona sat back from Ruby in the high chair and dabbed at the food splashes over the table that she knew had been there since breakfast.

'Yeah. I can see you weren't expecting anyone. Hi gorgeous Ruby. How's daddy's little flower?' Tommy was smiling through his sarcastic comments to Shona. There was a time when they would have spit abuse at each other but they were getting on better these days. She couldn't believe he was actually beginning to forgive her after everything she'd put him through. But she knew it was because she was Ruby's mam and that mattered to him.

'Oh, you're a hoot, Mr Farrell. We can't all be as perfect as you now, can we? The world would be a boring place.'

'Oh, thanks. That's only charming, so it is. I'm boring so. Well I'll tell you what. How's this for not being boring?' Tommy pulled out a chair, removed Ruby's mucky lunch bib from it and sat down. 'It's reading week from college and some of the students are heading to Belfast. I've managed extra hours in the library yesterday and today so I'm well on top of studies. I was talking to dad today and he says he'll give me a few quid, so if you and your mam can have Ruby for the next couple of days, then we're sorted. I could do with some time off. In fact I can taste the pint and feel the unfamiliar hangover coming on already. Oh the bliss of it!'

Ruby blew a raspberry at her daddy. 'Oh I'll miss you too, Ruby my love. But I'll get over it somehow.' Tommy reached over and tickled his daughter under the chin and they both giggled with the familiarity of each other's play. Then Tommy noticed the shocked look on Shona's face.

'What?' he asked.

'Well, there's something I need to talk to you about. Mum will definitely be around this week. I mean she's already agreed to look after Ruby while you're at college, when *I'm* away.'

'Away?' Tommy stared at Shona incredulously. 'Jesus, Shona. Where could you be going to? You're only beginning to settle into your new life as Ruby's mammy and she's nine months old. Where the fuck could you be going to, that might be more important than putting your feet on the ground and getting to know your daughter properly?'

'Tommy. Mum is on her way around now. Can I wait until she gets here to tell you? She won't be long. It's complicated and I know I'll get all caught up in explanations and get it all arseways if I try to say it by myself. And we'll end up having a row and I don't want that.' Shona picked up Ruby's dinner bowl and walked to the sink with it.

'Damn right we'll have a row. No, Shona. You can't let your mother do your dirty work for you. What's complicated? We've done complicated to bloody death this year. We're not going there again. Has this something to do with your new family? Because if they think that this is a good time for you to piss off on holiday with them, to get to know them better, then the answer's most definitely no.'

Shona didn't turn around. She stared out into the back garden at nothing.

'C'mon, Shona. What is it? Out with it, so I can explain to you why you should be staying right here and going nowhere except Ruby's side for at least a year.'

Shona still said nothing but her shoulders were slumped now.

'Ah, shit, Shona. What is it?' Then she caved in and let the tears fall and her whole body shook with sobbing.

'Dunno what to do, Tommy,' she blubbered. 'I know it's such bad timing… but I don't know if I can ignore it all… and I don't think I can face it either and I wish they'd never come looking for me… but I'm glad they did in a way… but it's the wrong time in my life to have to face up to these things. I want a quiet life… but if I ignore Fergal O'Gorman and don't go, then he might die and I'll never find out what the gift was that he has for me… and I'll never know what he might know about my mother and…' Shona hugged her arms around herself and turned to face him.

'Whoa. Stop there.' Tommy grabbed his stick and pulled himself to standing, while Ruby banged a spoon on the table as if she was trying to drown out her mother's words.

'You're not making any sense, Shona. What are you on about? What is it? C'mon. After what we've already been through in the past year, surely this isn't half as bad, whatever it is.' He used his stick to get over to the sink and to Shona. He then leaned the cane against the wall and took some kitchen roll from the windowsill. 'Here, blow,' he said handing her a few torn off pieces.

'You know what, Shona?' he said, 'I never thought I'd hear myself saying these words but I think we *will* wait for Norah to get here before you tell me what's gone wrong. The one thing I learned from before is that I'm never going to try to cope with crap by myself anymore. Now take Ruby from the chair and wipe her down for me and we'll start to clear up the day's mess. Whatever's happened won't be made any better by your mother coming in and tutting at how I can't even keep a small house tidy.'

Shona nodded, relieved to be given a reprieve on having to face up to more of life's crisis with Tommy.

It didn't take them long to put the worst of the mess to rest and as they were cleaning up Ruby's toys in the sitting room, the doorbell rang out Norah's arrival. Shona ran to answer it.

'Hi, Mum.' She looked pleadingly at her mother.

'Shona, what's the matter? You've been crying.' Norah came into the kitchen and saw Tommy with Ruby on his lap and a look of thunder on his face. 'Oh, so she told you then.'

'Hello, Norah.'

Ruby started doing a happy dance on Tommy's lap at the sight of her granny, so he held her up to Norah. 'No. She said she has something to tell me but with the state of her, I thought that it would be best left until you turned up.'

'How's granny's little princess?' Norah made funny faces at her granddaughter and then looked at the two teenage parents in the room and sighed. 'Oh, it's all too hard to put into the right words. I'll try to tell you what Shona told me, to help you to understand. But there's something else I want to say first, Tommy.'

Tommy shook his head and took a deep breath. Shona watched him brace himself for whatever it was that Norah was going to lecture him on today.

She spoke over the background music of her granddaughter's chatter. 'Tommy. I haven't always been good to you, I know. I needed someone to blame for everything that went wrong last year and you were in my firing line because I didn't know you well. I know that we spoke before and tried to patch things up, and you've been understanding with us all, especially with Shona. You're a wonderful father to Ruby, and your own dad as well as Des and I, are all proud of you. I think you're fantastic to go to college after what you went through with the car crash and everything. We're right behind you, one hundred percent.'

Shona and Tommy looked over at each other with the shock of what Norah was admitting.

'I know,' Norah continued, 'I've changed my tune, but I wanted you to know that before I said anything else. What Shona and I are going to tell you now, will sound like we don't appreciate how much you've had to endure already – but we do. And the timing of all this is nothing short of terrible but we can't change that.' Norah reached over for Ruby's bottle that was left on the counter from earlier and the baby clutched it and drank thirstily. Norah's voice relaxed her and her little eyes began to close over.

Norah went on to fill Tommy in on what he didn't know about Rory, Maria and O'Gorman; while Ruby slumbered in her arms, oblivious to the mayhem that continued to fill her first year of life.

'I'm lost for words. It's too much. You're a bloody stick of dynamite, Shona. All I want is a bit of peace and quiet for me and Ruby and now you throw this at us.' Shona's phone rang out over his words and she fished it out of her jeans pocket.

'Yeah?' Shona paled at the untimely sound of Rory's voice but she heard him out and said, 'Okay, Rory. That's good news, I think. Let it sink in for a minute. I'll call you right back.' She disconnected and turned towards her mum. She knew it was best to say no more in front of Tommy but she needed to convince him now of the importance of going.

'That baby blanket of mine, that Maria was holding when she died... I told you Rory sent it to the private lab. The results are positive. It *is* O'Gorman's DNA and the blood is there long enough to collaborate with Rory's story. It looks like he was right. That man *did* kill Maria. He murdered my mother.

'I'm sorry, Tommy. I have to go and see him. Rory wants to leave tomorrow. He wants us to confront Fergal O'Gorman ourselves before the evidence is passed over to the Gardaí. He reckons we won't get any information from him about Maria once he's arrested. I *have* to find out what he knows before that happens. I'll only be gone a couple of days. Do you understand, Tommy?' Shona walked over to where he was sitting and she hunched down, took his hands in hers and looked him straight in the eyes. 'I need you to be okay with this. You've suffered more than anyone in the past year. Please tell me that I can do this with your backing, Tommy? You've stood by me through so much already that I know I've no right to ask you to watch while the shit hits the fan all over again. But I'm asking anyway.'

Tommy looked at the two women waiting with bated breath. Then he looked over at his baby in Norah's arms.

'When she's older, you can tell her all about her background. She'll be delighted to hear what she came from.' Tommy hung his head.

'I'll leave nothing out either, Tommy, because there'll never be any more lies in this family.'

'God help Ruby with the story that's ahead of her so. Sure what's another bit?'

Norah was smarting at Shona's mention of family lies but she stayed on track nevertheless. 'At least this will clear Shona's head, Tommy and then we can learn to put the past behind us. And you can move on to that yearned-for peace and quiet. You do need a holiday and you'll get one this summer. I guarantee it. But right now Shona needs our support, not least to stop her getting into any more trouble.'

Shona looked at Tommy's face for signs that he was relenting. Ruby's dad had become her best friend. She trusted him totally. She would do whatever he decided. He looked at her and shook his head, and she thought he was going to say no.

But then he smiled.

'Go on to Spain, Shona but make sure that you come back in one piece. I'd be nearly tempted to come with you. A few rays of sunshine wouldn't go amiss. Don't ask me why I'm saying yes because I can't even figure it out myself. Rory sounds like a mad man on a mission, who'll stop at nothing to get answers. Ring every few hours and tell us exactly where you are and who you're with. And Shona, when you come back, be a mother first and everything else can wait.'

Shona reached up and gave him a big hug, and he amazed her by putting his arms around her and hugging her back.

Chapter forty-five

'BIT of a hangover, have we?' Fiona smiled over at her daughter as she scrunched up her face at the noise of the knife falling to the floor.

'Well I wouldn't have as much practice as dad in that scene. How did he manage to get up and go out today as if there was nothing wrong with him? And with whisky as well. Yeuk. I stuck to wine and I'm wrecked. He's back now this evening and he looks fine.'

'Ah, there's nothing wrong with sitting down and sorting out the problems of the universe over a pint. And isn't the world a better place for it today?' Fiona retrieved the knife from the floor and put it into the sink.

'Maybe so, but my head isn't.'

'You've reading week from college this week, Anna, so you picked the right day for it. Have you come to any decision about Rory?'

'Ah, don't pressurise me today, Mam. We've been all around the houses with the talking. *Rory is a good man... He isn't... He's a liar and a troublemaker... He's a man who's intent on outing the truth... He wants justice for the person he loved... He wants to bring down half the world with him...* We're never going to get our heads around this one.'

'Life isn't all about knowing who's right or wrong, Anna. There are times when we don't have the answers and I think this is one of them. This whole mess is too complex. Everyone involved is too busy getting it wrong while they're trying to get things right. Here. Mash the potatoes while I set the table.'

Anna was quiet for a moment as she took in the words of

wisdom from Fiona. 'What about Shona though, Mam? What should I do about her? It's all well and good telling Rory to get stuffed but Shona hasn't done anything wrong; well not to me anyway.'

'What's your instinct telling you to do, Anna? How do you feel about her?' Fiona held the kitchen door open, about to call Gerry for his dinner.

'She scares the shit out of me to be honest, Mam. I feel like I never know which way she's going to turn or what she's going to say next. That said, I love her. Already, I'd move mountains for her. I feel a strong pull keeping us together. I understand her motives behind what she wants to do. Like myself, she's trying to make sense of her birth family at the moment. My big problem is still Rory.' Anna plunged the masher into the potatoes with gusto. 'I'm beginning to understand and to accept, if not forgive him, for what he did but I can't forget what's gone before. To be honest, I never put much thought into anything to do with a birth father before. I thought that finding who Maria was with when she got pregnant was impossible and I grew up listening to Caitríona and Clodagh ranting about their father's treatment of them. I knew Rory was a friend of Dad's but I had no time for the man that I'd never met until he waltzed back into their lives.

'To be honest, love, there's no point in deliberating over what might have been. I think we're all in agreement that Rory had no option but to do what he did; and maybe it's time to give him the benefit of the doubt now, when he's trying so hard?'

'I know but still. It's this relationship we have… or don't have. I've known about him all my life but I've never given him much thought. Now suddenly I'm supposed to call him *dad*?'

Anna stopped short at the sight of her father at the kitchen door.

'Since when did you start to eavesdrop?' Fiona gave Gerry a hard look.

'I'm not eavesdropping. I came for my dinner if that's okay. Anyway. I've learned to listen out more. It's the only way anyone would find out anything in this house.'

Gerry sat down at the table.

'What's that supposed to mean? Are you still harping on about me not telling you about Rory at the beginning?' Fiona dragged her chair noisily and plonked herself down opposite him.

'And what about going off to Dublin without mentioning to me about Anna's sister? Oh, I'm going to eavesdrop on everything from now on.'

'Oh for God's sake, Gerry. At least I didn't go accusing you of having a bloody affair with someone. Don't go feeling all hard done by.'

Anna stared hard at her parents. 'Would the pair of you pack it in? You're supposed to be sorting out my problems; not creating new ones. I'm not sitting at this table if you're going to spend the whole of the dinner bickering.'

'She's right, Gerry. Sit down, Anna love, and don't be minding us. All this is getting to everybody. Let's leave it alone for now and eat.'

'Grand so,' said Gerry. 'We certainly don't need to throw any fuel on this particular fire. It's burning brightly all by itself.'

The three of them sat around the table in uncustomary silence as they each contemplated their own thoughts and tried to figure out what was for the best.

Fiona sighed.

'What now?' Gerry asked. 'Go on. Whatever it is.'

'Look,' said Fiona. 'Rory left the lab report with us before he left for Spain. I think we should go to the Gardaí with it; not wait for Rory and Shona to come back. I know it sounds mad and all that, but I started this little war with Rory and I feel I want to finish it. I'm going to go straight to them in the morning and get this thing sorted. I'm going to destroy the man who thought my sister's life was so worthless.'

'Where did all this come from?' Gerry put his knife and fork down, his appetite diminished.

'Nothing sudden about it. I want to put my sister to rest and, like Rory, I feel that this is the only way to do it. There's a whole gap in Maria's life that I know nothing about and I want answers.'

Anna shovelled her mashed potato in and spoke with her mouth full. 'I'm coming with you, Mam. You're right. We should support Shona and Rory in this. Fergal O'Gorman might be dying but we're all going to die some day and it doesn't make us any less responsible for our actions.'

'Does that mean you're forgiving Rory, Anna? Accepting him for who he is?' Gerry asked.

'No, Dad. Well… yes. In a way. I'm beginning to feel he's had enough punishment without me doling out anymore. I'm going to start this evening with talking to Clodagh and Caitríona. Try to get them to come around. Maybe they can talk to their mother. It's all very sad the way it's turned out for them. They've lost their dad, again.'

'And you've found one.' Gerry was stating a fact.

'No! I haven't. I have one dad and always will. I can't see myself and Rory getting that close, no matter how much blood we share. But we can learn to live around each other.'

'Fine,' said Gerry, not wanting to push it any further. 'As for going to the police, I'm in. Mad and all as I think you are, I'll not have the pair of you traipsing through the courts with no man but McGee to defend you. That said, I also think that we need to do something to help him out with the mess his life is in at the minute. I know he was an ass to lie the way he did but he had good reason. Let's help him to end this thing. Let's get O'Gorman back here and put him in front of a jury.'

Chapter forty-six

THE door of the airplane opened and the Malaga heat hit Rory's face like a slap. Shona had told him shorts and t-shirts but he hadn't believed her and had only brought long trousers. By the time he walked into the airport and down the long corridors with their pictures of exotic Spanish villages, his clothing had become part of his skin. But he would soldier on. He was here for Maria...

Pushing through the crowds of shouting people, Rory and Shona made their way towards the taxi rank and he handed the hotel address to the first driver. He ignored the constant babble as the guy drove away from the airport and out towards Benalmádena and Fergal O'Gorman. Not able to think about that yet, Rory concentrated on the mantra going through his head. Drink of cold water, shower, change of clothes, air conditioning... Water, shower, clothes, air...

Later, showered and refreshed, Shona sat on her balcony trying to remember the words of the letter that Fergal O'Gorman had sent her. The evening was overcast. Hot and heavy. She wished she had been given a room with a view of the sea. The mountains were lovely but had become very populated over the years. Too many people who wanted a piece of the sun.

She pulled the crumpled letter from her pocket and read the words he had written before he left Ireland. *This is my address in Spain. Come as soon as possible. Bring Rory. I have a gift for you.* When she first opened the envelope she wanted to scrunch it up or tear it into pieces. Who the hell did he think he was, summoning her and Rory to a villa in the south of Spain because he wanted to confess his outrageous sins before he died? The words had sat there, calling her, but she had no intention of obeying his commands. It was the last sentence that had stuck in her head and followed her everywhere. *I have a gift for you.* She knew it was bait and she also knew she would eventually bite. Fergal O'Gorman had something. It might be something belonging to her mother, so she had decided to come to Spain with Rory. They would take what he had and leave. Rory was delighted to have another shot at the bastard before he gave his evidence to the police. All the pent-up frustration and anger of the last eighteen years needed somewhere to vent.

It was time to call Tommy. She wished that she still had access to her social media pages but deleting them kept the media and doubters away from her. She missed the instant communication that they had given her, though. Shona keyed in his number and waited. She imagined him sitting in the kitchen where she had last seen him, his stick leaning against the chair, within easy reach for him.

She had tried to persuade him to go to Belfast with his friends, as planned, and leave Ruby with her mum and dad; but he had stood firm on staying home until she got back. This boy had been to hell and back because of what had happened in her life and he was still there, helping her through. She felt a pull towards him now and a yearning to be with him and sit beside him. Ever since her ordeal, she needed to be around someone she was close to all the time. She was frightened by the memories and worried about her future. He answered on the second ring.

'Hi, Tommy. How're things?'

'Yeah, grand. Are you alright? How's it going?'

'Fine. Hot. The weather's fab. We're heading to his villa now though. I'm nervous...' It was lovely to hear the familiar voice and Shona felt a warm feeling of something more than gratitude when she registered the tone.

'You'll be careful, Shona. Won't you? Has your man settled down at all or is he still like a centipede on speed?'

'Rory?' She laughed at his apt description of her travelling partner. 'He's okay. A bit weird but… ah, he'll be alright. How's Ruby?'

'Screaming blue murder. She's cutting a tooth. Hopefully she'll sleep it off for a few hours.'

'Don't skimp on the medicine, Tommy. It's only for a day or two until it comes through properly.'

'Listen to you, all know-how and domestic-like. I know how to look after my daughter.'

'Ah, Tommy don't. I didn't mean anything by it. Will you give her a kiss and a hug from her mummy? I'll give you a ring after I've spoken to O'Gorman. If Rory doesn't land the pair of us in the clink for murder ourselves.'

'For God's sake, Shona…'

'I'm only messing with you. Sorry. We'll be home tomorrow evening. No bother… Tommy?'

'Yeah?'

'Tommy… I… well I…'

'What?'

'I think you're amazing. I love you, Tommy.' Shona hung up before she could hear his reply. Had she actually said that out loud to him? Jesus. She must be jumpier than she thought.

It was time to go and meet Rory; get on with what they'd come here to do.

Shona walked out of the lift on the ground floor and over to where Rory was sitting in the lobby. He was watching two children playing with a set of dominoes on the floor nearby.

'Come on,' she said. 'The taxi will be waiting outside.'

'What if we can't get in, Shona? What if we have to turn around and come straight back? It's a long way to go for nothing, if that's the case. Maybe we should wait until the morning.'

'For God's sake, we've already come a long way. This is what we've come *for*. We want answers. You said so yourself. You even have evidence now, so what are we waiting for?' Shona was getting impatient. This man was impossible. One minute he was racing forward like a hare and the next he was running away.

Was it such a good idea, after all, to go back to visit his family before he travelled here? He was full of get-up-and-go before then. The man lived in two worlds. Well he had pulled her into this one and he could damn well stay with her.

'Rory. Stand up. We're going.' Shona moved. She looked back as she walked and he was still sitting on the chair.

'What's stopping you, Rory?'

He stood then and walked towards her. 'I was just looking at those kids and remembering something from when I was younger,' he said. 'I used to love to build up hundreds of dominoes; then go to the start, tip them over and watch one knock the other. I marvelled at how, once the first one toppled, there was no stopping the others; until there was nothing left standing and you had to start building them up all over again. I guess there's still a domino here that hasn't fallen yet. I suppose I can't rebuild the rest until that's done.'

Shona nodded and smiled. 'So let's go knock the last one down.' She gestured for him to get a move on.

By the time they were out on the street, Rory had caught hold of himself. Shona had travelled all the way to Spain, relying on him to justify his accusations. She had heard the politician speaking to the media, swearing that he had never murdered Maria; that he was dying of cancer and he appealed to them all to let him go in peace.

On the news later he had said that he wouldn't be taking a slander case. Yes, he was fully aware that he had one. No, he didn't have a problem with commenting. Yes, he was sure that he was innocent.

But Rory had seen the man murder his Maria; saw him leave that house with his own eyes. He had personally left the scar on O'Gorman's face before the man had threatened him with his life, and those of his family, if he said a word. He was the man who killed Shona's mother, no mistake, and Rory would make sure his leaving of this world was as awful as Maria's had been.

Chapter forty-seven

IT was deathly silent outside O'Gorman's villa. The air was warm but a fresh breeze was coming in from the sea. The view of the sun setting was breathtaking, and from up here Shona understood why so many people had carved out a space for themselves on the side of the mountains.

Footsteps disturbed the quiet as someone came through the house in answer to their knock. A man, who looked like he was in his late thirties and was well-tanned from years in the sun, opened the door to them. He showed no surprise at them being there but looked like he'd been crying. He went to shake Rory's hand first but was rebuked and so reached out to Shona. He seemed reluctant to let her go.

'Shona... you're exactly as Fergal said you were. Come in. My name's Danny.'

'Is he here?' Rory interrupted. He was keen to get down to business and get out.

'Come on in,' the man said, and they both followed him down the marble corridor towards the sitting room, where they settled themselves on soft leather chairs.

Rory tried again. 'Is he here?'

Danny closed his eyes and scrunched up his face as if Rory's words had physically hurt him. Opening them again he nodded slowly.

'Fergal's here. Yes. But you're... too late.' Danny said the last two words softly. He cleared his throat and spoke again to clarify himself.

'Fergal died today. I don't know how he managed to stay alive in the last week. I think it was the hope that you would come, that kept him going as long as he did. He didn't want to be in the hospital and he begged me to help him to stay here. Most of the time he refused morphine because he wanted a clear head when he spoke to you. This morning he lay in his bed, wasted, and he said, 'they're not coming, are they?' and then he closed his eyes. Over the following few hours he let the pain take him away.'

They were silent for a moment while the visitors took in all that Danny had said. Shona shook her head, obviously upset that she wouldn't get to speak to him, but Rory was hardened to Danny's soft words and the tears in his eyes.

'I hope he died screaming, the dirty shit.'

'Rory!' Shona said. 'That's cruel.'

'Cruel? *Me*?' Rory stood and began to pace the room. 'What about *him*? A friend of a murderer? What kind of person has friends like Fergal O'Gorman? Why would anyone want to associate with a man like that?'

'Look. Come on. Calm down.' Danny sounded sympathetic to Rory despite what he had said. 'Let me tell you what happened to Maria and to your father, Shona.'

Shona shot Rory a look that said *I want information. Let the man tell us what happened.* An uncomfortable silence followed as Danny turned towards the open window, but looking out at the sea he eventually spoke softly.

'Fergal loved this view. Especially at night when the stars came out. He knew all the names of the planets and the constellations and stuff. I can't believe he's gone. It was so quick.'

'Yeah, pity that,' said Rory. 'Go on with your story.'

Danny didn't turn around to face them. 'I'll give you the short version. And sometime, if you still want to hear it, I'll tell it to you in more detail.'

Shona followed his gaze. The sun had completely set now and the crescent moon was taking over the job of lighting the Andalucian coast.

'Fergal never killed Dónal.' His announcement was sudden and he turned to face them to show the conviction of his words.

Rory and Shona exchanged confused looks.

'Hang on a minute. Maria told me exactly what happened,' Rory said. 'I remember the look of horror on her face. She said O'Gorman had told her that he'd killed Dónal. *A bullet through the back of the head,* were his exact words.'

'It wasn't Fergal who said that to Maria.' Danny was adamant. 'You've no idea of the kind of people Dónal was working under. They would stop at nothing to make sure they weren't grassed up. It was Fergal's own brother Eoin O'Gorman who gave orders to Fergal to shoot Dónal. Fergal couldn't do it. *Wouldn't* do it. Fergal organised Dónal's escape to another country. A new name on a passport. He pretended to show Eoin the spot where he had *buried* Dónal, having dug a trench in the middle of the Dublin Mountains, near the Hellfire Woods, and filled it in with rubbish for authenticity. At first Eoin was convinced, and Fergal thought it would all work well.

'But then Fergal found out that Eoin was after Maria. Eoin believed that Dónal had given her information about them. Fergal sent her a note to ask her to meet him that night so he could warn her off, and to suggest a place to go to hide out for a while. He was hoping to send her over to Dónal. But she never made it to that meeting. Eoin killed her that afternoon.'

'No way!' Rory was standing again. 'I *saw* Fergal kill Maria. The scar he has on his cheek; I gave that to him before he left Maria's house.'

'No,' said Danny. 'You scarred Eoin. When he left you, he waited around to make sure there would be nothing left in the squat to incriminate him in any way. He watched the ambulance take Maria away and when he was sure she was dead, he came straight to Fergal. Apparently, he was raging like a wild animal. He had seen the note that Fergal had written to Maria and recognised the writing. He still had the syringe in his hand that you had used to stab him with…'

'…that was used to kill Maria first…' Rory shook his head at Shona's look of horror.

'I know. Eoin decided that Fergal couldn't get away with trying to warn Maria off. The man was a nutter. The only reason he had climbed so high in the organisation was because he was fearless and because others were afraid of him. Dónal had been terrified of Eoin. But Fergal thought that he could get away with some things because he was Eoin's brother, his twin in fact. Eoin lunged at him with the syringe and ripped his cheek, as he said you had done to *him* earlier. He laughed at Fergal's howls of pain and told him that they were a better match of twins for each other with their slashed cheeks. That's when Fergal lost it. You were right when you said that Fergal was a killer.'

'I knew it...' Rory was nodding.

'Fergal grabbed the syringe from Eoin and brought it down into his brother's heart. Eoin was dead in a matter of minutes and in answer to what you said earlier... yes, I heard he died screaming.'

Danny turned to Shona. 'It was Eoin who had told Maria that Dónal was dead when he met her in the park, and it was Eoin who killed your mother. Not Fergal.'

'You're wrong!' shouted Rory, standing up once more in his anger. 'I saw *Fergal* in that house. I'll never forget what he looked like. And I have proof! I have a match to Fergal's DNA on a blanket that was covered in his blood on the day that he murdered Maria.'

Danny stood and walked over to Rory and put a hand on his shoulder to try to calm him. 'He didn't murder her. As identical twins, Eoin and Fergal shared the same DNA. Maria's murder was Eoin's doing. At the time, Fergal was only as caught up with the struggle as Dónal was. He wanted out as much as Dónal did.

'Afterwards, Fergal brought Eoin's body to the mock grave, the one that he had built in the Dublin Mountains to convince Eoin that Dónal was dead, and he buried him there. Eoin was reported missing by their parents but the police were never going to do much about trying to find a man who they were glad to see the back of.

'After that, Fergal got heavily involved in promoting and maintaining the IRA's ceasefire. He never looked back. That's why he helped Dónal. Eoin may have been Fergal's identical twin, but when it came to personaility no two people could have been more different. Eoin was a total psycho. He made enemies with everyone.'

Rory looked at Danny who was staring at Shona. Eventually he found his voice and asked 'Did they ever find the body? I mean… to kill your own brother, that's terrible.' Rory could still see a fight ahead of him.

'No. They never found him. But when Fergal found out he was dying, he told me exactly where he had buried Eoin. And yes, it was terrible for him to have killed his own brother. He paid for that with the guilt he lived with all his life,' Danny answered, not taking his eyes off Shona. 'They had grown up together as kids and Fergal had hero-worshipped his fearless twin – until they grew as adults and he realised that Eoin was completely out of control. Fergal had to face his parents while they searched for his brother. They never gave up looking for him. They left Ireland eventually, to live here in Spain and get away from their memories, but they both died soon after the move. They wasted away.'

Rory nodded; an amazed but contented nod.

'And Dónal?' Shona asked. Her voice a whisper. 'What happened to him?'

She wanted to know but was scared of the response.

Chapter forty-eight

RORY tried to take in all that Danny was saying. The man was staring at Shona with yearning and Rory recognised that look. It was how *he* looked now at Anna when he wanted to reel back the years and make her his own daughter.

Rory spoke to Danny.

'Dónal is the Irish for Daniel. I'm right, am I not? You changed your name.'

Danny nodded, still not taking his eyes from his daughter.

Rory's fight wasn't finished. 'So you're the man who was the cause of Maria's death.' His voice was cold. 'He might as well have murdered your mother himself, Shona.' Rory wasn't ready to let it all go. He had psyched himself up to be angry and he still wanted someone to blame for Maria's loss.

'Yes. I'm Dónal. I'm Shona's father. Maria and I hardly knew each other when she fell pregnant. I was nineteen years old when all this happened; young and impressionable and wanting to change the world. I was in way over my head when I met Eoin O'Gorman and I wanted out before I met Maria. I remember seeing you, Rory, when I was first going out with her. I didn't realise then who you were but she told me a little about you later. She was miserable for ages after. She tried to dump me because she said that you had ruined her trust in men because you'd been two-timing her. She never told me that she'd had a baby by you.'

'Yeah. She never told me either. At least you knew you were going to be a father.' Rory was still fuming.

'When I found out about her being pregnant, I was beginning to realise how dangerous Eoin was, and I insisted that she go back to Donegal to her family. It wasn't that I didn't want to stand by her with our baby but I knew that they would both be at risk if she stayed with me. I was horrified when Fergal told me that Eoin had told her I was dead. I could only hope then that she would grieve, but be able to move on with her life; that she would go to her family and have our baby there. But it was too late. I didn't completely understand the horror that was Eoin O'Gorman's mind. When Fergal told me Eoin had murdered her I wanted to die. If he hadn't told me that he had done away with the bastard, I would have got him myself. I thought that Eoin had killed Maria when she was pregnant. We didn't realise that she had given birth to Shona already. We never knew you were alive until you turned up at the press conference with Fergal.' Danny went back to looking out the window to hide his stricken face. The years hadn't lessened his pain. 'I've never forgiven myself for what happened to Maria. I've never married or had a proper relationship since. Even with Eoin dead, I worried that there were others who would kill me if they knew I was alive. I would never put anyone at risk like that again.'

All the time he was talking there were tears running down Shona's face, but still she said nothing.

'But now that you're naming Shona as your daughter, aren't you doing exactly that?' Rory still couldn't back down from his fight for justice. 'You were bad news for her mother and you'll be bad news for Shona too.'

'I'll decide that, Rory.' Shona found a voice through her tears. 'Could you leave us alone for a few minutes? I want to ask Danny... or Dónal some questions and I don't want him to have any reason to hide the truth.'

'No way!' Rory was adamant. 'This could all be a trick. I'm staying right here, Shona. I told your family I'd be with you until we got you safely home and I'm not changing my mind.'

'Let him stay, Shona.' Danny turned back around, a little more composed. 'There's nothing I have to say that you can't hear as well, Rory. I don't believe that Shona will be at risk from me now. There's nobody left who wants to threaten me. Times have changed in Ireland. There are a few mad men still carrying the gauntlet but most of those who followed Eoin O'Gorman, way back then, are either dead or have faded into everyday living now.

'I won't hide any truth from anyone anymore, Shona, least of all you. Let him stay and you can both ask me anything. Maria's family have every right to know all the answers to the questions that must have been plaguing them.'

Rory stepped forward then. 'Danny. Or Dónal again is it?' he was almost sneering.

'Danny. I've been Danny as long as I was Dónal and I'm used to it now.'

'I loved Maria, you have no idea how much, and I regret every moment of my life without *her*. You took that from me. From us, and I will never forgive you for that…'

Danny looked at Maria's daughter, his daughter, before he replied. He shook his head.

'Maria always seemed to be miles older than me and she was clever. I think at that age I wasn't old or mature enough to understand about real love. But I think that Maria *was* and that she'd been there before. With you, Rory. I think that if she'd lived she'd have gone to find her babies and that you two would somehow have stayed together. I was a boy she hung out with and got pregnant by. And yes. You're right. By being with her I took away her life. I wish I had realised that in time. But time let us all down.

'I'll be bringing Fergal back to Ireland, Shona, for his funeral. He was a good man and he did an awful lot in his political career to help others. He was a great friend to me. He let me live in this villa that used to belong to his parents and helped get me set up as a caretaker for a number of local properties here. Going back means I'll be giving myself in too as I've been missing, presumed dead, all these years; and I'll need to go through all the crap of being arrested and questioned about our activities back then. I'll also give them the information that I know now about where Eoin is buried.

'There'll probably be a lot of media coverage, Shona, and I want you to go home now and get away from it all before it starts up. I want to be heralded as your father so much, but right now is not the time. I know all about what you've been through this past year. You and your family have put up with enough.'

'Excuse me, being my father for five minutes doesn't give you the right to tell me what to do, Danny.' Shona was getting over her initial shock. 'I've already been dragged into this and it's too late to turn back.'

'You need to think of Ruby,' Danny answered. 'Her little life has been marked with too much crap already. Sometime, when this all blows over, I want to be able to see her and to get to know you both, if you'll let me…'

Rory nodded and turned to Shona. 'We have the answers we needed. And for what it's worth, O'Gorman has given you what he promised. We should go now. As Danny says, he has a funeral to organise.'

'Rory. I want a moment with Danny alone.' Shona was insistent this time. 'Wait outside for me. I'm not in danger. You know I'm not. Now go.'

Rory shot Danny a warning look but then shook his head. 'Okay. I'll be the other side of that window.' He left them to absorb each other and went out to the garden. His phone bleeped and he read a text from Fiona.

We've passed the evidence on to the Gardaí. Decided not to wait 'til you came back. Not sure how long it might take before things get moving but get my niece the hell out of Spain before the shit hits. Fiona.

Now she starts to take action, he thought.

Rory could feel the adrenalin rush of the impending drop of the last domino falling neatly under all the others. He glanced back at the two in the villa. He should get Shona out, but once this all took off it would be some time before she got to talk to Danny again.

Danny? Dónal. That name had been on his mind for so many years. The last thing he wanted to do was spend any more time with the man who had set up Maria's death. Unwittingly or otherwise.

He sat on the grass and looked out over the horizon; the only sound disturbing the quiet was a distant siren. He looked up now, to where the Spanish sky was filling with stars, and he remembered a night so many years ago when Maria had sat with him in her sister's garden and talked about her interest in the constellations. There was a circle of stars tonight too. The *Winter Circle* she had called it. That was the first of many nights that they had made love.

He would hold all the good memories of Maria with him from now on. There was nothing more he could do for her except to keep her daughters safe. Anna, who they had created between them during a time when they had loved each other. And Shona, who was the living picture of her mother.

He had finally re-written Maria's eulogy and her memory could be cherished now by everyone who knew her.

Chapter forty-nine

RORY keyed in the number their taxi driver had given them and told him they were ready to go back. Then he found himself calling Fiona. He needed to talk to someone about what had happened today, a person who had known and loved Maria as much as he had.

'Hi, Fiona. I didn't disturb you?'

'No, Rory. How's it going? Did you meet him? What did he say? Is Shona alright?'

'No. We were a few hours too late to hear him say anything. He's dead. But he's left Shona one hell of a legacy.'

'No way! Tell me.'

And Rory filled her in on all that he had been told by Danny.

'So what are you doing now, Rory? I'll call the Gardaí here. Let them know what you said but I think it's too late to pull out completely. There'll be an enquiry and it sounds like that fella, who you say is Shona's father, is in for a grilling.'

'Good enough for him I say, but the first thing I'm doing is getting her out of here and back to Ireland to her family. She has what she came for and they can catch up another time. I couldn't spend another day here anyway. The heat is killing – and they call this winter!'

'It's been hotting up a bit here too, Rory. Your girls were over last night to talk to Anna and it seems that they're willing to see you when you get back and try to come to terms with what's happened.'

Rory couldn't hide his delight. 'That's wonderful, Fiona. Thank you for helping. I know it'll take time to sort out the mess I've made, but I think I'm getting there… You know, today has taken a huge burden from me. I feel freer than I have for most of my adult life. Listen, I'll call you when we get back. Let me know what the Gardaí say... And Fiona? I've caused trouble for you in so many ways and we've had our differences, but I had to see it through and I couldn't have done all this on my own. I mean it.'

'Yeah. No doubt we'll have plenty more rows about what was right or wrong in the future, but you did alright in the end, Rory. Now get yourselves to the airport and come home. Give Shona a hug from her Aunty Fiona. Bye now.'

Rory heard footsteps crunch on the gravel behind him and turned to find Shona walking towards him, linked with Danny. As he had his phone in his hand he quickly switched it to camera and clicked their moment.

'More evidence?' Danny was smiling, despite his earlier loss.

Rory shook his head. 'No need. I called Maria's sister, Fiona. I might as well tell you that the police are involved already. She brought the evidence to the Gardaí this morning. There'll be an enquiry.'

'Maybe I should call them myself. Start the ball rolling,' said Danny.

He turned to Shona. 'Looks like we're not going to get to catch up yet. No doubt I'll be charged with lots of old stuff from way back and it'll be a while before we meet again. I'm keeping you out of all this but I'll get through it knowing I have a relationship with you to look forward to when it's all over.' He reached over and hugged his daughter.

Eventually, Shona let go and smiled up at him. 'I've found my dad, my birth father, and I'm *going* to get to know him. Fergal O'Gorman promised me something worth coming all the way here for and he wasn't lying.' She turned and reluctantly headed for the car.

Shona waved back at Danny as the car drove out of the gate and down the mountainside towards the coast, not taking her eyes off him until he disappeared. Then she turned back to Rory, who was lying with his head back and his eyes closed.

'Are you tired?' she asked.

'No. I'm thinking about Maria. Right now, I can see her face as if she were beside me. She's laughing. She's beautiful.'

'What's she saying to us?'

Rory opened his eyes again and smiled at Maria's daughter.

'She's saying, *go and sort out your lives, you pair of gobshites and stop arsing around in the past… It's over.*'